Code Red

Books by Janie Chodosh

The Faith Flores Science Mysteries
Death Spiral
Code Red

*Wild Lives, Leading Conservationists
on the Animals and the Planet they Love*

Code Red

A Faith Flores Science Mystery

Janie Chodosh

Poisoned Pen Press

Copyright © 2017 by Janie Chodosh

First Edition 2017

10 9 8 7 6 5 4 3 2 1

Library of Congress Catalog Card Number: 2016949805

ISBN: 9781929345281   Trade Paperback
      9781929345298   E-book

Poisoned Pen Press
6962 E. First Ave., Ste. 103
Scottsdale, AZ 85251
www.poisonedpenpress.com
info@poisonedpenpress.com

Printed in the United States of America

*To Isabella, who keeps me on my toes
and who fills my heart*

Acknowledgments

Thank you to Ellen Larson, editor extraordinaire, for patience, time, and deep insight. Thank you to all the fine people at the Poisoned Pen Press for the magic of making a computer file into a book. Thank you to Emily Ruppell for balanced and thoughtful writing on controversial scientific issues and for an early read of a very rough draft. Thank you to Dr. Stephen Hanson of New Mexico State University for sharing knowledge of the New Mexico chile, plant pathogens, and genetic engineering. Thank you to the **Friday** writers: Deb Auten, Nadine Donovan, Jillian Brasch, Susan Rathjen, Catherine Coulter, Barbara Mayfield, Hope Cahill, and Jennifer Dewey, where it started. Thank you to Katharine Peters for friendship and excellent editorial comments, and most of all thank you to Callum Bell, my husband, co-conspirator, and source of all things science; my talented stepson, Liam Bell; and my crazy wonderful daughter, Isabella. Finally, thank you to my parents, Joan and Richard Chodosh

One

I should join the bevy of arts and academic interns bonding in clumps of polite, socially correct conversation. At least, if I'm going to be antisocial I should be harnessing the power of positive thought and thinking, *Wow! Here I am—St. John's College in Santa Fe, New Mexico! Or, wow! What an honor, out of all the science geeks around the nation, the Salazar Center for Plant Genomics chose me as their summer student scholar!*

Instead, I sit alone in a window seat overlooking a confusion of mountains and arroyos, no idea what to say to any of the other interns who look so at ease and whose off-resume experiences probably don't include waiting in the backseat of some beater while their mom scored a fix. Not to mention that if I were to actually open my mouth what would come out would likely have a high lab geek element. And then there's the nagging distraction of The Jerk, also known as The Sperm Donor, sometimes known as my father, who I happen to know was born here and could still be hanging around.

"Faith, cool name," someone says.

I spin around, absolutely no idea how long I've been staring out the window, to gape at a tall guy standing in front of me who might be Hispanic, might be black, and might be in

1

competition with Jesse, my Philly boyfriend, for the cutest boy I've ever seen. To make up for the fact that I seem to have forgotten how to speak, I jam my hands on my hips and demand an explanation for how he knew my name.

"Um. That would be your nametag?" He nods at the Hi! I'm FAITH FLORES label stuck to my chest. "Artist?"

I have no idea what he's talking about, so I don't respond, and he repeats, "You're an artist, right? You're here for the O'Keeffe internship. It's your hair. Gives you away."

I consider my hair. Long. Dark. Square-cut bangs. In no way artistic unless you consider self-styling with a pair of dull scissors, artsy. "Guess again."

He scrutinizes the rest of me—one-dollar Fleetwood Mac tee, camo-print shorts, Converse lowtops decorated in rainbow-colored Sharpie, five silver hoops in my ears. His gaze is a once-over that would feel creepy if it weren't part of this game we're apparently playing. "Film production?" he finally says.

I slash a finger across my throat like a knife. "Wrong. Science. And your internship? Let me guess."

I inventory the guy and input the following: curly dark hair, brown freckled skin, amber eyes, perfect teeth, no visible piercings or tattoos, plain blue tee, jeans, Keds. *Abercrombie model?* Doubtful modeling is one of the internships the ten of us teens have slogged to New Mexico for, I snoop for some other clue. And there it is, a small, gold treble clef dangling from a leather cord around his neck.

"Musician," I say.

"Lucky guess," he retorts, but I can tell he's impressed.

"Maybe." I raise my eyebrows and try not to smile. "Or maybe I have psychic powers." I close my eyes now and make a spooky Ouija-board-meets-fortune-teller kind of sound.

"And you play the...it's coming to me...wait for it...your instrument...it's...violin." I cock open an eye and look at him.

"Not bad," he says, staring at me as if I just invented Pop-Tarts. "How'd you know?"

I point at the instrument case with the name Clem (also on his nametag) written on it. "It was either a violin in there or a submachine gun and you're here for the terrorist internship." The joke falls flat, so I clear my throat and attempt embarrassment-recovery. "I knew a dog called Clem once. Man that thing farted a lot," I say, realizing too late that a farting dog sharing your name isn't exactly a winning statement. "Oo-kaay. I'll just shut up now."

But he's smiling. Not that I care what he's doing or thinking. Why should I? I'm here to learn. Not to flirt. And he's too good-looking to be smart. Or funny. Or...are his eyes really amber or would you say honey?

"My mom's an old hippy," he says, interrupting my digressing synapses. "I guess violin was in my destiny. She named me after Vassar."

"Huh?" I say, hoping my expression isn't as stupid as my word choice.

"Vassar Clements?" he says, as if the name should mean something to me. "The Grammy-award-winning fiddler? Bill Monroe and the Bluegrass Boys? Old and in the Way with Jerry Garcia?"

I fold my arms. "Isn't Jerry Garcia dead?"

"Don't tell my mom that." He laughs. "Dead in body, not in spirit, that's what she says." A trio of interns passes, two girls and a guy. "What about her?" he says, changing subject and pointing to a rail-thin blonde with long, straight hair and cut-off jeans. "What internship do you think she's here for?"

"Vegan activism," I say, without missing a beat. "And him?" I point to an Asian guy with dyed blond hair.

"Filmmaking," he answers, just as quick. "Him?"

"Web design. Her?"

"Organic farming."

"Really?" I say, checking out the girl's spunky red frizz and freckles. "I was thinking more like children's museum assistant director or camp counselor."

"No way. Check out the shoes. The organic farming interns always wear hiking boots."

"Always? As in you've done this before?"

He laces his long fingers and cracks his knuckles. "I'm a local, and the best violinist under eighteen in the state, so I get the Pro Musica internship every year."

"And very modest, too, I see."

"Yeah, well, big fish, small pond." He sighs and rakes those long fingers through his curls. "I'm hoping to go to Julliard in the fall. I'm accepted a year early, but I'm waiting to hear if I get a full ride. So what's your story?"

I don't want to get into it with a stranger. My story sounds like a trailer for a sappy TV drama in the telling. I can just hear the voiceover and the cheesy music: *After her ex-junkie-mom's murder, a young city girl's aptitude in science propels her out of obscurity and lands her in beautiful Santa Fe, which also happens to be the birthplace of her absentee father.* "No story," I say, with a shrug.

"In other words, a huge story, but it's a secret and you don't want to tell me." His eyes are playful, teasing, would I say flirting? I'm about to brush him off with a "whatever dude," when a dark-haired, twenty-something woman with a pierced nose walks in and calls us to attention.

"Welcome interns!" she bellows. "My name's Guadalupe. I'm the internship and dorm supervisor. Grab a chair and let's begin orientation."

Clem snatches his violin case and plunks into the chair next to me, forcing the redhead, whose chair he's abducted, to relocate and setting off a ludicrous round of musical chairs. Much as I hate to admit it, I can't say I'm not a tiny bit pleased.

When everyone's found a seat in the circle, Guadalupe begins. "If you have any problems over the next six weeks, you can see me. You're all in for an excellent summer. This internship program is a model for community outreach, educational enrichment, and job development throughout the country. We have high school interns at magazines, in charitable foundations, in leading scientific and arts organizations. Before I go over rules and answer questions, I'd like you each to introduce yourself."

"I'm Rejina with a j," the bubbly blonde to Guadalupe's right says with a drawl. "I'm from Texas, and I'm here for the O'Keeffe internship."

"I'm Bill with a B," the next boy says. "I'm here for an internship with Challenge New Mexico, therapeutic horseback riding for people with physical and mental disabilities."

The red head is next. "Hi!" Her voice matches her hair— cute and spunky. "I'm totally excited to be here! I'm Dahlia from Minnesota, and I'm totally excited to be here!" She giggles. "Oops, I already said that. I'm here for the organic farming internship at Camino de la Paz."

I catch Clem's eye and smile.

The rest of the interns introduce themselves, and sure enough, the Asian guy is here for film production, the tall blonde for a magazine, the short, frizzy-haired Bro Boy ("Yo, Bro, I'm from Boston") for a charitable foundation, the African

American girl for costume design at the opera, and the shy, pale girl for a Canyon Road art gallery. I'm the only one here for science, and Clem the only one for music. When we finish introductions, Guadalupe goes over rules—don't have sex or get pregnant or take drugs or drink alcohol or stay out past ten.

"Finally," she says, "in celebration of the tenth anniversary of the internship program, today's paper has a feature article about you all, what you'll be doing, and where you're from. I only brought one, but you can buy a copy or see it online."

The paper gets passed around the circle. When it's my turn, I skim the article, but before I hand it off another news story catches my eye: *A New Drug for Northern New Mexico*. With a dead junkie mom and sixteen years around the whole Philly drug scene, I can't help but pause to read.

May 1, 2014

By Julia Martinez, *Santa Fe New Mexican*

The sleepy town of Chimayo, fifteen miles north of Santa Fe, known for its towering cottonwoods, flowing creek, and Santuario with its holy dirt, has a darker side—a history of heroin abuse and overdose.

Now, a new drug has infiltrated this town. Liquid gold, a Schedule 1 illegal substance, is making its way into this small community as a recreational drug. However, it is not just the recreational use of liquid gold that worries the police. Santa Fe officer Virgil says liquid gold is also known as a date-rape drug, slipped easily and without detection into drinks and rendering the person who drinks it unable to perceive their surroundings.

Holly Redding, community activist and founder of the environmental group, UpsideDown!, voiced her concerns about the drug and its impact on the

community. "As if we don't have enough environmental and social concerns to worry about in New
Mexico with the rise of GMOs, drought, mining, the
use of dirty coal in our energy economy, heroin, and
poverty, now we have another new drug. The health
of the land and the health of the people, it's one and
the same."

Liquid gold comes from a rare Peruvian plant in
the genus *Brugmansia*. Until recently, its high price
tag has made it an elite drug without widespread
use. However, the past few months have seen an
influx of liquid gold in the communities of Northern
New Mexico.

Bro boy to my left clears his throat, as in "you gonna spend
all day with that thing or can I have a look?"

"Sorry," I say, and hand him the paper.

Rejina with a j is saying something to the group, but my
mind is on the article. It's not that there's a drug around. I
can handle that. Growing up with a junkie was about the best
stay-off-drugs campaign imaginable. I'm so clean I squeak.
The government should start an anti-drug campaign: "Want to
keep your kids off drugs? Spend a day with a junkie! It's free.
It's easy. Just dial 1-800-junkie." What my thoughts stick on is
the name of the plant the drug comes from: *Brugmansia*. I've
heard that name before, but I can't remember where or why.

I'm still distracted and trying to figure it out when Clem
leans over and says, "Dinner?"

Two

I load my tray with pasta, a few token pieces of lettuce, a double helping of soft-serve chocolate ice cream, and take a seat with Clem in the back of the cafeteria by the bathrooms.

"So, you've been playing violin long?" I ask, as I dig into the soft-serve—eating dessert first, a decree from when my mom was alive, and one I currently abide by whenever I'm out of the organic, gluten-free clutches of Aunt T, my legal guardian.

Clem's face lights up, a radiant, from inside smile. "Just since I was three."

"Wow, you started old. I spoke Urdu and Finnish by the time I was two," I say, keeping a straight face. "What kind of music do you play?"

"Classical." He ignores my joke and rocks onto his knees. "I plan on being a soloist in the Chicago Symphony or the New York Philharmonic. Only four percent of all orchestra members in the whole country are black or Hispanic. I'm going to up that number."

"Cool. So, which are you?" My own mixed race too-brown-to-be-white-too-white-to-be-brown ethnicity often prompts similarly rude questions, so I should know better than to ask, but given it's too late to have not asked, when he doesn't answer, I push. "You said only four percent are black or Hispanic, and you're going to up the number, so you have to be one or the other. I can't really tell."

Now he gives a sly smile and relaxes back into his seat. "Guess."

I shrug and swipe my bangs out of my eyes. "Fifty-fifty chance. I go with Hispanic."

He laughs, showing off a set of impossibly straight, white chompers. "It was a trick question. My Dad's half Venezuelan, half Chinese. My mom's half Nigerian, half white."

"Wow," I say, slurping down a spoonful of ice cream. "You're like, international man. You have what, four continents covered?"

"Local wherever I go, that's me. My mom took me to Alaska when I was twelve. They thought I was Inuit. What about you? What's your ethnic bubble?"

"Someone once asked me if I was Filipina. I didn't even know what Filipina was. I thought it was some kind of drink."

We both laugh, but my strategy of avoiding the question does nothing to deter him. "So? What is it? What's your bubble?"

"White mom. No idea about my dad, but I like to think he was a cross between Che Guevara and Crazy Horse, so usually I just go with 'other,'" I say casually, as if the answer's no big deal, but the question of my parents brings up that nagging issue of The Jerk again, my father who I never met. A blast of pop-rap music spills into the cafeteria from some passing hipster. Someone shouts a joke about the person's musical taste followed by a burst of laughter and musical retaliation by an increase in volume. "So, anyway, big day tomorrow," I say, thankful for the interruption. I stand and pick up my tray. "I have to go unpack and get ready."

"Me too." Clem stands up with me.

"You're staying at the dorms?" I ask, surprised.

"Yep. I convinced my mom to let me live here, like a stay-cation, so I could get in on some dorm life. I'm an only child. My mom's kind of overly protective. It was a compromise as long as I promised to have dinner with her twice a week."

"What about your dad? What does he think?" I'm prying, but fair's fair. I told him my paternal history—or the absence thereof. His turn to spill.

"No idea what he thinks," Clem says with a shrug. "He lives in LA. Vacation parent. I see him twice a year for three days."

"Hey!" Rejina calls from across the cafeteria, beckoning us over to her table before I can reply. "Y'all ready for tomorrow?" she asks when we get there. Clem and Rejina banter a bit about first day jitters, though Clem doesn't appear to actually have any and seems to be making them up for Rejina, who talks too much and seems totally nervous. "You guys want to party tonight?" We're both standing there, but clearly she's only talking to Clem. "A few of us are meeting at Dahlia's room, then walking to town."

"Nah," Clem says, and although he's looking at Rejina, I feel his attention on me. "It's cool."

She looks disappointed as we walk away, but I notice that she doesn't ask for my answer.

Clem and I leave the cafeteria together and head to the dorm where the interns are housed. As we enter the building and walk down the hall, we pass door after door, some decorated with hand-drawn signs, announcing names of the occupants, others with cartoons or posters for bands, personal badges of introductory statements: *Hello. I'm a metal head, who are you?*

We reach the end of the hall and Clem stops outside a closed door with no personal deco. "This is me," he says. I'm about to say later and take off when he adds, "Would you like to come in, so I can play you a song? A good-night serenade, milady?"

"Cute, but I seem to remember a 'no opposite sex in your rooms' rule."

"Live dangerously," he says and unlocks the door.

I can't resist a challenge. I follow him in.

He opens his violin case, adjusts the pegs, and bows each string in the magical act of tuning. Then he starts to play. And there you have it, ladies and gents. Faith Flores melts. I don't even like classical music, but this is something different. This music is silk and clouds and butter and…well, just really freaking amazing. Standing there listening to him play I think how there's who we want to be, and who we try to be, and who others think we are or should be. And then there's just the truth—who we actually are. That's the space Clem's music comes from.

He finishes and takes a bow. I'm too stunned to do anything but stare at him.

"So, you didn't like it, then?" he says, taking my silence for disapproval. "I can play other stuff, too. Not just classical. I can—"

"No," I interrupt, finding my way back to the physical world, the room, my feet on the floor. My voice. "It was…magic."

I would think someone with this kind of talent would have arrogance written all over their face, but Clem's smile is shy and grateful and modest, and when we say goodnight, I leave his room with the gift of not just his music, but of his smile, too.

The second I start huffing up the steps to my room on the second floor, though, gifts and magic are replaced by altitude-induced aerobic distress. *Hello, body! You can start producing a few extra red blood cells and capillaries any time now.* I get to my room, breathless, and collapse onto the bed. I zone and stare out the window as the sun dips lower in the enormous turquoise sky, turning the distant mountains a shade of pink I've never before seen. I'm beat from the journey, starting early this morning in Philly. My eyes are just drooping shut, Clem's violin lingering in my mind like a yummy musical aftertaste, when I hear laughter and talking in the hall.

"Come on!" a girl's voice I recognize as one of the arts' interns says.

Her summons is met with giggles and a discourse on where the intern gaggle should go and what they should do. I remember Rejina inviting us—well, inviting Clem, anyway—to go party, and I imagine wherever they're going and whatever they're doing will involve some first-night-rule breaking. And with this thought of partying and rule breaking I'm back to the newspaper article: *A New Drug for Northern New Mexico.* I'm contemplating *Brugmansia* again, when my FaceTime ringtone sounds.

I swipe and see Jesse's blue eyes. "Christmas," he says when he sees my face.

"Chanukah," I retort. Ask Jesse what day it is and instead of an answer, he might tell you, for example, that the name Friday comes from the Old English meaning the day of Frigg. Or that The 4-Skins are a working class punk band from the East End of London.

"No. Not Chanukah," he snorts. "Chile peppers. That's what they ask you in New Mexico when you go to a restaurant: red, green, or Christmas. Red chile, green chile, or both? Get it? Christmas. The whole chile thing is confusing if you ask me," he goes on. I didn't ask, but before I can elucidate this fact, he continues. "What's up with calling them chile peppers anyway? Did you know they're not even in the pepper family? And why in New Mexico is chile spelled with an e at the end and not an i?"

"Shouldn't you be studying?"

"Nah. I'm good." He flashes a big grin. "Studied for twenty minutes already. I have ten days before the ACT. So, how was it? Your big first day in the Land of Enchantment. Enchanting?"

I flip onto my side and stare out the window at all that space and too much sky. It's like the opposite of claustrophobic. It's open-o-phobic. Where's the corner store? The DQ? The Wawa? "Pretty good, I guess."

"'Pretty good?' Could you possibly give a duller answer? That's like saying good job or nice work or not bad or—"

"I found out something interesting," I cut in, more than anything to stop his rant before it really gets going. "I saw an article in the paper today." I tell him about *Brugmansia* and the drug making its way through the area.

"Faith," he says, and now his tone is serious, "you have that voice."

"What voice?"

"The one that says you're going to stick your nose in something that has nothing to do with you, as opposed to sticking it into something that does have to do with you, like your father. Have you started looking for him?"

With this reminder of The Jerk, my thoughts jump to my just-in-case file (just in case I do decide to look for him), a manila envelope with two things I found in Mom's stuff after she died: a blurry photo of The Jerk and an article torn from the Santa Fe newspaper dated two years ago, saying he'd been arrested here for drug possession. "No," I say, turning from the window.

"Why not?"

"Because if I look for him I might find out he's a worse jerk than I already think he is. Or that he's a drug addict like mom was and I have two sets of junkie genes. Or he's part of some fundamentalist, right wing cult or he's a Satan worshipper or a polygamist."

"Or a right wing-Satan-worshipping-polygamist-murderer who sucks the blood of small children."

"I'm serious, Jesse. I didn't come here to find the guy. I came for the internship. I'm just not sure looking for him is a good idea."

"And neither is letting fear make your decisions."

"It's not fear," I say defensively.

"Then what is it?"

"I don't know. Self-protection. Common sense."

"Well, you're there for six weeks. A lot can happen in that time." He pauses. Even though our FaceTime eye contact is an illusion, I feel the intensity of his gaze. "I miss you. Stay out of trouble."

"What trouble could I possibly get into?" I tease, resorting to default mode when it comes to expressions of sincerity, but then I add, "I miss you, too."

We say good night and hang up. As I strip off my clothes and climb into bed I can't help but wonder if the possibility of finding out something horrible about a parent is worse than having no parent at all.

Three

I wake up recharged the next morning, ready to check out the seriously ass-kicking molecular miracle of plant genes. The lab isn't exactly a place most kids my age fantasize about, but for me, total dreamville. Adventures in microbiology day one, here I come.

I slug down a quick breakfast, then take the cross-town bus and arrive fifteen minutes later at the Salazar Center for Plant Genomics. A thin woman I'd guess to be in her mid-twenties, dressed in jeans and a plaid button-down, with academic-chic round glasses, wavy blond hair, and freckles, meets me in the lobby.

"You must be Faith. I'm Esha Margolis," she says, extending her hand.

"It's nice to meet you," I respond with the polite and practiced greeting drilled into me by Aunt T when she saw me toss my head and give a "Wuzzup?" to a teacher I saw at Walmart. Looking at Esha, though, I get the feeling that a "Wuzzup" wouldn't bring about the end of civilization. She has a hip, laid-back vibe, the kind of cool you don't try to be, you just are.

"It's great to finally meet you, too," she says with a comfortable smile. "I'm glad to have you here. You know, Faith, over 300 students applied for this position, but as soon as I saw your application I had a feeling you were the brightest of the bunch. And then after we spoke, I knew I was right. I think you'll be a great help to me this summer. You're just the person for this job."

Instead of basking in the glow of her praise, I fizzle with anxiety. I reach into my pocket and finger Mom's Zippo to calm my nerves. *What if she's wrong? What if I'm not just the person for the job? What if I'm not good at detailed lab work?* The cool metal of Mom's Zippo in my fist helps me relax. I've kept the lighter since her death—and why not a lighter? Little kids have blankets and stuffed animals. Adults have Xanax. I have a Zippo.

"Before we head down to the lab, I want to introduce you to Dr. Richmond, the president of SCPG." Esha leads me down a hall and knocks on the door of a corner office. A moment later a woman with a blond, blunt-cut bob and a sharp, angular face like a geometry lesson comes out to greet us. Esha introduces her as Dr. Richmond and says something about her big project with the New Mexico chile, the details of which I don't hear because as I shake this polished professional's hand, the president of the entire company, my anxiety spikes to an even higher level. Dr. Richmond looks at me like she's expecting Esha's new teen intern—who's been chosen out of 300 applicants—to speak and not just stand there, mute.

"So, why are they called chile peppers, anyways?" are the mortifying words that come out of my mouth, an uncharming regurgitation from Jesse. I should leave my verbal vomit at that, but with both women looking at me, nerves keep me talking. "They're not even in the pepper family, and why do you guys spell chile with an e at the end and not an i?" *And thank you very much, ladies and gentlemen. I will now die of embarrassment.*

"Those are great questions," Dr. Richmond says, preventing my untimely demise. "In answer to your first question, we really don't call them peppers around the lab for just for that reason. They're in the *Capsicum* genus—from the capsaicin alkaloid that makes them so hot. At least one story about why they're called peppers has to do with Christopher Columbus."

"What, like he wanted to commit genocide against them?" I bite my lip and think this time my mouth really has gone too far.

Esha laughs and answers for Dr. Richmond. "It's that he was the first European to discover them. He was looking for another type of black pepper and he found small, hot pods that were used as seasoning by the Native Americans. He called them *pimientos*—meaning 'black peppers' in Spanish. The name stuck I guess."

"Well, the dude had a real problem with getting names of things correct."

"Can't argue with you on that," Esha responds, fiddling with her necklace.

"As for the spelling," Dr. Richmond says, picking back up my other question. "In New Mexico, chile with an *e* refers to a capsicum pepper. Chili with an *i* is the Texas chili dish—*chili con carne*—chili with ground meat, beans, and spices. The Spanish who immigrated to New Mexico changed the indigenous name *chilli* to chile."

"And not only that," Esha pitches in, "in 1983 a New Mexico senator had the chile with an *e* spelling actually entered into the Congressional Record."

"Wow. You guys are like serious hardcore chile historians." I give a double thumbs-up and flash a smile, hoping I look enthusiastic and not psychotic.

"Not just historians. We're about the future," Esha says. "Dr. Richmond is going to change the future of the industry with her genetically modified seed."

"Modified for what?" I ask, hoping she hadn't explained that before when I was shaking Dr. Richmond's hand and too nervous to listen.

"For a chile resistant to an insect called the beet leafhopper that's been decimating the crop for the last five years," Dr. Richmond replies. "With climate change and warmer winters, it seems we've created conditions for them to thrive. The chile is vital to New Mexico. Not just to the culture and food, but to the economy as well."

"Right! I got this one! Red or green? The state question. I didn't actually know states had official questions. Like what's South Dakota's question? Or Arkansas'? And why's there an *s* at the end of Arkansas anyway?" I reach into my pocket for the lighter, clear my throat, and make myself stop rambling. "Have you finished the project?"

"We're in the final stage of field-testing now. In one month we're having a board dinner to celebrate their official release to the public." She smiles at Esha. "Esha's in charge of that event. I'm sure she'll benefit from your help with the dinner. She's been working day and night to help me get this off the ground."

"Of course," I say. Then I contemplate the whole genetic engineering thing. Aunt T, having donated to save the bees and the sea turtles, gets gobs of requests for money from environmental groups. I've seen more than one letter coming to her with slogans touting the evils of GMOs. "So, are people into the GMO thing around here? I've heard they're dangerous."

"Everyone has something to say about genetically modified foods these days," Dr. Richmond responds.

"What, like you turn into a mutant if you eat one?" I'm trying to be funny, but this time nobody laughs.

"Let's just say there's a lot of misinformation out there." It's Esha who replies this time.

Dr. Richmond nods thoughtfully and looks at me. "You have to be careful about your sources and what you read and who you talk to. When it comes to GMOs, people easily let their emotions get in the way. There are plenty of people out there with kneejerk reactions to anything GMO, people who might say you're putting yourself at a risk for cancer if you eat them. Tumors. Allergies."

"What do you think?" I ask.

"I base conclusions on research, knowledge, and evidence. Let's say you saw a graph that showed the rise of autism with the rise of organic food, would you say organic food causes autism? Or if someone does yoga every day and gets cancer, would you say yoga causes cancer?" Dr. Richmond looks at me, but I don't think she's expecting an answer. "Just because two events happen at the same time doesn't mean one caused the other. That's what happens all the time with GMOs. People get scared. They think a GMO causes some symptom and they leap to conclusions. It's easier to know what to believe when you make things black and white. Science and media can easily be manipulated to scare people into believing anything. But there's no scientific evidence that GMO foods pose any risk to the consumer." She walks into her office and motions me to follow. "Look at this," she says, and points to a world map that's covered with red and green dots. "The red dots represent the Earth's current population of seven billion people."

I nod and study the clusters. "And the green ones?"

"Projected population of 2050. Nine billion."

"That's a lot of people," I say, the ultimate "duh" answer.

She turns away from the map and looks at me with those sharp and focused eyes. "You think we can feed all those people the way things are?"

"I don't know," I admit. "I'm guessing not?"

"Not if we want to have trees and forests. Genetically engineered food will play a critical role in addressing global food security." She looks like she wants to say something more, but her phone rings. She checks the screen and tells me she has to take the call. I leave and she closes the door behind her.

Esha leads me down a flight of stairs and into the lab, a brightly lit, clean white room. Stainless steel counters line the walls. Big box-like machines sit on tables. From the lab I visited back in Philly when I was investigating my mom's death I recognize the machines as DNA sequencers. "So, here it is," she says, gesturing into the space. "Your home away from home for the next six weeks."

As she gives me a key and a swipe card for the building and the lab, a black guy with short, tight dreads, and wearing a Green Day concert T-shirt looks up from his computer. "You play volleyball?" he asks in the kind of extremely cool British accent that reminds me of the Orcs from *Lord of the Rings.*

I flash on an unpleasant image of a school gym and a volleyball net and vigorously shake my head.

"We have a game today at five," he goes on. "I'm captain of the SCPG team. We're playing the guys from Los Alamos. They beat us last year, so if you can serve it up, you'd better let me know."

"Don't worry about volleyball," Esha says, noticing the horror on my face. "It's not a prerequisite for working here. Faith, this is Jonah, operations manager. Jonah, meet Faith, our intern." Jonah reaches out with a fist bump and starts in again on volleyball, but Esha cuts him off. "Your basic job for the next few days will be to enter bar codes and sequencing instructions for DNA samples into the database and then work on quality control of the samples," she tells me. "After that we'll move into bioinformatics." She leads me to a desk separated from the sequencing machines by a cubicle partition covered in blue fabric and taps a computer to life. "We get an average of fifty samples a week. The work isn't the most exciting, but it's important to be thorough and not make any mistakes. Working in a lab is all about precision. A mistake could mean ruining years and years of someone's research."

"Yeah, but no pressure!" Jonah calls.

"Shut up!" Esha lobs back, but there's a smile in her voice. She enters one bar code as an example, hands me a glass vial filled with clear liquid, and asks if I understand. I tell her I do. She fingers her pendant, a tribal-looking thing hanging from a beaded chain, as I enter the first bar code on my own.

"Cool necklace," I say when I've entered the information.

"This?" She looks down as if just remembering it's there. "Thanks. Gift from an old boyfriend. Now, why don't you get started? I'm around if you have any questions."

Jonah pokes his head around the divider the second Esha sets off for her own desk. "You like music?"

"You like to breathe?"

He laughs. "Excellent. Because everyone gets a day to choose tunes, and it's a tradition that the newbie gets to choose their first day. So you bring anything? Again, no pressure. If I don't like what you picked I'll send you into deep freeze with the samples."

Most of the music I listen to has a painful, tragic honesty to it, songs that feel somehow too personal to share, as if my musical taste will reveal an insight about me I don't want others to see. So I go with Jesse's song collection. "I have this,"

I say, taking my iPod with Jesse's playlist from my pocket. "It's kind of eclectic."

"Eclectic's good. As long as it's not American country. 'I lost my girl and I drank a beer then I crashed my motorcycle and now I'm broke.'" He attempts to sound twangy and Southern, but the British accent gets in the way.

"I heard that!" Esha calls from the other side of the room. "And for the thousandth time it's *alt* country, not country."

The two tease each other about music while Jonah plugs my device into the sound system. As the first rock-meets-reggae track sings to life, everyone goes back to work.

I zone in on my task, becoming one with the vials, descending into a trance of bar codes and numbers. Entering bar codes might not be the most monumental scientific task, but the process of DNA sequencing is a scientific assembly line—the whole only as good as the sum of its parts. I imagine the work and research these flasks represent, what knowledge awaits discovery. I enter the information with a mechanical precision that's a relief from the imprecision and chaos of the outside world. Before I know it, it's time for lunch and Esha's back at my side.

"You got all these done this morning?" she asks, examining the rows of vials in the ice buckets, waiting for storage in deep freeze.

"Yeah. It wasn't that hard. I mean, I don't think I ruined anyone's research." I don't want to sound like I'm bragging, so I add, "Entering bar codes isn't exactly complex genetics."

"You'd be surprised how many ways there are to screw it up," she says. "You ready to eat?"

I tell her I am, and we go outside and park ourselves at a picnic table under a big shade tree. The sky is a moody mosaic of clouds and light. I'm watching a funnel of rain across the valley, listening to the crackle of thunder, when Esha asks me how I got interested in genetics.

"I had a biology teacher who said genetics was the forefront of scientific discovery. I liked the way that sounded." I rip open a bag of Doritos with my teeth and leave out the rest of the story—the real story of how I actually learned genetics, which had nothing to do with school and everything to do with a fake clinical trial and murder. "What about you? How'd you get into it?"

She contemplates her answer as she picks through leafy greens in a Tupperware container. "After my PhD I traveled for a while. I went to South America, and I became fascinated with the tropical forest," she says, spearing a blade of spinach. "Twenty-five percent of our medicines come from the rainforest, you know, and only about ten percent of the plants in the jungle have even been studied. There are so many things to learn about them, so many ways they can help us, and like you, I wanted to be part of the discovery." She puts the salad to the side, unwraps an expensive-looking protein bar, and looks out toward the distant mountains. "I got sidetracked for a while," she says without elaborating on how or why, "but eventually I knew what I wanted to do, so I came to New Mexico to work here." She takes a bite of the protein bar, then holds it out to inspect, nose wrinkled. "Tastes like sawdust," she says, inspecting the wrapper and the list of gluten-free, soy-free, anti-oxidant, no-creature-harmed-in-the-making-of, planet-saving list of ingredients. "GMO-free is listed as a health benefit," she says with a sarcastic laugh. "I think I paid three dollars for this thing."

"So, I guess you're on the side of GMOs? I mean, duh. Obviously. You work here." A few drops of rain plunk down hard on the table. Thunder rumbles.

"I'm certainly not into big agricultural companies manipulating our food economy," she says, "but there are uses for genetic engineering beyond agriculture that could help us in ways we can't even yet imagine." I wait for her to say more, but a cloud directly above us lets loose, and now it really pisses down, a deluge that makes me think of building arcs and counting animals by twos. "Ahh! Welcome to New Mexico!" Esha shouts over a clap of thunder. She shoves her food into her lunch sack, and we race for the building. "Don't like the weather? Wait five minutes!"

She's right. By the time I dry my hair under the hand drier in the bathroom and get back to the lab, the sun's gloating over a double rainbow. Jonah's spinning the tunes now, but I'm too absorbed in my work to listen. I enter DNA data for professors and research scientists all over the country. Even Esha's gotten in on the act, I notice, as I input a vial with her name on it.

Like the morning, the afternoon flies by. I'm so busy with bar codes and sample storage that I have no idea what time it is until I hear Jonah inform Esha it's time for volleyball and to go crush the opposition, which he says in an Orc-meets-the-Terminator-mash-up-Euro accent that makes me laugh.

"I don't think I'm up for it," I hear Esha respond.

I try not to listen to the argument unfolding, but unless I stick my fingers in my ears and sing, there's no avoiding overhearing. I hear Jonah when he tells Esha it's the second time she's used this excuse. I hear her insist she's too tired. I hear Jonah concede with a grumble, and finally, I watch as he leaves for the day.

I follow Jonah's lead and pack up, expecting Esha to call it a day, too, but when I pass her desk, she's hunched in front of the computer, no signs of quitting. I say good-bye, and head for the bus back to the dorm, wondering, despite myself, if Clem will be around.

Four

Rejina, Bro Boy, and a few other interns are hanging around in the dorm entrance when I get back. Rejina's telling the group about her Amazing! First! Day! at the O'Keeffe Museum, and how she'll be going to Ghost Ranch, the real Georgia O'Keeffe country, for a two-day study with the art curator, and how Georgia (apparently she and the famous dead artist are on a first-name basis) was just the Most! Inspiring! Painter! To prove it she points to a print of some O'Keeffe painting of a white flower hanging on the wall. A few others tell about their first day, and then the conversation hits the inevitable topic of evening plans and who's doing what and going where. I join in a bit, but this is the happiness brigade—the metaphorical high school cheerleaders with their aggressive joy and parties and streams of selfies on Instagram and Snapchat—and I feel like a cactus, all spines and prickles, in a sea of sunflowers.

I keep an eye out for Clem as I half-listen to them plan, telling myself I don't care if he shows up, but when he doesn't show up, I take off, telling myself I'm not looking for him, then I detour by his room on the way to mine.

Violin music drifts from behind his closed door. A beautiful, complex piece, and then the music stops, and I hear, "Shit!"

followed by more expletives. A minute later the music resumes, repeating the part I just heard. I'm tempted to eavesdrop on the practice session, but it's too stalkerish to stand outside the door, so I head up to my room.

I consider calling Jesse when I get there and responding to his voice mail, but I don't. Instead I call Aunt T to check in and update her on my first day. I tell her about meeting Esha and Dr. Richmond and the lab work and the dorm, but I specifically don't mention The Jerk. Aunt T thinks digging into the past to find a guy who abandoned my mom when she was three months pregnant will only lead to hurt. Still, the topic lurks in the background, its omission only shedding more light on its presence.

When we hang up, the energy of avoiding the subject has placed it in the forefront of my brain. I take out my father's photo from the just-in-case file and study it, trying to imagine the features blurred by an unsteady hand. Do we look alike? Are his eyes the same brown as mine? Staring at the photo, I realize Jesse's right. Screw it. I'm not letting fear guide me. Alvaro Flores, I'm going to find out about you.

I decide to take a shower—as good a place as any for planning a mission. As I soak under the hot water, I ponder the best place to start the search. I have no idea how one goes about locating a person they've never met. I finally reason that the library's as good a place to start as any.

I'm heading back to my room, clad in a bathrobe, hair wrapped turban-style in a towel, when I smack into Clem.

"Hey!" he says, ignoring the fact of my near nakedness. "I was just coming to find you."

I clutch my toiletries to my chest, wondering what the protocol is for bumping into a cute boy while dripping wet and one step away from unclothed. I power up a smile. "Well, looks like you found me."

"I'm hungry," he says, apparently oblivious to the awkwardness of the situation. "You want to get something to eat?"

"I was actually thinking about going to the library," I say, wondering if we're going to have an entire conversation in the hall while I'm in my bathrobe.

"Cool, we have three libraries. The closest is downtown. I could show you."

I study the small puddle pooling at my feet. "I guess so. Sure."

"Great. Let's go."

"Um, one small problem," I say to the floor. "I might need to get dressed first?"

He blasts out a string of apologies, as if only now noticing I'm a step away from naked, says he'll wait for me out front, and rushes off.

I dart back to my room, terrified of bumping into someone else in the hall, and throw on my clothes still crumbled on the floor from yesterday, then slip into my Converses, run a brush through my hair, and set off.

"It's about a fifteen-minute walk to the library," Clem tells me when I join him in front of the dorm.

I wait for him to say it's a fifteen-minute walk and therefore he'll drive. I'm a city girl, or a formerly city girl before I moved to the suburbs last December with Aunt T. To get from point A to point B, I took a bus or a train, and on the rare occasion I had cash on hand, a taxi. If I had to walk it meant city blocks. Traffic. Noise. Rude dudes with rude gestures. Buildings. Stores. Not this lip-cracking heat and backdrop of mountains and sky and houses in an unvarying palette of brown and beige.

When Clem doesn't say anything about driving, I lie through my teeth. "Walking's cool," I say and start down the hill.

There's something elemental and in-your-face about this place, with its mountains and thin air and dry heat, a reminder that no matter what, nature has the final say. I'm not sure I like it, but I respect it in the way you respect a hornet or a rattlesnake.

When we arrive at the library, I unglue my lips from my teeth with a long guzzle of water, then we find a seat at one of the tables in the front room. "You didn't say why we were here," Clem says and pulls up his shirt to wipe his sweaty forehead. I try not to notice the flash of taut brown skin, but trying not to notice just makes me notice more. "You like to read?"

"Huh?" I say, quickly pulling my eyes from his abs to his face. "I mean, yeah, but I'm not checking out books." I glance around as if someone might be listening. I don't want the guy with the huge backpack using the computer, or the blue-haired girl with the dog, or anyone for that matter, to overhear. I sigh and frown down at my fingers. "Okay, here's the deal. My would-be father was born in this town, and I know that two years ago he was here. I never thought I cared or wanted to know about him, but I guess I'm curious, so I thought…" I stop talking because truthfully I have no idea what I thought I'd find out in a library.

Clem seems to read my dead-end conclusion. "If he was born here, maybe he grew up here. And if he grew up here, he might be in a high school yearbook," he suggests.

The idea is good, but I slump into my chair still unsure how much, if anything, I want to know. It's too hard to explain the back-and-forth tumble of my feelings, so I just say, "I have no idea what school he went to or where I'd even get a yearbook."

"That's easy," Clem says. "There are only two public high schools here, or at least there were only two five years ago. They donate yearbooks to the library each year, so if he went to public school, we should at least be able to find out which high school he went to. Not that I'm helping or interfering," he quickly adds. "I'm just saying."

"No." I sit up, reinvigorated by the idea. "I mean, you're not. I mean, that's a great idea."

Clem leads us past the circulation desk to a reading room, several shelves of which are dedicated to Santa Fe and Capital High yearbooks. The yearbooks go all the way back to the nineteen seventies. I have no idea how old my father is, but assuming he's about the same age as Mom was, I start with the nineties. I show Clem my father's photo, tell him his name, and we start to search.

Side-by-side we scan photos of sports teams, thespian clubs, and all the various high school cliques and groupings. We study individual portraits of freshman, sophomores, juniors, and seniors. After scouring three yearbooks and matching columns of photos with names, I realize this search could take hours.

"We should focus on just the senior photos," I say, shutting a Santa Fe High yearbook from 1993. "Those pictures are big and the names are underneath. I mean, assuming he graduated and didn't drop out, it'll be faster."

Clem agrees, and I start pouring over senior photos. About fifteen minutes in, I'm tired and frustrated. It's been a long day. I'm hungry, and I'm back to doubting this enterprise. I halfheartedly open my sixth yearbook, ready to quit as I turn to the F's in the senior photos.

That's when I freeze.

In the Capital High graduating class of 1995, I stare at my father's face.

Although the one photo I have of him is fuzzy, although this guy is just a year older than I am now, although there could be more than one Alvaro Flores in Santa Fe, I know without doubt that it's him. I gape at his picture, too overwhelmed to speak, trying to reconcile the image of this handsome kid with my father.

Like all the other senior photos, his has a caption underneath, but unlike most of the others with their song lyrics and inspirational quotes, his says: "Remember the Cowgirl." I'm disappointed at the non sequitur, but then again what was I expecting? Was his picture supposed to be accompanied by his autobiography? So he went to high school here. Big deal.

"You got something?" Clem asks, sensing the fact I've gone rigid and looking up.

"Remember the Cowgirl," I mutter, turning the page to him. "That's a freaking weird thing to put under your senior picture. What, did he have a thing for some girl with spurs? Sounds kinky." I shove the yearbook away from me and get up. "This is stupid. Forget it. Let's go eat."

Clem considers the picture a minute longer and then says, "I know the perfect place."

Twenty minutes later we're standing on the sidewalk outside a restaurant with a crowded outdoor patio filled with young, hip beer-drinkers and a band getting ready to play. When we go inside to find someone to seat us, the first things I notice are the walls—they're plastered with photos of cowgirls and their horses. Every space displays black-and-whites of rodeo gals, horse gals, gals with spurs. It's a veritable cowgirl museum.

"Welcome to the Cowgirl Hall of Fame," Clem says. "Known locally as the Cowgirl, one of the more famous bars and restaurants in Santa Fe." He waves at a few people as we make our way to the hostess. "Maybe your father liked hanging out here with his friends. Maybe he was talking about this place and not about an actual person."

I consider this possibility as the hostess, a girl dressed in a studded Western shirt, jeans, and cowboy boots and hat, leads us to an outside table. Maybe Clem's right, I think as I take the menu from the faux cowgirl. Maybe my father hung out and partied here, and his quote didn't refer to romance with spurs. Senior photo tag lines aren't just inspirational quotes and song lyrics, they're inside jokes, private reminders of good times and partying, as if you need to be able to look back at your eighteen-year-old self and think, man was I sloshed.

"I think it's great you're looking for your dad," Clem says, tossing a what's-up? nod to one of the guys in the band. "I mean it would be cool to know about him, right?"

"I guess," I say, hiding my doubt behind the menu. The closer I get to him—his geography, his place in the world— the more unsettled I feel. What if he sat in this chair? Listened to this band? The idea makes my stomach hurt, and when the waitress (a cute new cowgirl) comes to take our order I'm not hungry. I don't want to let on to Clem how I'm feeling and ruin the meal, so I order Frito pie because, seriously, who can resist a plate of Fritos, chile, and cheese, no matter how low they're feeling?

The band starts up and Clem goes all bobbleheaded, nodding in time with the beat, grinning. When the first song ends, the fiddler, an old guy with a long gray beard, shouts out to Clem, asking him if he wants to play a tune. Clem raises his eyebrows at me. I nod and shoo him away. He jogs to the stage and takes the guy's fiddle. A few words to the band, and a second later they're busting out a tune straight from Appalachia.

At first I think of Jesse, who'd have some random historical detail about the music, but then I'm not thinking of anything.

I'm just here—a girl on a summer night, having dinner on a patio, listening to music. My feet, appendages not normally inclined to keeping rhythm, take off on a toe-tapping hoedown. I'm not thinking or worrying or angst-ing. In fact, I'm watching Clem and smiling. His fingers on the violin neck are giving the speed of light a run for its money. The crowd loves him. They beg for another song when he finishes, but he waves them off, promising to return later if they'll have him. He hands back the fiddle to its owner and rejoins me at the table.

"You really are international man," I tease when he sits down. "You've got Appalachia written all over you. You sure you want to go into classical?"

"Why? You think I'd make a good hillbilly?"

"I don't know. Let's hear your country twang."

He's twanging away like the best of them when a pretty, middle-aged woman with gray hair and a similar skin tone to Clem's, sidles up onto the bench next to him and bumps him with her hip. "Now that's the music I'm talking about," she says with a wink. "You and Vassar really are blood brothers."

Clem lights up and gives the woman an affectionate hug. "Hey, Ma. 'Orange Blossom Special,' just for you." He turns to me and his eyebrows shoot up his forehead. "I hope you don't mind. When you went to the bathroom before we left the library I texted my mom and asked her to come by."

"No, of course I don't mind," I say, despite the pang of jealousy. Not jealousy at having his mom here. I'm cool with the mom thing. It's that he has a mom to be here at all. And a sober mom he obviously adores and who adores him.

"Great." He looks relieved. "Faith, meet my mom, Dolores. Mom, meet Faith."

I'm about to return Dolores' warm smile with a handshake, but before I have a chance, she wraps me up in a bosomy hug as if she's known me all my life. "Nice to meet you, Faith," she says when she releases me. "Clem says you're here all the way from the East Coast to study genetics. If you need anything, you just call me, okay?"

Normally I'm unreceptive to invitations to call on strangers, but somehow in this woman's presence, I drop my defenses and agree.

"I can only stay for a minute, Sweetie," she says, turning her attention back to Clem. "My shift starts in half hour."

"I thought you weren't doing the night shifts anymore," Clem complains. "Your back?"

"I know, but one of the nurses called in sick, and I could use the overtime." She gives him a playful pinch. "I'm fine, Clemmy. Stop worrying and have fun with your friend. Don't forget, dinner Wednesday?"

Clem sighs and agrees. "Just be careful," he tells her.

She chuckles. "I'm supposed to be the one telling that to you." She winks and picks herself off the bench. "Love you, Sweetie. See you Wednesday."

She says good-bye, and we watch her make her way across the patio to the street.

"She works at the hospital," Clem tells me when she's gone. "She's a nurse. I worry about her, you know? Maybe…"

"Maybe what?" I prompt.

"Nah." He looks down. "It's nothing"

"If it was nothing then you wouldn't have said it."

He looks up again. His eyes seem troubled. "I just worry about going to New York City for music school. Leaving my mom. Maybe I should stay closer to home." Before I can respond, he reaches into his backpack and puts the yearbook with my father's photo on the table. "I checked this out while you were in the bathroom."

"Wow, you accomplished a lot while I was in the shitter. Imagine if I'd been constipated."

We both crack up, and as the food comes, his mood seems to brighten. The Frito pie does the job, sparking my salivary glands and returning my appetite to full force. *Frito pie, you are no challenge for me,* I think and dig in.

We listen to the music as we eat. People dance. A pack of kids spins around in unabashed musical glee. A woman, who has to be eighty, dressed head-to-toe in tie-dye, waves her arms above her head and shuffles her feet. There's a cheerful, laid back vibe about the place, and when I'm done eating, I feel light and unburdened. So light, in fact, that before my turbulent emotions surrounding Alvaro Flores have the chance to return, I decide to take action. I push back from my seat, tell Clem I'll be right back, and head inside to find someone who works here.

I find the hostess talking to a waiter, also in Western garb (apparently the Cowgirl is for cowboys, too.) "Excuse me," I say interrupting the adorable cow-people. "I'm looking for someone who used to hang out here, or maybe still does. Alvaro Flores?"

"I've only worked here for a few weeks," the cute cowgirl tells me. "Griz might know. He's worked here forever and knows everyone."

She points me to the bartender. I head his way and instantly understand why he's called Griz. The guy is huge and his face is covered with thick brown hair—eyebrows, beard, mustache— a grizzly bear in human form.

"You have ID?" Griz asks as I approach the bar.

"No," I say, pushing up against the crowded counter between two guys, drinking beer. "And I don't want a drink. I just have a question."

"Well then I have an answer," he says, a smile emerging from his downy cover.

"Okay, well, it's kind of weird."

"Right up my alley."

"So, there's this guy," I begin.

"Uh oh."

"No, it's not like that," I quickly add. "This guy's old, like in his mid-thirties. His name is Alvaro Flores." I show Griz the yearbook picture. "This is kind of an old photo, but I'm wondering if you recognize him or if you've seen him around."

He looks at the photo and then up at me. "I might. Who's asking?"

"He's a friend of my uncle," I say, blurting out the first thing that comes to me. "I'm spending the summer here and my uncle told me to look him up."

A customer asks for a gin and tonic. Griz turns and reaches for a clear bottle from a shelf above a crackled mirror and TV. "You ask if I know Alvaro and if I've seen him," he says when he turns back to me. "The answer is yes and no."

He starts pouring the alcohol into a glass, his attention on the drink now. I'm not sure if he's going to elaborate on the yes and no statement, so I press. "Which part is yes and which is no?"

He stops what he's doing and raises his eyes to me. "I know Alvaro well. Known him since before that picture was taken. He used to hang out here all the time. As far as if I've seen him?" He wipes a hand like a bear paw across his wrinkled brow, then he sighs as if he'd rather say anything than what he's about to tell me. "That's the no part. I haven't seen him because he's dead."

Five

"Dead?" I repeat, choking out the word.

"Yep. Sorry to say. He died about eight months ago."

The customer who ordered the gin and tonic asks where his drink is, another wants a beer. Griz's attention goes to his patrons, but he's back to me a moment later, wiping his hands on a towel. "Your uncle didn't know about this?" he asks, lowering those furry brows.

"My uncle?" I say, momentarily spacing on my story. "Yeah. I mean, no. I guess not. They were..." My voice trails off. "Kind of out of touch. So, anyway, thanks for telling me. I'll let my uncle know." I turn from the counter and start to leave.

"Hey! What's your name?" Griz calls after me.

"Faith Flores," I reply, and scurry away before he can ask any more questions.

Instead of returning to the table, I go to the bathroom where I lock myself in a stall and perch on the edge of the toilet. The memory of finding my mom dead on the bathroom floor smashes into news of my father's death, a head-on collision without a seatbelt. I bury my face in my hands and take a few deep breaths, telling myself that his being dead shouldn't matter since I never even met him. The thing is, though, my mom's death left a hole in me, not just a hole of having lost her, but a hole that emphasized the absence of my other parent, and the word "orphan" pops into my brain—the fact that I'm now officially parentless.

Two girls stumble into the bathroom, chattering loudly in giddy, drunken voices and bursting my privacy bubble. I can't hide in here forever, so I force myself out of the stall and head back into the restaurant.

I stop a few feet from our table. A part of me wants to tell Clem what I found out, but the bigger part wants to keep it in a locked box and throw away the key. I was stupid to bring Clem into my drama in the first place. I clear my throat, smooth my hair, as if hair smoothing can remedy my mental state, and head to the table.

The second I get there, Clem looks at me and asks if I'm okay.

I look away, but I feel his gaze on me. "Yeah. Of course. I'm fine. I just don't feel that great all of a sudden."

The gray-haired band dude calls out to Clem, asks if he's ready to play another tune. Clem holds up a finger, keeping his focus on me.

"No, go ahead," I say, using the music as a chance to make my break. "You should play another one with them. The crowd loves you. I'm going to head back to the dorm and call it a night."

"Then I'll go with you." He leaps out of his chair and swings around to my side, as if he's going to pull out the seat for me. The guy's got serious old school manners like when "please" and "thank you" hadn't yet hit the endangered species list.

"I'm good," I say. "I know the way back." I put on a showcase smile, which the skeptical expression on his face tells me he knows is crap. "I'll see you tomorrow, okay? Here." I reach into my pocket for my wallet and hand him some money for dinner.

"It's on me," he says, refusing the cash and sounding hurt. For a moment I hesitate, thinking I'll stay and tell him what I found out, but then, no way. I want to forget about Alvaro Flores, not broadcast his death to a kid I've known for approximately twenty-seven hours.

I turn and dash across the patio without looking back. I can't get away fast enough.

Back in my dorm room I don't bother turning on a light. I lie on the hard mattress, pinned to the bed like an insect on an entomologist's tray. At least I don't have a roommate to have to make small talk with, I think, as I study my father's yearbook photo. What were he and Mom like as a couple? How'd they meet? Did he love her? Wondering these things gives me a strange, unmoored feeling. They're both dead and I'm still here, tumbling blind through a dark, parentless universe. The sole Flores offspring to carry out the legacy of a junkie mom and a who-knows-what of a father? I guess I'll never know.

I don't know how long I lie there in the silence, pierced only by the occasional voice in the hall, but at some point the tightness in my chest loosens and I'm no longer looking at the yearbook. In fact, at some point I'd stopped thinking about him, and my mind arrived in a zoned-out, empty state some people call enlightenment, others call stoned, and I just call calm. Whatever it is, the end result is when I blink back to hello-I-need-chocolate consciousness and go to the desk for my stash, I flash on something unexpected. Relief. And with that feeling comes something else. Closure.

As I unpeel the foil and break off a square of milk chocolate I realize something else—I no longer have to wonder if my father's out there somewhere, if he's thinking about me. I no longer have to be pissed off, knowing that he isn't thinking about me, that he doesn't give a shit. I can let go and move on with my life. Still, the O-word pops up again.

With the orphan word rattling around in my brain, I remember the life skills class I had in ninth grade. "What is family?" I hear the soft, pleasant voice of a narrator say in a video the nurse showed us in the family and friends section of the class. "Some families have two moms." Flash to smiling lesbian couple with baby. "Some families have two dads." Flash to smiling gay men with baby. "Some families…" Montage of divorced/single/grandparent led/adopted ethnic child families. "What all these people have in common is love."

The word love leads me to Aunt T. The janitor of my existence—picking up the pieces of Mom's mess. The CEO of my life—making executive decisions regarding my well-being when Mom couldn't. She's been nurse and nutritionist, guidance counselor and shrink. If love is the definition of family, then Aunt T's the real deal. Aunt T and me, a cozy family of two, and come to think of it, that's pretty freaking awesome. No family baggage to carry around. Light traveling. No complicated relationships. For the first time in my life, there's nobody to be angry at.

I guess I fall asleep with this thought, my clothes on, my teeth unbrushed, so when morning light wakes me it's with a terrible taste in my mouth, like something crawled in there and died. I Crest away the taste, shower away last night's haze, and as a lighter, and also hungrier, person, head to the cafeteria.

Organic-farm Dahlia, who looks so content with the simple fact of being alive, is sitting alone. I load my tray with sugar and carbs (hello, cafeteria food!) and slip into the chair next to her.

"Hi, Faith! How are you?!" she exclaims. Everything Dahlia says is an exclamatory sentence. There are no

declarative statements in Dahlia-speak. I wonder if she's this
enthusiastic about getting out of bed in the morning, about a
visit to the gynecologist.

"I'm fine," I say, testing out my newfound lightness with
words. "How are you?"

"I'm great! I love working at the farm! Don't tell anyone, but
I smuggled a chick into the dorm!" She's not exactly whisper-
ing, so I'm thinking I don't exactly have to tell anyone for the
whole world to know. "She's so adorable. I named her Free
Ranger. I just couldn't part with her when I left yesterday."

"Chicken smuggling, huh?" I say with a smile. "I hear you
do hard time for that."

Her eyes widen and for a minute she looks panicked, but
then she realizes I'm joking and giggles and punches my arm.
It feels so good to delight in the pleasures of weightless conversation. I could listen to Dahlia talk about organic carrots
and baby chickens and goat milk all day, but alas, there is one
thing on my mind: Clem.

I'm a pretty good pretender at most things, but I can't
pretend I don't notice that he's not at breakfast. And I can't
pretend I wasn't a shit last night, ditching him at the Cowgirl,
not saying thank you. I finish my chocolate chip muffin, wish
Dahlia a good day, and head up to his room.

"Hey," he says, cracking open the door a few seconds after
I knock.

"Hey," I reply, not exactly the deepest exchange, but it's
a start.

"You made it home last night, I guess?"

"Yep. Can I come in?"

"No opposite sex in the rooms, remember?"

I shrug. "Live dangerously."

He cracks the tiniest of smiles and opens the door wider. I go in and sit on the edge of the bed, atop a rumpled blanket, next to an iPod and earbuds and a scattered assortment of sheet music. It's then I notice that his hair is uncombed and he's in a T-shirt and boxers.

"Just wake up?" I ask, trying to pretend I don't notice what he's wearing—or not wearing.

"Nah. I've been listening to music since five." He plops down next to me and picks up the earbuds, letting them dangle over his finger. "I'm trying to learn Paganini."

I nod, attempting to look informed. Apparently I'm not looking informed, more like I have no idea who or what a Paganini is, because he says, "Nicolo Paganini? Italian violinist. Born in Genoa in 1782?"

"Oh! That Paganini. I thought you meant the other one."

"I'm trying to learn 'Caprice No. 1' for the concert with the Dallas Symphony at the Lensic over the Fourth of July weekend. I'm a soloist," he says without any humor. He tosses the earbuds back onto the bed and rakes his fingers through his hair. "I might as well play 'Twinkle Twinkle Little Star,' at the rate I'm going."

"What's wrong with 'Twinkle Twinkle'? It's a great song. It's the same tune as 'Bah Bah Black Sheep' and the 'ABCs.' I mean how clever is that? Three for the price of one?" He's not amused, and I get that violin isn't something Clem jokes about. I clear my throat and continue. "Right. So. Anyway, I wanted to say sorry about last night." I twist the bed sheet, clear my throat again, and tell him what I found out about my father, hoping he doesn't try to hug me or console me or in any way act like I'm to be pitied.

"Man," he says when I'm done talking. "That blows. Want some chocolate?"

I laugh. "Yeah. Chocolate sounds perfect."

A bar of chocolate later we're back to being friends. We agree to meet up at the end of the day and I head out for work, but not before I pick up my iPod from my room and download a tune by Paganini.

———

I try to call Jesse as I wait for the bus to SCPG. He doesn't answer. I leave a voice message, and as the bus arrives, dial Aunt T, who answers on the first ring as if she'd been waiting all night for me to call. I tell her a lot of nothing stuff as I ease into the information about my father, and then I drop the bomb of his death because sometimes a thing isn't real until you say it out loud. The second I finish explaining, she's all on about if I'm okay and if I want her to come out here and if I need anything. I swear I hear her fingers on the keyboard, searching flights to Santa Fe.

Once Mom died and Aunt T became my legal guardian it was like she was making up for lost time in the parenting department. She delivered nervous lectures on birth control and teen pregnancy and underage drinking. It was like the A-to-Z of mandatory mother-daughter talks. I half expected her to start teaching me about my period and growing breasts. Never having had this kind of relationship with my mother, I wasn't sure how to react, but I discovered I liked my aunt's concern.

I assure Aunt T that I'm okay and that I don't need her to come to Santa Fe. After much convincing, she agrees to stay put in Haverford, but I'm sure I still hear typing.

We finish talking and the bus drops me off in front of SCPG, the lonely building plunked in a field sprinkled with scraggly orange flowers and prairie dog holes against a sky of cloudless, uninterrupted blue. I take a moment before I go inside to stare at this alien landscape. With no trees or buildings to block the horizon, I have that feeling again of too much space. Without anyone to bump up against and remind me I'm here, it almost feels as if I'm not. An ant with razor sharp mandibles bites the exposed flesh between my Converses and my jeans and with that little reminder that, yes, I'm here all right, I hurry inside before his friends can join the attack.

When I get to the lab Esha isn't there, but Jonah's at his desk, some sort of electronic trance music playing.

"How'd the game go?" I ask, stopping as I head to my cubicle.

He looks up with a huge smile and says, "We creamed 'em," then proudly recounts the details of the game, including a replay of his own stellar serves.

He finishes the play-by-play and turns back to his work. Esha still hasn't arrived, so I plop into my swivel chair and spin around a few times, seeing how fast I can make the thing go. I'm in the midst of a chair-spinning race: Faith Flores vs. Faith Flores, when Jonah politely suggests Esha might have left a note for me outlining my morning tasks. I grind my feet to the ground and stop mid-spin to check my desk. No note. I start to spin again when Jonah suggests that perhaps she forgot to put the note on my desk and left it on hers.

"Good thought," I say, and vowing to finish the race later, I get up to check.

Esha's desk in the corner of the lab is neatly organized, one pile of paper, an inbox and outbox, a few photographs, several phone numbers attached to the corkboard cubicle, but no note. I sit in her non-swivelly chair and bide my time by checking out the photos: A cute dog. A cute guy. Three photos of a cute monkey wearing a U2 baseball hat—okay, weird, but whatever—the pictures make me laugh.

"Find anything?" Jonah calls above the electronic drum-beat, a steady pulse like being inside a heart.

"Just that Esha has a thing for monkeys."

Jonah gets up and comes over to Esha's desk. He unpins one of the monkey photos and stares fondly at the animal. "This, Faith, is Waldo. He was sort of the lab mascot before you got here."

I lean forward to take a closer look at the monkey. "He's pretty cute with the long tail and the big eyes, but wouldn't it be easier to stick with a dog or a cat?"

Jonah laughs. "He wasn't a pet. Sonya—Dr. Richmond—had a fondness for him when she was in Peru. She e-mailed photos all the time. He'd sometimes show up when she was Skyping."

"And the hat?"

"Esha gave it to Sonya before she left for Peru. They both love U2. Sonya always put it on Waldo's head as a joke, but go figure—monkeys don't like hats. Usually he'd throw it off, so getting the photos with him wearing it was kind of a big deal." He sighs with a pining love and pins the picture back up. "We felt like we knew Waldo. Kind of miss the little fellow."

What was Dr. Richmond doing in Peru?" I ask, steering the conversation away from hat-wearing, non-human primates.

"Working on *Brugmansia*."

Brugmansia from the newspaper article. I close my eyes and remember now where I'd heard the name of the plant. It was when I was learning about SCPG and Dr. Richmond. "Something to do with developing an anti-seizure medicine?" I say, opening my eyes.

"That's right."

"And isn't that also the name of the plant that the drug liquid gold comes from?" I ask, thinking again of the newspaper article.

"That's right," he repeats. "Plants are amazing. They can have many different uses."

I wait for him to say more about the drug. When he doesn't, I go back to Dr. Richmond. "So, what happened with her research?"

The music changes to some sort of experimental jazz that could be confused with noise. Jonah perches on the edge of Esha's desk and folds his arms. "She spent a year in Peru working on the project. When she sequenced the whole genome, it turned out that the same chemical responsible for the anti-seizure properties is responsible for hallucinogenic properties," he says. "She couldn't isolate one from the other. A few million dollars later, she had to give it up. The board wasn't happy. They'd invested a lot of money in *Brugmansia*."

"That sucks. So will the GMO chile make up for the loss?"

"That's the idea." He lets out a breath. "We're all working our asses off. That's why the board meeting next month is such a big deal. Sonya has to showcase the financial feasibility of her project and get their approval for more funding. If she doesn't…" He shakes his head and lets me fill in the rest of the statement, which I imagine goes like this: if she doesn't, the place could close.

At that moment, the door flies open and Esha flutters into the lab, looking harried and apologetic. I scoot out of her chair as she scurries over to her desk. "Sorry I'm late," she says. "I was up north in Chimayo."

Jonah stays perched on the edge of her desk, his eyes fixed on Esha. "Everything okay with the chiles?"

"Everything's fine," she says, waving away his concern. "Just a distribution issue. We have to be careful with the GMOs and Holly monitoring our every move."

Jonah nods gravely and goes back to his desk. Esha turns on her computer, and I'm left wondering why they have to be careful and who Holly is. The GMO chile isn't on the market yet. Isn't that what Dr. Richmond said? So how could there be a distribution issue? Maybe they're planning ahead, I think and turn my thoughts to today's tasks, ready to delve into my work. But alas, delving in is impossible because I have nothing to delve into. I'm left stranded on my own little taskless island. I clear my throat, hoping Esha will look up and remember me, Faith Flores, her faithful intern.

"So," I say, rising to my tiptoes and clapping my hands when her eyes stay glued to her computer. "I finished all the samples from yesterday."

Now she does look up, eyebrows raised. "All of them?"

"Yep."

"You're fast. I'm not sure I've ever seen someone pick up the procedure this quickly. I guess it's time to move on to something new." I can't tell if she's happy about my fast learning ability or annoyed because she hadn't planned the next task and has to come up with something for me to do. "I guess I'll start you on QC today."

"QC, great!" I exclaim, wanting to be agreeable, though I have no idea what QC actually is.

QC turns out to be quality control. I learn how to use instruments called a Qubit and a NanoDrop to make sure there's enough DNA in each of the vials to be sequenced. I pick up the routine quickly, and as I work, I hunch over the NanoDrop, conjuring up ways to toss the word into conversation: *Hey, what's up? You need any nucleic acids measured? No prob, I've got the NanoDrop for you!*

The day passes quickly. Jonah leaves early for a meeting, and by five o'clock it's just Esha and me in the lab. I'm busy

NanoDropping my time away, when I hear her talking on the phone.

"Yes, you'll pick up the chiles at the Farmers' Market this Saturday. That's the plan until further notice. It's more efficient than going up there and harvesting them."

Hearing her discuss the chiles, my earlier questions come back, and being the trained eavesdropper I am, I listen.

"Rudy will meet you," she says to whoever's on the other end. "Don't worry. He'll have them all."

I should mind my own business, but I'm the curious type. Minding my own business isn't really my thing. *Dr. Richmond's genetically modified chiles, being careful, not everyone's for it, some person named Holly, a distribution issue.* None of this, of course, has to do with me, which means, of course, I want to know everything. I'm pondering the situation when my phone rings with the guitar-riff ring tone that means Jesse.

"What's up in La Villa Real de la Santa Fé de San Francisco de Asís—the Royal Town of the Holy Faith of Saint Francis of Assisi?" he says when I pick up.

"I'm fine, thanks, you?" Hearing Jesse's voice reminds me that I haven't yet told him about my father, and with this realization my attention is diverted from chiles to personal matters. I pack up for the day and wave bye to Esha. As I step outside into the warm late-afternoon, though, I decide I don't feel like getting into the whole dead father thing. Jesse deserves to know what I found out, but I can't bring myself to go there. Instead, I tell him about working in the lab, taking the opportunity to drop in my beloved new words, NanoDrop and Qubit.

"Nerd girl," he says fondly when I'm done talking.

I smile at the name. "Nerd Girl at your service."

I feel the familiar affection for Jesse as we talk, but I also feel the distance. It's just geography, I tell myself when we hang up. He's there. I'm here. End of story. But somewhere deep in that locked box, I know geography isn't the whole deal. Jesse makes me laugh. I can be myself with him. I'm attracted to him. I mean we haven't done it, but that's more to do with my past and mom's revolving door of guys and one-night stands and heartbreak than with him. Maybe I just can't get over the fact of how different our backgrounds are. Or maybe I can't do commitment. Or maybe it's just my age—I'm not even seventeen. Why do I need to decide on one boy?

The rest of the week passes quickly. Clem is busy with my new dead musician friend, Paganini. We see each other for meals and agree to hang out more on the weekend. I read, explore around campus, hang out some with Dahlia, who keeps me up on the intern gossip—like that Rejina and Bro Boy are a thing, and that Brian, the Asian with the blond hair, met a cute boy whose room he's been sneaking into at night.

On Friday, Esha moves me away from the Qubit and the NanoDrop. I'm sad to leave my treasured tools behind, but she tells me it's time to move into bioinformatics, the analysis of DNA data, and this new thing gets my nerd-girl adrenaline levels spiking.

While Jonah picks the tunes—a Norwegian punk band called Oslo Ess—and interjects musical factoids about Northern European alternative rock and rock venues (the INmusic festival in Croatia attracts 25,000 people a year—who knew?), Esha shows me sample DNA data that comes off the sequencing machine. I've seen this kind of data back in Philly, but then she shows me the real heart-pounding magic: how to access the data through the central server, where we can call up anyone's research.

"Bioinformatics has many definitions depending on who you talk to," she explains. "But in all cases it has to do with extracting meaning from biological data using computers." She peers at me to see if I'm following. I nod, and she goes on. "In our case it means looking at a set of DNA sequences from a sample we've sequenced in the lab. We then find the locations of those sequences, in a reference genome."

"Reference genome," I repeat, cool new words with a secret thumbs-up for Nerd Girl. "Meaning?"

"Meaning a standard to compare against. So, we have a reference corn genome, for example. Soybean. Wheat. Anything in the DNA of what we're looking at that's reported as a difference, is a difference in respect to this reference. Make sense?"

A bolt of music electrifies the room, causing us to take cover, at least to cover our ears. Jonah pumps a fist in the air with a shout of yes! as our eardrums ring.

"Don't you have work to do?" Esha calls out to him.

"Tons. Just getting warmed up." He laces his fingers and cracks his knuckles.

Esha rolls her eyes, mutters something about his music, and continues explaining. "What we do in bioinformatics, and what you're going to learn how to do, is to look for mismatches between the sequence reads in the data being analyzed and the reference."

"And those mismatches are from variations in the genome, right?"

"That's right, and we can explore those variations and what they might mean using statistics, and then identify the genes that contain the variants. Got it?"

"Sounds fun."

Esha teaches me the basics and I spend the rest of the day looking at sequence reads from a sample corn genome, comparing the reads to the reference and, okay, having a blast looking for variants. So, hey, some people get off on sports or chess or acting in plays or going to Renaissance fairs and dressing up as kings or queens (nobody ever dresses as toothless, syphilis-ridden serfs), scrapbooking, playing an instrument, or model trains. For me, it's DNA variants, those packages of letters that reveal worlds of hidden meaning.

When the day ends, the first week having flown by, I'm bummed to leave the lab. When I get back to my dorm room, though, I realize I'm exhausted. I lie down and wait for Clem to finish practicing and come get me for dinner. I'm chilling out, looking at a graphic novel Dahlia lent me, when there's a knock on my door.

I assume it's Clem and fling open the door with a raucous, "Nerd Girl at your service!"

It's not Clem, though. In fact, it's nobody I've ever seen. The person standing in the hall is a small, thin woman with a long, gray braid, a face as wrinkled as an unmade bed, and anxious brown eyes.

"Can I help you?" I ask, once I've stopped staring and wondering if she's some intern's grannie looking for her grandkid.

"Are you Faith Flores?" she asks tentatively.

The question takes me by surprise. How on Earth does this woman know my name? "Uh, yeah," I say in a guarded voice.

"*Dios mio,*" she cries. Her face screws up with an emotion I don't understand. She clears her throat, same as I always do when I'm about to communicate something difficult, then says the most impossible thing I've ever heard. "I'm Alma Flores, Alvaro's mother. I'm your grandmother."

Six

I laugh at the absurdity of the statement, but she doesn't seem to be kidding so I say, "I don't have a grandmother."

"Don't have a grandmother?" she repeats, a distressed arch in her eyebrows. "Everybody has a grandmother! You mean you just never met yours, but I wrote to you, *Mija*."

Something inside me twists. I don't speak Spanish, but I've been hearing the word *mija* since I got to New Mexico. I had asked what it meant and discovered that even though it literally means "my daughter," older people use it all the time for younger people they feel affection for. I reach for the Zippo lighter, my breathing shallow and fast.

"You did get the letters, right?" she asks when I just stand there, *mija* reverberating in my brain.

I stare at her, trying to unscramble her words, decipher the hidden code, uncover the punch line. When she doesn't crack a smile or tell me she's kidding, I shake my head and mumble "no." Her eyes widen. She lets out a little gasp, and her hand flutters to her chest.

Despite the static clogging my head, I realize I'm keeping her standing in the hall like an unwelcome missionary coming to sell me salvation, and I manage to ask if she'd like to come into my room. She nods and follows me through the door. I throw my clothes crumpled on the desk chair to the floor so I can offer her a seat, then plunk down on the bed, too tongue-tied to speak.

"I sent them to your address in Philadelphia," she says, studying me with wide, worried eyes. "Alvaro wrote to you too."

My breath does this funny wobbly thing in my chest. I squeeze the lighter in my fist, no idea what to say, thankful when she speaks again and I don't have to.

"That's why you never wrote back," she says. The emotion in her voice is contagious, infecting my heart and stinging my eyes. "I thought it was because you were angry with Alvaro for leaving and didn't want anything to do with us. About two years ago I stopped." She reaches into her pocket for a tissue, blows her nose with one sharp blow, then squashes the tissue in her fist. "I thought I'd give you space and someday if you were ready...and then you showed up here."

I watch, stupefied, as she reaches into her purse and pulls out a photograph. She hands it to me without speaking. I lower my eyes. "Oh my God," I gasp, my hand flying to my mouth when I see the image of a wispy blonde, my mother, nestled against a tall, dark man, who I match with the blurred photo of Alvaro.

"Your mother was Augustine Archer," the woman says, getting up and slowly lowering herself to sit on the bed by my side. She's so small her weight hardly registers, but her presence is enormous. "Everyone called her Auggie. She married my Alvaro." She gives a hard sniffle and turns to face the window. "But he had a problem with drugs, and he left her. Abandoned her and his child. I never forgave him for that."

I've gone black hole. Sucking in all words and sounds. *How can this be? How can I just suddenly have a grandma? How is it possible I never knew a thing about her?*

I know how it's possible, though. Mom. She never wanted me to know anything about Alvaro. She must have stolen the letters to keep me from finding out. A feeling I haven't felt since before she died arises. Fury. All these years I could have had a grandmother and Mom took that from me? I don't know what to do with the rage, the nuclear emotion about to explode. I glare at Alma, but this isn't her fault—even in my rage I know that.

"How did you find me?" I manage to say.

She turns from the window and takes my hand in hers. Her hands aren't soft cookie-baking, grandma hands. They're strong and wrinkled, the fingertips hard and calloused— working hands. People say eyes are the windows into the soul. I say it's the hands.

"Last week I read in the newspaper about the interns coming to Santa Fe. I'm always interested in the internship program because every year I hope Amelia will apply," she says, tightening her hold on my hands. I have no idea who Amelia is, but in this weirdly altered state, I don't care. "When I saw your name, I thought it must be a coincidence. And then Little Timmy called me."

"Little Timmy?"

"The bartender at the Cowgirl. You met him, no?"

"You mean Griz?"

She nods and laughs, a buoyant, cascading sound like a seedpod catching wind, and I join in. There's nothing light or airy about my laugh, though. My laugh is loud and harsh, a semi-hysterical release of all the other emotions knocking around inside me.

"He was little about twenty years ago," she says with a sigh. "He said Faith Flores had been there and was asking about Alvaro, so I did some investigating and called the college. I found out you were almost seventeen, which is just the right age, and that you were from Philadelphia, just the right place, and I knew it had to be you." She pauses, draws in a long breath, and then says, "There's something else."

I'm not sure I can handle a "something else" but I glance at her.

"It's not just me."

"There are two of you?" I blurt, stupid with shock.

"No, *Mija*. I have two other granddaughters."

I don't comprehend what she's saying, and I guess this shows on my face because slowly, and with the patience of a preschool teacher, she says, "Alvaro left behind two other girls. Amelia's sixteen and Marisol's fourteen. They live me with me. You have two half sisters."

 Seven

"Half sisters?" I repeat, or at least I think that's what I say. I might have said laugh-misters or path-blisters or I might not have said anything at all and just imagined it in my head.

"I know it's a lot to take in, *Mija*, but you'll come over and meet them as soon as possible." She writes something on a piece of paper. "This is my phone number," she says and stuffs the paper into my hands. "You have to promise to call and come for dinner. This week. I'll pick you up."

I nod, unable to speak.

"I've thought about you for so many years. I'm not going to let you slip out of my life again." Without warning, she turns, grabs me into her arms, and hugs me. The hug takes me off guard and I receive it like a plank of wood, arms pinned to my side. "I have to go now, Faith," she whispers into my hair. She lets go of me and slowly rises. "I wish I didn't have to leave, but the greenhouse where I work falls apart without me." She emits a little of her seedpod laugh. "You'll promise to call," she says in a firm voice, and I get that this is an order. "I don't want to lose you again, not after I finally found you."

I lock the door when she leaves and don't answer when Clem knocks. How can I answer when I can't talk or move?

I lie on my bed where minutes before Alma sat, gripping the paper she left with her phone number.

A lot to take in? It's like trying to swallow the Grand Canyon. Balance the Empire State Building on a spoon. Fly an airplane to a star. It's like someone said, "No really, we made a mistake. The Earth is actually flat." Or "Ptolemy was correct! The sun does revolve around the Earth, not the other way around."

Am I supposed to just waltz over to her house and say, "Hey, how are you three, oh long lost family of mine? It's really nice to meet you after almost seventeen years." Then I jerk back to the other major revelation. Mom conspired to keep Alma from me, which brings me to an even worse thought: Maybe Aunt T did, too. Maybe both of them united against me. I grab my phone from my pocket and punch my aunt's number. I don't care that it's midnight Back East.

"Are you okay? Where are you? Are you hurt?" are the first breathless words out of her mouth.

"No. In the dorm. No," I say, rattling off the answers to her questions. I tell her what happened and what I found out and then, unable to contain my anger, blurt, "Did you know about the letters? Did Mom tell you?"

"I swear to God, Faith, I didn't know anything about this." She sounds genuinely horrified. I imagine her twisting a blond curl around a finger the way she does when she's worried or upset. "I never heard of letters or a grandmother or half sisters. I would never have kept something like that from you, and I never would've allowed your mother to, either."

Almost a year ago when Mom died and I didn't trust anyone, I wouldn't have believed Aunt T. After living with her, though, after knowing her better than I even knew my mom, I believe what she's saying.

"Maybe your mom never got the letters," she suggests. "You two moved a lot, right?"

Aunt T, always rational. When Mom was puking up her guts and I called my aunt for help, she stayed calm. When I crashed her car last winter, she never lost her cool. Still, although what she says is a logical suggestion, I don't buy it. "I always went to the post office and left a forwarding address."

"Always when you were old enough, but not when you were little. You guys started moving around when you were just a kid, so it's possible your mom just never got them," she says. She doesn't push me to accept her theory—which I don't—and doesn't say anything else on the topic. She leaves me with the question of the missing letters to consider, asking only if she could have Alma's number and if she has my permission to call her. I tell her she does, give her the number, and we say good night.

I meet up with Clem the next morning at breakfast after a restless night's sleep. Feeling bad about blowing off dinner last night, especially after my behavior earlier in the week, I sit down next to him, about to apologize for not opening the door when he came to get me, when he beats me to it.

"Sorry I didn't come by last night," he says.

"Huh…oh…you didn't?" I'm off the hook, but now I'm pissed at him for breaking his dinner promise, and besides, who knocked?

"I'm just having a hard time with Paganini," he says, sighing at his breakfast tray. "I've never tried to master something so difficult so quickly. I'm a soloist. Did I tell you that? It's a benefit concert, and…" He stops talking and looks at me when he realizes I'm not listening. "I can tell this is really meaningful to you."

"It is. Sorry. I'm just distracted." I apologize again and pick at my cereal.

"Distracted because?"

I sigh, put down my spoon, and without looking up, tell him what happened last night.

"Wow, there's never a dull moment in your life. I've known you for one week, and in that time you've lost a father and gained two sisters and a grandma. That's crazy."

"I know," I mumble and turn my attention from my cereal to my toast, letting my hair sweep across my face and hide my eyes.

"My dad remarried and had two kids with his new wife," he says, picking at the crumble top of a blueberry muffin. "I never wanted to know them, but when they got older I decided it was stupid to pretend they didn't exist."

A memory creeps up as Clem tells me this, something I haven't thought about in years. Mom passed out drunk. Me alone, sitting on the couch next to her, wishing more than anything I had a sister. Even though I'd never been taught to pray or seen anyone do it—and I had no idea who or what I was praying to—I remember praying and asking for a sister.

"We have nothing in common," Clem goes on. "They're total jocks, but still. It's cool having brothers. Like knowing there are other people around with the same messed-up dad, and maybe that means they'll get you more than other people do. And then there's the fact we're related and that has to mean something, right? Like when the world sucks and there's nobody to turn to maybe I can turn to those guys. My bros, you know?"

Just then Dahlia scoots by the table with an empty tray. She stops when she sees me. "Hey, Faith! I came by last night to see if you wanted to have some dinner. I knocked, but you didn't answer. Everything okay?"

So it was Dahlia who knocked, I think, feeling guilty for ignoring her and happy now to see her. "I'm fine," I say. "Sorry I didn't answer. I must've fallen asleep. How's Free Ranger?"

"Oh, she's great!"

"How do you know it's a she? Can you sex a chick?" I tease.

Dahlia considers this with all the serious weight of gender politics. "She just seems like a she. Anyway, I'm helping out at the Farmers' Market in town the next few Saturdays. I'm heading down there when I'm done eating. We sell eggs and goat milk and goat milk cheese. You should totally come by."

I beg out of going today, but promise to check it out next week.

"Sure," she says, and takes off with a peppy wave, leaving Clem and me to finish our food. Once we're done he disappears to practice, and I head to my room. Despite Clem's advice and my obsessive wondering about Alma and my two half sisters, I don't call them. I pick up the phone three times during the day, but every time, I lame out and hang up.

I do, however, call Jesse. I tell him about The Situation, as I've been referring to the arrival of my long lost family, a euphemism that helps me distance myself from the reality of their flesh and blood existence. As expected, Jesse is all Go for it! Meet them! Cool! Wow! Amazing! and Did I hear the story of the long lost family reunited after sixty years despite living two streets away from each other? Our conversation curdles inside me, leaves me feeling empty, like his words are more of a performance than a real understanding. Again, I try and persuade myself that being so far away makes it hard to relate, hard to have the same intimacy as you get in person. Like with texting and Facebook and Twitter—all that connecting and I just feel more alone.

Going for walks isn't really my thing, but when we hang up, I take myself out for one anyway. I need to clear my head, and my room's starting to feel like a prison. I wander down the hill to town, with no particular destination in mind. The weird thing is I see sister duos everywhere—in the gelato shop, the card shop, the organic, healthy juice shop—and grannies? Forget it, they're like popping out of the woodwork. Were there always so many sisters and grannies hanging around, or am I just noticing them now that they're on my mind? Like when someone says don't think of a pink elephant, and that's all you can think of. Even YouTube's gotten in on it. When I get back to the dorm, sweaty and tired from the walk, I flop onto the bed and watch a mind-numbingly stupid video called "Famous Sisters." Stupid, yes. But do I turn it off? Do I find something more meaningful to do? No. I watch the whole thing, then go back to the beginning and watch again.

Would I be friends with my half sisters, I wonder as I watch a third time. It's possible, but then again, what if we hated each other? What if they're awful? What if we have nothing in common and can't stand each other? I tell myself I shouldn't complicate my life. Aunt T's all the family I need. My life is simple. Clean. Streamlined.

But.

The truth is what Clem said really resonated with me. The thing about there being someone else in the world who gets you in a way others can't. The fact that swap spit and 50 percent of our DNA's the same. And then there are a million questions I'm dying to find out. What do they look like? What do they like to do? What are they like?

As a new YouTube video loads ("Things Only Sisters Would Understand") I can't stand it anymore. I don't think. I just act. I pick up the phone and call.

Eight

All day Monday I'm jumpy and preoccupied with the fact that Alma (can't quite get used to calling a stranger grandma) will be picking me up after work and taking me to her house for dinner. Jonah teases me about too much caffeine. Esha also seems distracted, which is good for me because it means her distraction negates noticing mine. I try to focus on bioinformatics, lining up sequence reads from one genome to another, checking the output files to see how the data's accumulating, but I can't concentrate.

When five o'clock finally comes, I shoot up from my desk and race outside as a light blue pickup truck pulls into the parking lot and Alma gets out. I'm relieved it's just her, and I have some time before meeting the girls.

"Your aunt is very nice, *Mija*," she tells me as we leave SCPG. "We had a very nice conversation. Over an hour."

I don't respond to what she's saying because nerves have glued my tongue to the roof of my mouth. Alma thankfully doesn't force a conversation and instead turns on the radio and hums along to Spanish music. About twenty minutes later, the truck coasts down a steep dirt hill, takes a sharp left, and pulls up to a shoebox-shaped house plunked down on a stretch of red-hued earth dotted with squat green-needled trees. An assortment of gardening tools and bikes in various states of disrepair, along with recycling bins and garbage cans are strewn along the side of the house.

"Here we are," she says and opens the door to two barking dogs that come barreling up the driveway to greet us.

The second I step out of the truck, both dogs are on me, paws on my thighs, tongues lolling, tails wagging. The smaller of the two whines and moans while I stroke her pointy ears and rub my hand down her surprisingly soft mottled fur.

"Cattle dogs," Alma says. "They're supposed to live on a ranch, but instead they live on the couch." She laughs and pets the larger one. "The little red one's Biscochito, and the large bluish one's Sopapilla."

"Mom wanted to change his name," says a girl of about fourteen who's just appeared. She has an unruly mane of long, dark curls and big brown eyes. She's wearing cut-off jean shorts, a blue tie-dyed tank, and too many string bracelets to count. "She said that non-Spanish speakers around here would see the name and pronounce it the Anglo way—Soap-a-*pill*-a," she says, pronouncing the *l* sound of pill, instead of the Spanish *ee* sound. "But after she died, the name stuck, and so there you have it."

As I fumble for words and try to take in this information, I notice an older girl with an aggressively slumped posture lurking in the doorway. Her mutilated pixie cut has a chemical burn look to it. Her right eyebrow is pierced with three silver hoops, and she has an expression that manages to look both bored and pissed off. The younger girl goes to the doorway and nudges the other girl in the rib cage. She scowls and reluctantly joins us on the driveway.

"Girls," Alma says, turning to my two half sisters and making the introductions for us. "This is Faith." She nudges the one with the curls forward. "Faith, this is Marisol."

"Call me Mari," she says. "Everyone does."

I have no idea what the protocol is for meeting the half sister you just found out about, so I reach out to shake her hand. Instead of taking my hand, she pulls me in for a hug. The hug takes me off guard—again—but this time I return the embrace.

"I have a shitload of things to ask you about!" she exclaims, releasing me and reaching down to pet Sopapilla.

"Mari, language!" Alma scolds.

"Sorry, Gran." She stands and clears her throat dramatically. "I have many interesting questions to which I'd like the answers, Ms. Flores," she says, laughing in delight at herself— a contagious laugh that has me joining in.

Alma turns in the scowling girl's direction. "Mia," she says pointedly to the girl. "Introduce yourself to Faith."

"Hey," the scowler says with a chin jut in my direction. "My friends call me Mia. You can call me Amelia." And with that, she turns and walks back into the house.

"Don't worry about dork-butt," Mari says once Alma finishes apologizing for Amelia. "She's just mad that Gran won't let her go out tonight with her pot-head boyfriend." She turns to the door and shouts when she says the words "pot-head boyfriend."

"I heard that!" Amelia calls from inside. "And he's not a pot head."

"Oh. Excuse me! *Cannabis cabeza*!" Mari fires back, rolling her eyes at me and air quoting the words.

Amelia flies back outside. "Don't mix Latin with Spanish. You sound like a nerd."

"You're just jealous because I speak Spanish and you're so busy getting high with your wastoid *vato* boyfriend you never bother going to class and *tu sabes nada!*"

"You're one to talk about getting wasted," Amelia snaps.

Mari starts in on another comment, but Alma interrupts, hands out, separating the sisters as if they might come to blows. "Girls," she says, giving them each a look. "Enough. We have a guest. Let's all go inside."

Verbal disarmament. Cease-fire. Enter house.

The room I enter is amazingly cool compared to the outside temperature. With the low-beamed ceiling, white tile floor, and thick earth-toned walls, there's something timeless about the space. Even the long wood table has an ageless quality about it, not fussy like over-priced antiques, but worn, like old work boots. The kitchen and living room are one big room, so I see Amelia go to the stove and pick up a skillet. I see the pissed off look melt from her face and a more tranquil expression move in to take its place.

Mari plops onto the couch and pats the cushion, indicating I should join her. I sit down and she stares into my eyes. Yep," she says, after studying my face. "You definitely have his eyes."

"Whose?" I ask, stupidly.

"Dad's."

The statement leaves me tongue-tied with a million questions, but all that comes out is, "I do?"

"Totally. They're like so dark they're almost black. Mine are much lighter, see?"

She leans forward and widens her eyes, so I can inspect the color.

"Do you look like him?" I ask.

"Same nose," she says, rolling her eyes and sinking back against the cushions. "That's what everyone always says, but that's just stupid. They might as well say we have the same toenails."

She laughs, then starts shooting off questions, rapid-fire, one after the other, hardly giving me a chance to answer. I squeeze in a few superficial questions of my own, like what bands she likes, but she's all about the asking and doesn't respond. What do I like to do? Where do I go to school? Do I have a boyfriend? Who do I live with? When the questions transcend the mundane and delve into the personal (why do I live with my aunt and not my mother?), Alma intervenes and calls Mari into the kitchen.

"Give Faith some space, *Mija*," she says. "Come help your sister with dinner. We have all evening to ask questions." To me, Alma says, "Make yourself at home. Dinner will be ready in ten minutes. Hope you like chile."

Mari slides off the couch with a sigh and tromps into the kitchen where she and Amelia work side-by-side at a corn-flower blue counter, two heads dipped over a stainless steel bowl. Alma stands at the center island in front of a cutting board, her hands a work of art as they manage a knife in quick movements. She slices through an onion and a potato, throws everything into a frying pan and adds some seasoning.

"Needs more cayenne," Amelia says, dipping a finger into the bowl.

Mari nods, adds the spice, and goes back to mixing.

"I can't believe Marcus got booted off 'Teen Chef' last night," Mari complains, as she carries a stack of dishes to the table.

"Totally," Amelia agrees, following Mari with silver-ware and glasses. "The judges completely got it wrong. They should've chopped that *chica* from Atlanta who used tofu as her main course. Tofu! Does that even count as food?"

"Mia is going to make it onto the show," Mari explains to me. "Can you imagine if she gets on and wins? Five thousand dollars! She totally beat out that nerd-butt from Flagstaff at the audition."

"Mari," Alma scolds.

"Sorry, but he was. Did you see his pants? Talk about a wedgie!"

Both girls laugh as they finish setting the table.

I feel like I should participate in the action, but I stay parked on the couch, looking around the room at the photos on the walls that belong to someone else's life, the dogs that belong to someone else's family. A mix of resentment and longing rises in me. What would my life have been like if I grew up here? What if Mom hadn't confiscated those letters and I had two half sisters and a grandma all along? How would it feel to be part of that kitchen tribe?

Amelia is back at the stove now, working the skillet. Alma's moved to the oven, and Mari's tossing salad. Unless you count boiling water for mac and cheese, I have no idea how to cook, which means I have no idea how to break into the conversation or activity and join the hive. An outside bee doesn't just show up at a foreign hive and ask for a job. A guard bee would assassinate it at the entrance. Maybe that's Amelia's role. She's the guard bee of the family, keeping the queen safe from marauders. Maybe that's why she's so pissed at me. I'm the marauder. The interloper. The one who's come to invade the hive.

"Dinner's ready," Alma calls out, waving me to the table and pointing me to a seat.

"Looks good," I say, admiring the spread: gluten and dairy to die for!

"Amelia's our chef." Alma smiles and lifts a tortilla smothered with melted cheese and green and red chile sauce from a glass dish and slides it onto my plate.

I dig in, scarfing too big a forkful for decent table manners. Instantly my eyes start to water and my mouth is on fire. "Water," I gasp.

Amelia laughs and hands me the milk carton.

I think she's being a jerk and I reach for the water pitcher, but she intercepts and says, "No, *Guera*. Not water. Milk. It cuts the heat."

"What's a *guera*?" I ask, guessing from the tone it's not a compliment.

"White girl," Amelia shoots back at me.

"She's hardly a *guera*," Mari interjects. "She isn't a blonde and she's not exactly white."

"Well, she isn't one of us either," Amelia snaps, giving Mari a look.

"Uh, I'm sitting right here and, like it or not, Amelia, we're fruit of the same loins. Same sperm. Different birth canal."

I glance at Alma to see whether using the words *loin* and *sperm* and *birth canal* at the dinner table is acceptable, but she doesn't appear to have heard. Her face has crumbled into a horrified expression and she's giving Amelia a talking to in Spanish—apparently Amelia can't speak it, but sure as flies on shit, she can understand it.

"I'm sorry, *Mija*," Alma says to me when she's done with the lecture, but she's still glaring at Amelia.

Amelia shrugs off her—our—grandmother and narrows her eyes at me. "I hear you have some hot-shot internship," she says, which coming from another person could be taken as nice. Coming from her, it's anything but.

I could verbally nail Amelia's ass into submission. Verbal ass-nailing is one of my special talents, but out of respect for Alma, and because Mari looks so upset, I keep my more colorful comments to myself. "Yep," I say, playing it cool. "It's pretty great."

"So that's what happens when you grow up Back East? You go to some fancy *guera* private school and get the best internships? What, is your white mom loaded?"

"I see you've never been to North Philly," I say over Mari and Alma's protests.

The question catches Amelia off guard. For a second she looks confused, but she quickly recovers. "Why'd I want to go there?"

"You wouldn't. That's my point. It's the ghetto. That's where I grew up. Not with mountains and open space and bikes to ride around on. With rundown bars and abandoned buildings and nightly drug deals outside my window. My public schools—I went to five because my mom was a drug addict and we moved so much—were so overcrowded that most of the time nobody cared or noticed if I showed up. Oh, and my mom? She's dead. Murdered." I smile sweetly at Amelia and help myself to some potatoes.

A mountainous moment of silence in which forks clatter on plates and ice clinks in glasses follows my little speech. And then Amelia's instincts kick in.

"I don't even know what you're doing here or why you showed up!" she fires at me, fiercely twisting one of her eyebrow rings. "You can't just walk into our lives and act like you're family!"

"Amelia!" Alma snaps, sliding a hand onto Amelia's wrist. "That is enough."

Amelia jerks away her hand and turns her huge, anger-filled eyes on me. "Well, it's true!" Then she pushes away her plate and storms out of the room.

The second she's gone, Mari whirls around to Alma. "You have to do something about her! She's so flipping mean all the time. All she ever does is hang around her jerkazoid boyfriend and act like everyone's her enemy! I'm sick of it! Can't she just be nice for a change?"

"You just need to let her be," Alma says in a tired voice. She reaches across the table and brushes a curl from Mari's eyes.

"Let her be?" Mari huffs. "Why? So she can ruin my life?"

"No, *Mija*, so she can figure out how not to ruin hers."

I can tell Alma's furious at Amelia, but instead of chasing after her, she turns to me, smiles sadly, and says, "Welcome to the family."

Nine

"Your mother was murdered?" Mari says when dinner's over, Alma's gone to the top of the driveway to check mail, and we're clearing dishes. "Jeesh. I thought our story was sad. What happened?"

When I use the M-word most people get all weird and tongue-tied and don't say anything—a highly awkward response situation that makes me feel like I've turned green and sprouted horns. Mari's lack of shyness on the topic is refreshing. As I carry plates from the table I tell her about the clinical trial that killed my mom. It's weird how not-weird it's become to talk about it. Distance plus time equals not quite detachment, but almost like I'm telling a detective story about some other people.

"What about your mom?" I ask when I finish my story. "What happened to her?"

"Nothing like that." She stops clearing the table and stands at the sink, staring into the soapy water. "I mean total suckville, but it was natural at least. Cancer. Four years ago."

"What kind of cancer?" I ask, determined to match her in frankness.

"Ovarian," she mumbles.

"Sorry. That must've been terrible."

She nods without speaking, and another mountainous silence follows in which the natural extension to the dead mom question is the dead dad question. Nobody's said a word on the subject, but it lingers, waiting to be asked.

I clear my throat and squeeze the lighter. "And what about your...our..." I can't bring myself to call him our father and go instead with Alvaro. "What about Alvaro? How'd he die?" The question sparks all the smoldering feelings I've had since meeting Alma last Friday—how my world was one thing and how suddenly it's become something else entirely—a world in which I'm a sister and a granddaughter and part of a family.

"He drowned," Mari says in a flat voice. "He was a good swimmer, so he was probably drunk." She stops talking and goes stiff and small and silent. I can practically see her disappearing—there goes the hair, the nose, the eyes—until all that's left is shadow. I don't know what she's feeling exactly, but I know what she's doing. I, too, have mastered the disappearing act. I ask a few more questions, but it's a lost cause.

Mari mutters something about having things to do and goes outside. I watch her through the kitchen window as she sits beneath a tree, hunched over a sketchbook, pencil furiously scribbling across a page.

Amelia's nowhere to be found and Alma hasn't yet come back. I'm solo in the kitchen, feeling unanchored and out of place, unsure how to occupy this unfamiliar space on my own, so I follow Mari outside. I know she's trying to be alone and I'm bordering on creepy lurking, but screw it. I sit down next to her without saying anything. She keeps drawing and doesn't look up, but she doesn't move or ask me to leave either. We sit in side-by-side silence, each lost in our own world, until Mari turns the open page of her sketchbook to me.

"Wow," I say, studying the drawing she's done of a hummingbird. "You're really good."

She shrugs off the compliment and shows me the rest of the sketchbook, more drawings of birds, followed by pages and pages of cartoon sketches—big-eyed Anime girls, cartoon animals of every sort, fantastical creatures. "I'm trying to get into the charter art school for fall," she says. "I have to do a portfolio. I'm focusing on hummingbirds." Her voice brightens as she tells me about her art and her portfolio and the birds she's drawing. "My favorite hummer is the Calliope. They're hard to see, though. I've been trying to get a picture of one. Did you know it's the smallest bird in North America north of Mexico? The males have these amazing magenta stripes on their chest and…" She stops talking and blushes, as if her love of birds is something to be embarrassed about.

"My mom was really into birds," I say quickly, wanting to assure her that in my book, digging birds is nothing to be embarrassed about. "Are you any good at identification?"

She shrugs and looks at her sketch with a critical gaze, erasing some of the lines. "I can tell the hummingbirds apart, and I can tell a sparrow from a pigeon." She blows eraser dust from her paper. "You?"

"A little. My mom had a thing about identifying birds. She said knowing their names made her feel less lonely, so she was always teaching me what they were." *When she was sober* I think, but I don't want to get into that. I stop talking and stare at my hands, picking at my fingernails that I allowed Dahlia to paint lime-green the other day. Sitting in the shade of the tree, the sun winking through the branches, flecks of green polish settling on my lap like Martian dust, my thoughts drift back to Alvaro. I get this uneasy feeling, this sense of being an alien invader dropped onto Planet Family Flores. I don't even know the basics about my father, The Jerk, and here I am supposed to just be part of this family? "So, I have kind of a weird question," I say.

"Okay. Weird's cool."

I crack my knuckles and spend a minute chewing the hell out of my lip. "Well, I don't really know anything about Alvaro and you guys speak Spanish, so..." This is as far as I get because as soon as I speak I feel green in my gut, like I'm about to skydive and I'm unsure if my parachute will work.

"You mean you don't know where you're from? Your mom never told you?" I shake my head and she lets out a soft whistle. "Jeez. That's crazy. So you never knew you were half Mexican?"

I feel my eyes widen. "Mexican?"

"Yep. Gran and Pops—he's dead now— came from Morelia, but Dad was born here." She pauses and now she's the one to chew her lip. I notice her hand tightening around a pencil. "A lot of people around here are jerks about Mexicans. They think anyone who speaks Spanish is illegal. As if a person can even be illegal."

We go quiet after this statement. My thoughts converge on this new information about my ethnicity. *Mexican. Mexico.* A word. A place. A country. A geographical statement. A geopolitical thing in a world of geopolitical things. What does that mean for me? Do I have to speak Spanish? Do I just become Mexican because that's what someone before me was? I'm too overwhelmed to speak, and fortunately I don't have to. Any further conversation is interrupted by the sound of a door slamming and Amelia shouting. Mari jumps to her feet and races into the house. I'm a step behind.

Amelia and Alma are standing in front of the door, Alma's arms out, blocking Amelia. Amelia's laughing, but the laugh is off-kilter, like a scale that hasn't been calibrated. It's too loud, too aggressive, and there's nothing in it that sounds funny.

"You're high, aren't you?" Alma says in a forceful whisper that carries far more weight than a shout.

"What if I am?" Amelia counters, all hands-on-hips attitude.

"Damn it, Amelia!" The whisper has increased in volume now. "You will not be doing marijuana under my roof."

Amelia rolls her eyes. "I didn't 'do' it under your roof. I 'did' it outside. And for your information, you don't 'do' marijuana. You smoke it." A horn honks. I look out the window to see a boy in a truck waiting in the driveway. Amelia tries to brush past Alma, but Alma grabs her arm.

"Okay, *Mija*. We can deal with this later, but please, I don't want you going out with Rudy. He's a bad influence." She speaks gently, changing tactics, going for a reverse psychology, kindness approach.

Amelia doesn't take to the kindness or to the statement about Rudy, who's apparently the one honking. "You're not my parent," she hisses, a cut that even I can feel. "You can't tell me what to do." And with that, she jerks free of Alma's grasp and shoves past her. She lunges through the door and climbs into Rudy's truck. He peels out of the driveway, a puff of black smoke as a parting gift.

I turn to glance at Mari, but I'm surprised to find she's gone. It's just Alma and me, standing by the front door in the icy aftermath of Amelia's departure.

"This must be very overwhelming for you," Alma says, turning to me. "But you're family now. There's no use hiding anything. I don't want to make you uncomfortable, but you should know about us. We're not without troubles. I'm very sorry about Mia's behavior. Come." She gestures me to the sink and together we start washing dishes. There isn't a dishwasher, so Alma washes and I dry. "These girls—you girls—are *mi vida*, my life, but I worry so much," she says as I dry a frying pan. "Amelia's such a talented chef, but she dropped out of her cooking class at school this spring, God knows why, then she started failing all her subjects. And that Rudy." She brings a soapy hand to her forehead and holds it there for a second. "He got arrested for selling marijuana. After everything that's happened with Alvaro, I don't want her around that stuff."

I'm not sure if "everything" refers to the newspaper article about my father's drug arrest or his dying or both, but even though I'm curious about my deceased father, I'm more curious about my living sisters. "What about Mari?" I ask.

Alma leans her hands wearily on the counter and shakes her head. "Mari used to tell me things. We were close after her mother died, but lately she's been so distant. She doesn't tell me anything." She pauses and looks out the window. "Last month she snuck out of the house. I was sleeping and didn't hear her leave. The police brought her home drunk. She'd found out about a party some high school kids were having. And this spring at school she started cutting classes." I hear both the pain and the strength in Alma's voice, how hard all of this is for her, how she's not giving up. "She's a follower and she wants so bad to fit in, but she's gotten in with the wrong crowd. I just pray she gets into that art school for ninth grade. I don't know what will happen to her if she stays in the public school...." Her voice trails off. She stares out the window, hands lingering in the water as if I'm not there, but then she straightens and dries her hands on a dishtowel. "And you, *Mija*, we have a lot to catch up on," she says, turning to me with a warm, tired smile. "But it's getting late, and I have to get up early tomorrow for work, and you, too, no? I'll get my purse and keys and take you back to the dorm. We'll talk more very soon." She squeezes my hand and leaves the kitchen to gather her things.

Mari comes in as Alma departs, earbuds dangling around her neck. She opens the fridge and pours herself a glass of lemonade. "Did my jerk sister scare you off?" she says without meeting my eye, as if I've done something to piss her off and now she doesn't give a crap if I stay or go. I'm wavering between being offended and being mad when something occurs to me. She's acting like she doesn't care, in case I don't come back. I know because I've acted this way plenty of times.

"It takes more than a few stupid comments to scare me off," I say. "It's just late. I have to get back to the dorm."

"Good. Because I'd kill her if she did." She offers me a glass of lemonade and when I decline, puts it back in the fridge. "Maybe we could do something on the weekend?" she says, returning to her earlier enthusiasm. "Sometimes I go to the Farmers' Market with Mia if she's not being a total butt. Rudy works there on Saturdays. He sells chiles. You could come?"

"Rudy sells chiles?" I say instead of responding to the invitation. I sound like a jerk, but I think of Esha on the phone, telling someone to pick up the chiles from some guy named Rudy this Saturday at the Farmers' Market, and it can't be a coincidence.

"Yeah, so?" Mari says, folding her arms defensively. "Is that a problem?

"No," I quickly say. "I just heard the name somewhere, that's all. Of course I'll come."

"Great," she says, as Alma returns. "See you in a few days."

Ten

"You sure you don't want to come?" I ask Clem for the third time on Saturday, a couple of minutes before Alma and Mari are set to pick me up. I waggle my eyebrows. "Dahlia's selling goat cheese."

"Oh, well, if there's goat cheese…" he jokes. "Nah. Seriously. I have things to do."

"Okay, but you don't know what you're missing."

"Actually, correction," he says, picking up his violin. "I live here. I know exactly what I'm missing." He bows a few lively notes. "I used to play at the market on Saturdays when I was little. The cute kid in a bow tie, playing classical music. It earned me enough to buy all the candy and comic books I wanted."

I give in and accept that he isn't coming, thinking maybe it's better anyway to spend the morning on my own with my sister. But when I say good-bye and go outside to wait for Mari and Alma, I'm struck by a wave of insecurity. Eight days ago I knew nothing about these people. Suddenly we're all insta-family—just add water! What if there's more to being a family than "just adding water"? What if I don't have what it takes? What if I blow it? What if Mari decides she doesn't like me? What if—

Two short, impatient honks startle me out of another "what if?" I'd assumed Alma would be driving, but when I look up, it's Amelia behind the wheel. She's driving a truck that should've never been allowed off the ranch. If the thing were a horse, it'd be one step away from the glue factory. Four colors of paint show through its New Mexico suntan, and the clatter the engine makes is like someone's dragging something metal by a chain or like an elephant's chomping on a mouthful of ball bearings—not to mention the fact the front tires move more or less independently of each other, which I'm guessing is a pretty good indication of the state of the suspension.

I open the door and squeeze into the jump seat behind Amelia. "Where's Alma?" I still can't bring myself to call her Gran, a word that implies history and relationship.

"Gran works at the greenhouse in the summer. She's the plant whisperer," Mari says.

"That's stupid," Amelia retorts. "How can you be a plant whisperer?"

"Maybe plants have feelings," Mari says defensively. "Ever think of that?"

Amelia's response is a mocking snort.

Mari twists in her seat to look at me. "All I'm saying is Gran's really into plants. She knows everything about them and can make anything grow. The summer is crazy busy in the greenhouse, so she works there all day and then takes care of Mrs. Gonzales for her home health-care job at night. She doesn't get home until midnight on Saturdays. Poor Gran."

"And I got assigned the task of driving." Amelia grunts and eyes me in the rearview mirror.

"You were going anyway," Mari says. "It's not like it'll kill you to drive one more person."

"Don't be so sure," Amelia mutters.

Ten minutes later we park in an underground garage and head into the Farmers' Market, a festive atmosphere of vendors lining a narrow, outdoor corridor, their stalls covered with white canopies like sails against the blue sky. Crowds of people with colorful shopping bags and clothes mill up and down the corridor, drinking coffee and poking at the various fruits and vegetables and bundles of lavender and sage.

Amelia weaves through the crowd and stops at a stall where a guy, who looks just a little older than me, hunches over a scale, weighing a bag of green chiles for a waiting couple.

"Hey, Babe!" she calls in a girlie singsong that makes me wonder if Amelia hasn't been abducted by aliens and replaced by a boy-band loving, #OMG, teen-girl cult member.

Babe, who must be the alleged Rudy, looks up and smiles. His freckled brown skin and sunburned nose gives him a rugged, outdoorsy look, and his smile oozes a laid-back-California-surfer vibe. The backwards baseball cap adds to the impression.

"Babe!" he responds (do they wear matching underwear, too?) and wraps a tattooed arm around Amelia's waist, bringing her in for a kiss. When the tongue action subsides, he lets go and sends out a fist in Mari's direction.

Instead of reaching out for a bump, Mari puts her arm around me and blows air from her bottom lip, sending a curl skyward. "This is Faith."

Rudy tosses his chin toward me and I toss mine back—introductions for the twenty-first century. "Man, it's been sick busy all morning," he says, turning his attention back to Amelia. "Can hardly keep up with all the sales. You ladies want to help?"

Amelia looks torn, like the word "help" might kill her, but also like she'll do anything for her guy.

"I'll help," Mari pitches in, surprising me, since seconds ago she wouldn't give Rudy the time of day. "For a free bag of chiles!"

Rudy takes off his hat and scratches his head in comedic introspection of the request. "What the hell," he says, putting the cap back on. "Ernie will never know if I give a few away. Just stay away from those." He points at the sealed crate on the ground behind the table.

"Why?" she asks and goes straight for the crate.

"I said stay away!" Rudy snaps. "Premium goods. Special delivery. No touching."

"Jeez. Take a chill pill. What's so special about them?"

"Extra capsaicin, engineered to be extra hot. Ernie's leasing his fields to a scientist who sells them to the specialty chile market. She grows these bad boys and today I started delivering them to her buyer who brings them to his uncle's restaurants. They're way too hot for you, girl."

"Nothing's too hot for me," Mari counters.

"Yeah, well these are. Trust me. Extra hot. Extra special."

At that moment there's a shout from the far end of the corridor. Rudy and Amelia turn to see what's happening. I turn too. It's like a wave, carrying with it a raft of unusual creatures, in this case the human sort, but all of them costumed as if for some bizarre fruit-and-veggie-themed Halloween parade. Many of the paraders carry signs, and all of them chant the same slogan: *Hey. Hey. Ho. Ho. GMOs have got to go!*

I turn back to Mari just in time to see her prying open the crate and slipping one of Rudy's special chiles into her pocket. I catch her eye and she winks. I wink back.

"I'll share it with you later," she whispers. I give her a subversive thumbs-up, then jump as the paraders close in on us.

"There he is!" the blond chile leading the parade shouts. She stops in front of Rudy's booth, and I read the sign she's brandishing like a machete: Save the New Mexico Chile!

"Holly Redding, what a surprise. Always a pleasure," Rudy says, invoking the god of sarcasm.

"Where's Ernie?" she demands.

"At the farm. Not coming today."

"Well then I have a message for him." Holly scrutinizes Rudy with fierce blue eyes. "You tell him we won't stand for genetically engineered chiles in New Mexico! Tell him we'll do whatever it takes to stop him."

"Like dress up like corns and chiles and wave signs in our faces? I'm trembling, *pendeja*."

"Well, you should be!" a tomato in the back of the group calls. "We'll do what it takes. GMOs aren't welcome in New Mexico!"

The protestors raise their signs and march off, shouting their anti-GMO slogans as they part the shoppers like an organic Moses splitting the Red Sea. They might look weird, but I have to admit, you wouldn't catch me dressed up in a chile suit. Those guys have guts.

"What was all that about?" I ask when the last chile and a kindergarten-sized ear of corn have passed.

Rudy leans on the open tailgate of a small truck backed up to the stall. Amelia sits beside him, texting. "Let's just say me and her don't see eye-to-eye on the future of the chile and the roles of the farmers here in New Mexico." He slings an arm around Amelia, and I look over at Mari, bent down in front of the stall, petting a dog. "My family, they've been here on the land a long time, since my great grandfather. We know chiles. And they're dying. We lost our farm due to these *pinche* insects that destroyed the crop, so I had to go work for Ernie. He's got a deal with this scientist lady, Dr. Richmond. She leases land from him to grow her chiles. He gets a good chunk of change out of it. Not a bad deal, if you ask me. She's got a project to make a genetically engineered chile that's going to save the industry."

"Engineered to be extra hot?" I ask, even more confused. "But how does that help fight off an insect?"

"Nah. Dr. R does the bug chiles. The extra-hot ones come from Dr. Margolis, the other scientist lady."

"You mean Esha?"

"Yeah, that's her. Dr. R's chiles aren't on the market yet. Dr. M started harvesting hers a few months ago. She asked me to bring them into town for her buyer and collect the cash." He looks longingly at the crate of chiles, which Mari has managed to reseal, and lets out a low whistle. "These beauties are worth a lot of money."

So Esha has a chile project, too. Maybe that's what she was sequencing when I saw her name on one of the DNA vials, and that was the distribution issue I heard her talking about on the phone. Jonah says everyone's been working their butts off. I guess this is Esha's contribution to keeping SCPG open. And Holly Redding is none too happy. She doesn't just have one GMO to deal with. She has two.

Amelia yawns and tucks her phone into her pocket. "Boring," she says to Rudy. "What do you want to do?"

"I have to work until four," he says. "But there's a party tonight. You want to go?"

At the mention of a party, Mari stops petting the dog and stands up to join us. Amelia glances at her sister and rolls her eyes. "Can't. Gran's working late. I'm in charge of Mari. She'll kill me if I take her to a party after what happened last month."

"Come on, Babe. Mari's a big girl. She can take care of herself."

"I have an idea," Mari interjects.

Amelia folds her arms and sighs as if the mere suggestion of an idea is an irritation.

"Faith can come to the party with us," Mari goes on, not letting Amelia's irritation deter her. "She can keep an eye on me if you're so worried."

"Um, no," I say, holding up my hands. "Sorry. I'm not a babysitter, and I don't do parties."

"Pleeease, Faith," Mari begs, clasping her hands in front of her.

Looking at this skinny girl with the big eyes and messy curls, this girl who wants to fit in and who has ribbons of sadness coiled inside her, I feel something I've never felt. For a second I can't put a name to the feeling, and then I get it. Affection. I want to hang out with her, even if it means going to some party where I don't know anyone. Because she's my sister.

"Fine," I say. "I'll go, but I'm not a chaperone."

Amelia groans, but I barely notice because Mari throws her arms around me and lets out a loud whooping sound in my ear that makes me go deaf. *Whatever*, I think, as she chatters excitedly, *hearing's overrated.*

Rudy explains where the party is and we agree to meet there at seven-thirty. Mari skips off to the bathroom. I move over to the shade. As I sit on a bench across from Rudy's stall, waiting for Mari to return, I see Amelia and Rudy huddling. Their huddle has a different vibe than their earlier lovebird grope fest. There's something secretive and exclusive about the hunch of their shoulders. My nosey gene kicks in. I reposition myself to see what they're doing.

I can't hear what they're saying, but I see Rudy handing Amelia a shoebox sealed with blue duct tape. Something about how guarded and stiff he seems makes me think back to what Alma said about Rudy getting arrested for selling pot—worse, it calls up the other night at Alma's when Amelia admitted she was high. Is he giving dope to Amelia now? A dizzying rush of worry about my half sister and drugs has just rocketed up in me when a silver truck with big, jacked-up tires and a Broncos plate squeezes into the stall next to Rudy's truck and a bulky, twenty-something guy with pale, acne-scarred skin, a flattish bulldog face, and a tattooed bicep steps out. My worry over Amelia screeches to a stop because I'm all about the Bulldog guy now. Sometimes you don't need to open the refrigerator to know something's bad inside.

Rudy gives Bulldog the crate of extra-hot chiles and Bulldog hands Rudy an envelope. The deal happens in a blink of an eye, and call me paranoid, but first the box now the envelope, and I'm thinking how many times have I watched a scene like this on some rundown Philly street corner? Rudy said he was selling a box of extra-hot chiles for Esha. Their little transaction looks more like a drug deal to me, like maybe it wasn't just chiles in that box. Maybe Rudy's still selling dope.

"I hate parties," I complain to Jesse via phone a few hours after Amelia drops me at the dorm and I've explained the situation to him. "I suck at small talk. I don't know anyone. I don't drink. I don't dance. And the music is always crap."

"Man. Sounds like a blast," he says. "I'm jealous. Wish I were you."

I groan and bury my head beneath my pillow.

"If it's that bad, don't go," his now muffled voice tells me.

"But I want to see Mari. Besides, I promised."

"Isn't there anyone else you can invite? Any of the other interns?"

I yank the pillow off my head and sit up. Great idea. Why hadn't I thought of it? "Well, yeah, actually there is," I say, not telling him who the other intern is. I should tell Jesse about Clem, but what exactly is there to tell? Hey, Jesse, there's a boy here with whom nothing has happened. It's like turning on the TV and the anchorperson saying, "Today in the news we have nothing to report!" But that's a lie and I know it. Just because nothing's happened with Clem, doesn't mean nothing's there, at least not in my mind. You don't need to cheat to be disloyal.

"Hello? You still there?" Jesse asks, and I realize he's waiting for me to elaborate on who I'm inviting.

"Sorry. Yep. Still here." I change the subject. "You still coming out for the Fourth?" I ask, even though just yesterday we talked about his plan to spend the Fourth of July weekend in Santa Fe.

"Nothing's changed in twelve hours." He pauses and then, in this uncanny ability Jesse has, he reads into everything I'm not saying. "Do you still want me to come?"

"Totally!" I say, a little too eagerly, and then—"Why wouldn't I?"

"I don't know. You tell me."

For a second I consider again telling him about Clem. This is my chance, but instead I say, "I can't wait to see you."

Because that's also the truth.

Eleven

"You finish practicing, Maestro?" I ask when Clem opens his door.

"Never and yes."

"So...that means?"

"It means 'Twinkle Twinkle' is starting to sound like a good option. Or maybe 'Yankee Doodle Dandy.' Maybe they could set off fireworks and nobody has to hear me play."

I peer into his room. The window is closed. The blinds are down. The smell of socks and armpits wafts into the hall. "You get out at all today?"

"Yep. Went to the bathroom three times."

"Right. That's not what I meant. Go change your clothes."

"Why?"

"Because we're going to a party. Even world-class musicians need a break, don't they?"

"Not really."

"Okay, forget that. Just come on. It'll be..."

"Fun?" he asks when I don't finish the thought.

"No. I hate parties, but it's something I said I'd do." I explain what happened at the Farmers' Market and conclude by saying, "I need moral support."

His face breaks into a tired grin. "Who could resist an invitation like that? I'll be ready in five."

———

Amelia picks us up a few minutes after Clem finishes changing, and I repeat this morning's routine of climbing into the truck, this time with Clem climbing in behind me.

"What's that?" I ask, moving two large bowls covered with tinfoil off the jump seat, so Clem and I can squeeze in, me on the tiny jump seat and him on the floor.

"Food for the party," Mari says, as I put one bowl on my lap and hand the other to Clem to put on his. "Rudy said people would be bringing stuff. Amelia made her famous *mole*—"

"It's not famous," Amelia interrupts.

"Yes, it is, after what happened," Mari retorts, and I pick up the snide in her voice.

"What happened?" I ask.

"Nothing!" Amelia snaps, throwing me a look in the rearview mirror.

O-key dokey. Tension. Knife. Change of subject. "What's *mole*?"

Clem's the one who answers. He explains that *mole*, sometimes called the national dish of Mexico, is a sauce made with chile peppers and chocolate and about twenty other ingredients. Although Amelia acts disinterested, I can tell she's listening to every word, that there's more to the *mole* than meets the eye.

"So what's in the other bowl?" I ask Mari when Clem's done explaining.

"Amelia couldn't be the only one bringing food."

"Yes. I could," Amelia mumbles.

"So I made green chile stew. Extra-hot," Mari says, ignoring Amelia. She turns and gives me a knowing look and a wink, and I get that she's made the stew with the special chile she took from Rudy. "It's super good. Super spicy. Onions. Chile. Garlic. You want to try it?"

"Not right now," I say.

"You want some?" she asks Clem.

"I wouldn't if I were you," Amelia warns, a dig at Mari's culinary skills, and I'm getting that all this food-making has more to do with sibling rivalry than with providing sustenance for a bunch of soon-to-be-smashed teens.

Clem, the diplomat, smiles. "No thanks. I'm sure it's great," he assures her. "But I'm not hungry."

Mari shrugs. "Okay, but you don't know what you're missing."

———

The party's in a neighborhood of small brown and beige stucco houses. Some are surrounded by chain link, some are manned (dogged?) by pit bulls and Chihuahuas, others are enclosed by walled-off courtyards. A few of the houses have gardens, but mostly the landscaping is a back-to-nature theme: rocks, weeds, dirt, and a few thirsty-looking cacti.

Amelia parks along the curb behind Rudy and the five of us walk up to the house together. Rudy pushes open the door and we make our entrance to a round of "S'up, bros?" and complicated handshakes. The smell of beer and pot is overwhelming, and the fact of far too many bodies packed into far too small a space, not to mention the thumping electronic beat—which played at a normal level would be bad enough—does nothing to improve the situation.

Amelia, our fearless party guide, is ramming through the mob when she stops so suddenly that Mari bashes into her. I follow Amelia's gaze to see what's causing the holdup and find her staring, with an expression I can only interpret as horror, at a skinny, redheaded girl wearing a sparkly green, doll-sized dress.

"You okay?" I say, tapping her shoulder.

Without answering my question she thrusts her *mole* dish at Mari and takes off in the opposite direction of the redhead, disappearing into the crowd.

Mari sighs and says she's going to bring her stew and Amelia's *mole* to the kitchen and see what other snacks they have. I check out the keg, the beer bongs, the empty bottles of wine coolers—mandatory party paraphernalia—as she too, gets swallowed up by the swarm. I'm totally not here to babysit, but the second she's out of sight, I think of Alma's story, how Mari snuck out and the cops brought her home wasted. How she's in with the wrong crowd at school. I think of all Mari's sadness, the way she disappears, and I have a twinge of unease because I know the easiest way to evade all that sadness. I was indoctrinated into the escapist school of Mom. When the going gets tough, the tough get wasted.

The song changes, some kind of ganster rap played too loudly to be enjoyed. I mean rap is cool when it's not all bitch this and bitch that. It can be poetry, but whatever this is, it's just bad.

Clem is saying something, but I can't hear him. I cup my hand to my ear and he points toward the door. I give him the thumbs-up and follow. He stakes out a place just outside where the breeze carries the smell of rain and diffuses away the stink of beer. Clouds have stacked up over the mountains. The sky is a moody gray. Any minute now it's going to pour.

"So, these are your half sisters." Clem says, now that we can hear each other. "The older one's…interesting."

"Jerk would be another word for it." I sigh as I hear the first crack of thunder. "I don't know what her deal is, but she really seems to hate me."

"I doubt that."

"Why?"

He shrugs and steps aside as three guys brush by. "I could see the way she was looking at you. She kept checking you out in the rearview mirror as she drove. Maybe she's just jealous."

"Of me?"

"No, of the wall." He laughs and slaps my arm. A zing of electricity charges through my belly, and I slap him back. We have a brief, promiscuous slap fest as inside the music changes again. This time it's Latin salsa.

"You like to dance?" Clem asks.

"No." I back away, fearing he's one of those guys who know a few moves and like to show off on the dance floor.

"Good. Neither do I."

I breathe a sigh of relief that I won't be forced to dance and make a fool of myself, but then the door opens. Three people stumble out and stagger toward the street, and Clem asks if I drink.

"Nah," I say, hoping that not only doesn't he dance, but that he doesn't drink either. "You?"

He shakes his head. "Sometimes I wish I did. It would help to fit in or whatever." He seems embarrassed to admit this, and I'm surprised that he cares about such things. "Being a violin geek doesn't exactly make you popularity king."

I consider saying "but you're so great and talented and cute." Instead, I bite down on my lip and say, "I know what you mean, but screw it. Fitting in's overrated."

So, the Latin music actually isn't salsa. It's a horrifying mash-up of Latin meets rap meets electronica meets whiny-girl pop. Clem and I both start to laugh.

"What do you say we find the person in charge of the tunes

and teach them a thing or two about music?" he says and leads me back into the house.

That's when I see her.

On the other side of the room, my fourteen-year-old half sister is accepting a beer from a pretty-boy blond who looks to be about twenty. There's something predatory about his posture, too close, too confident. I'm not a chaperone, but I'm also not into a perverted older dude hitting on a younger girl, no matter who she is. And more than that, the idea of Mari drinking, of making the same screwed up choices as Mom, awakens a beast in me I had no idea was there.

Without a word to Clem, I push through the crowd in their direction.

"I'm Thomas," I hear Pretty Boy tell a doe-eyed Mari as I get closer. I see now that she's holding an empty plastic cup of beer she's already finished and is reaching out to Pretty Boy for another.

"Hey," I say, stepping in between Mari and the out stretched hand and grabbing the cup. "Thanks for the drink."

"Whoa, man, I was giving that to her," Pretty Boy says, somehow managing to flex and show off his sculpted and tattooed biceps as he draws his fists to his waist.

I smile sweetly. "Yeah, well, she's fourteen, so, like I said, thanks anyway."

"I think she's old enough to make her own decisions," Pretty Boy says, lowering pale eyebrows over bleary, drunken eyes.

"And I know judo. Back off."

"Whatever. She's not that hot anyway," he says and walks away.

Mari's mouth drops open. I'm about to apologize for the assholes of the world and for my outbreak of motheringitis, but she laughs and says, "God, what a major jerkazoid. Like

he's so hot! I'm not exactly into grandpas. I just wanted a beer."
She imitates him flexing his muscles and now we both laugh.

"Total jerkazoid," I agree.

"Hey," Clem says, wandering back to my side as the music
changes to something quiet and moody. "I saw Thomas stagger
off. What'd he want?"

"You know that guy?" I ask, setting down the confiscated
beer on a table.

"Kind of. Not really." He jams his hands deep into his
pockets. "My mom helped his mom out a few times and I had
to go to his house with her. I think he might've said what's up."

Two girls brush past us, talking loudly. "This chile stew's
so good," Girl One, who's carrying a bowl in one hand, a beer
in the other, says to empty-handed Girl Two. "You should
totally try some."

"Ugh. No way, Eslee. My butt's like the size of Texas," Girl
Two, a skinny blonde, says.

"What-ever. Probably just as well. I think I ate like all
of it, " Girl One, apparently called Eslee, says with a bitchy
eye-roll as they merge into the crowd.

"Yes!" Mari pumps her fist in the air. "I told Amelia people
would like it! I wonder if anyone ate her food?" She picks up
the beer I put down and takes a few sips. "I'll be back soon."

She sways a little on her feet, and I wonder how much
she's had to drink. "Hey," I call after her. "Can I finish that?"
I indicate the beer still in her hand.

She looks at the cup as if she'd forgotten what she was
holding, shrugs, and hands it to me.

"I thought you didn't drink," Clem says when she's gone.

"I don't." I toss the cup into a trashcan. "But she doesn't
know that."

Clem and I park ourselves on a mattress someone's dragged into the room. Someone's dimmed the lights. Cliché romance rock has come on and apparently it's hook-up hour. I glance around at the bodies entwined on couches, in doorways, on the dance floor. Embarrassed by the suggestion of what everyone else is doing, I avoid looking at Clem, and instead, turn my eyes to the window, surprised to see it's gotten dark. Even without looking at Clem, I'm consumed with awareness of his presence, his knee brushing mine, the heat of his arm. I'm also consumed with awareness of Jesse, and the fact he's texted me three times to ask how the party's going.

Maybe I should say something to Clem about boyfriend-girlfriend stuff, but what? What if I tell him about Jesse and he doesn't want to hang out anymore? Worse, what if I tell him and he doesn't care because he doesn't like me in that way and I make a fool of myself? Then again, words are overrated. I could just turn and kiss him. Then again, the shoulder bump and leg brush could mean nothing. And then again there's Jesse.

Clem clears his throat. I get he's about to speak, and more than not speaking, whatever he might have to say terrifies me, so I whirl around and blurt, "Game show host!"

Of course I can see how this non sequitur would take anybody off-guard, and I'm horrified at the when-did-this-girl-go-off-her-meds? expression on Clem's face. I quickly point to a charismatic guy with long black hair, who's leading four or five others in a drinking game and add, "You know. His thing. He's a game show host."

"Nah," Clem says, nudging my ankle with his foot. "Used car salesman. See the way he got that girl to do a shot?"

I look around for some other party victim to examine, and as I do, I catch Mari's eye. From across the room she waves and holds up a finger, indicating she'll be over in a minute.

She's talking to Rudy, who's giving her another beer. I'm trying not to be overly interested in the Mari-plus-beer-equals-a-wasted-fourteen-year-old situation, trying not to return to my previous outbreak of motheringitis and intervene, when the voice of Marta—the school counselor I saw for a year in Philly—goes off in my head.

"What happened to your mother wasn't your fault," Marta says. "You can't take responsibility for other people's actions."

Thanks, Marta. Mari lived her life without me until now. It's her deal if she wants to drink. I smile weakly, ignoring the urgent signals my brain is sending to make Mari stop, and return to the game. Clem's pointing to the front door where a trendy girl with skinny jeans and streaked green hair is skulking. I'm trying to decide on a fit for the girl when I see Bulldog, the guy from the Farmers' Market, come in, beer in hand. I look back to Mari, but it's Rudy who catches my attention. He's staring past me at the door, frozen and wide-eyed. I follow his gaze to Bulldog. When I turn back to Mari, Rudy's gone.

Mari shrugs and starts over toward me. Bulldog reaches her first.

"You seen Rudy?" I hear him ask her.

"Maybe," she slurs, coy and a little drunk.

He seems to find her slurring and coyness charming. He hands his cup of beer to her, leans against the wall with a smirk and watches her drink. It's not the same lecherous vibe as before with Pretty Boy, more like he's having fun with her, teasing. Ply someone with alcohol and shave off their eyebrows kind of thing. I have to make an effort not to leap up and make it stop.

"So maybe yes, or maybe no?" he asks.

"Maybe yes." She points to a side door, leading outside.

Bulldog turns away from Mari without saying anything and takes off in the direction she pointed.

Mari mumbles something, wobbles a bit, then collapses into a chair.

"I'd keep an eye on her if she were my little sister," Clem says, noticing where my attention has gone. "She's not looking too good."

I nod. "I'll be right back." Instead of going to Mari, though, I follow Bulldog.

It's raining. Hard, angry drops send up puffs of reddish-colored dust. Rudy and Bulldog don't seem to notice, or if they do, to mind. They're standing on a buckled sidewalk under a streetlamp, their hair and clothes getting drenched. I can see that they're angry, but with the rain and the inside noise, I can't hear anything. I edge closer and slip behind a car, hoping to hear what they're saying.

A small white dog I hadn't noticed before whimpers and sniffs at me. "Hey, there," I whisper, reaching down to pet the animal. The dog starts barking and I quickly retract my hand, hoping my cover isn't blown. Rudy and Bulldog look up. I duck lower and hold my breath. Something tells me I don't want those guys catching me listening. Satisfied nobody's there, they go back to business.

"You ripped me off," I hear Bulldog say.

"You're full of it, bro," Rudy snaps back.

"Nah, man. I'm not. You got twenty-four hours to make this right and get the rest to me, and if you don't, there's gonna be trouble."

A clap of thunder drowns out Rudy's response.

"You've been warned," Bulldog says, and climbs into his truck. He sprays Rudy with muddy water as he guns it down the road.

Alma said Rudy had been arrested for selling dope. I'm thinking now that my earlier suspicions were right. It wasn't just chiles Rudy sold to Bulldog. It was pot. I'm overcome with a fierce urge to find Mari and Amelia and Clem and get out of here. I dash back inside, but when I get there I realize I haven't seen Amelia since we arrived, and the chair Mari had occupied is empty. Clem's the only one I can find. He's in the middle of a conversation with a guy wearing artsy glasses and a bow tie.

"Hey," I interrupt, tugging at Clem's sleeve. "We have to go."

"You read my mind. I tried to talk to Mari, but she was all spaced out and wandered off," he says as we strand the guy by an impressive vinyl collection.

"Okay, here's the plan," I say. "You search that side of the house." I point down a long hall going in one direction. "And I'll go that way." I point down the hall going the other way. "Text me if you find her."

I squeeze between a pair of hipsters in retro Seventies glasses, then worm around a pack of red-eye burnouts, cigarettes dangling from their fingers. I bump through a pair of dirty dancers and open the door to a bedroom where a couple is making out. I don't find Mari anywhere, but I do find Amelia, lurking by a closet door as if she's contemplating going inside.

"Your boyfriend left," I say.

"Duh, *Guera*. You're not the only one with eyes."

"Well, I'm ready to go," I say, refusing to give into whatever angry little psychological game she wants to drag me into. "Have you seen Mari?"

"Um, no. That would be your job. Remember? You were the chaperone. Not me."

I fight back a stitch of nervous guilt, even though I hadn't agreed to the position. "Fine. Whatever. Let's go look for her."

I text Clem and tell him I found Amelia and ask if he's found Mari. He texts back that he hasn't.

Amelia and I are walking back into the main room when she stops abruptly and veers left into the kitchen. "This way," she says, indicating a sliding glass door leading to the back of the house.

"It's raining. Why would she be out there?"

"She wouldn't, but we can get into the other side of the house that way."

I'm about to protest and tell her that Clem's already searched that side of the house, but I peer into the main room and see that redhead she'd been avoiding earlier. For whatever reason Amelia doesn't want to confront the girl; now isn't the time to push it. I shrug and follow her outside.

The rain is pounding down now. We're crossing the yard, holding our hands over our heads, when I make out a shape on the ground by the back wall. A guy stands over the crumpled figure.

"Come on, *Guera!*" Amelia shouts. I don't move and she gives and exasperated sigh. "Fine, whatever. You have a thing for rain, stay out here and catch pneumonia and die. See if I care."

I don't answer. I inch closer to the crumpled figure and the guy. As I get closer I see that the guy is Pretty Boy, and sprawled on the ground—curls flattened, dirt spattered, soaking wet—is my fourteen-year-old half sister.

Amelia sees her, too. "What the fuck?" She shouts and runs toward Mari. Pretty Boy takes off as Amelia and I reach her side.

Twelve

I hardly remember calling 911 or Alma, but I know I did because here we are, the four of us, Alma, Amelia, Clem and I, sitting in the ER waiting for news. I hunch over my chair, elbows on my knees, face buried in my palms, thoughts racing between this being my fault—that I should have been watching Mari—and that I'm going to kill Pretty Boy.

After what seems like hours, a tall Asian woman in scrubs enters the waiting area. She identifies Alma as Mari's guardian, introduces herself as Dr. Kendall, and leads us to the back to a curtained off cubicle where Mari is asleep on a bed with wheels. Tubes and wires dangle from her arms, nose, and chest. She looks so tiny in her hospital gown, so helpless on the thin mattress. I want to cry, but I fight back tears, not wanting to cry in front of these people who are both family and strangers. Amelia, on the other hand, who hasn't stopped crying since we found Mari, rushes to her sister's side in a flurry of snot and sobs.

Doctor Kendall stands by the cardiac monitor, clipboard in hand. "She's out of immediate danger," she tells us. "She's resting now, but her heart rate was extremely high when she got here, and she was disoriented." She pauses, and in that pause I dread whatever news is coming next. "Preliminary tests indicate a drug that goes by the street name of liquid gold was in her system."

"The date-rape drug?" I burst out, remembering the newspaper article. Clem and I exchange glances. Then, with sickening horror, I flash on the image of Pretty Boy kneeling over Mari in the rain.

Dr. Kendall looks from me to Alma and back to me. "In some instances, yes, liquid gold has been used as a predatory drug to assist in sexual assault, but it's not always used that way. It's also a recreational drug." I back up against the wall and keep my eyes glued to a cart of medical equipment, unable to meet Alma's gaze. "Mari spoke to the sexual assault nurse once she'd gotten her bearings. She said she doesn't think she was assaulted, but she can't remember what happened." Doctor Kendall inhales slowly. "I think it's best if we perform a rape test, but we need her consent. As soon as she wakes up we'll ask."

I peek now at Alma who's taking the blows with unflinching warrior strength. I also notice the strain in her jaw, her knuckles white on the rails of Mari's bed when she asks if Mari can come home tonight.

Dr. Kendall shakes her head. "I'm sorry, but her blood oxygen was dangerously low, and she was short of breath when she arrived. She'll have to stay here for observation and treatment."

Alma nods, her face a mask as she strokes Mari's hair, speaking softly to her in Spanish. A splintering of love rips through me. More than anything I want to join Alma at Mari's side. I want to bury my face in her curls and tell her I'm sorry. I don't. I stand by the counter with the bandages and rubber gloves without moving because who do I think I am? I don't belong here. This is between Alma and her real granddaughters. I'm the uninvited guest, the proverbial fifth wheel. If it weren't for Clem, I'd be so out of here.

"Since we found an illegal substance in Mari's system, we had to call the police," I hear Dr. Kendall say, and I realize she's speaking to me. "You were at the party and the one who called the paramedics, so the officer would like to talk to you first, and then to Amelia, and then to the other boy."

Cops. Of course. I close my eyes and recall all the useless interactions I had with the cops back in Philly. How they never got it right, not even the circumstances of Mom's death.

"Are you okay to see him now, or do you need a few minutes?" Dr. Kendall asks.

"I'm okay," I say, opening my eyes and reaching into my pocket for the lighter.

Doctor Kendall slides open the curtain and escorts me to a small, windowless room. A middle-aged guy with closely clipped gray hair, a tired smile, and a weathered face greets me. "I'm Officer Virgil," he says. "Please, have a seat." Instead of the usual cop thing—him on one side of a desk, me on the other—he pulls up a chair next to mine. "Can I get you anything? Water? Coffee?"

I shake my head and focus on my hands folded in my lap.

"I'm hoping you can help me understand what happened tonight," he says.

Besides the fact that if I had been watching over Mari none of this would have happened, I think, but I don't say that. I don't say anything. I wait for an actual question before responding.

"Do you know if Mari's had trouble with drugs in the past?" he asks.

"I have no clue, Virg," I say, sinking down and pulling my hoodie over my head. "I just met her."

"Did you see anything weird at the party?"

"You mean other than some really bad outfits?"

He narrows his eyes as if deciding how much of a smartass I'm going to be. "Yes, other than that. Any drugs?"

"Besides alcohol, no."

He taps his fingers twice on the arm of his chair and doesn't take his eyes off me. "Do you know if anyone offered her drugs?"

I think about the newspaper article again—*Liquid gold can be slipped easily and without detection into drinks*—and consider all the drinks Mari had, from Rudy, from Bulldog, and especially from the perv, Pretty Boy. He could have done anything to her. If he slipped her liquid gold and assaulted her, it was my fault. And my fault means it's up to me to make this right. I'm not handing out details to some cop, so he can go mess things up like they did with Mom, writing off her death to an overdose when she'd been murdered.

"I didn't see anyone offer her drugs," I say, presenting just the right amount of information to satisfy the appearance of cooperation. "But a lot of guys were giving her beer."

Virg considers this as he gets up and starts to pace the tiny, windowless room. "I don't know how much you know about liquid gold. It comes from a Peruvian plant. Some South American cultures use it ritually, but when it gets turned into a street drug, we have a real problem. It's lethal if you take too much, and it's extremely difficult to regulate the dosage. We saw a lot of it around here about ten years ago, but it was expensive. Too expensive to take a real hold. It's been coming in cheaper recently. The trouble is, we don't know where it's coming from, and from what happened to your sister, it seems much more pure. It's a bad thing. This valley has already suffered hard from heroin. New Mexico has the second-highest drug overdose death rate in the country." He reaches into his pocket and hands me a card. "If you hear or see anything get in touch with me. I can't emphasize enough the seriousness of this drug." He looks at me as if he's about to say something more, but a knock interrupts whatever was coming next. He opens the door, and Dr. Kendall is back.

"Another case of liquid gold OD just came in. The girl is in critical condition. She was picked up at the same party."

———

We leave the hospital sometime around midnight after Virg talks to Clem and Amelia. As we walk to the parking lot, I realize Alma hasn't said anything in a long time. I glance at her and see that her face is tight and pinched with dark shadows beneath her eyes. She's exhausted, obviously, but there's something else, too, and then I get it. Anger. Back in the emergency room she hadn't said a word about Mari ending up at a party, passed out in the rain with liquid gold in her blood. I avoid her eyes as we weave through the maze of cars, waiting for her to tell me how I failed Mari, how she had expected more of me. She'd be right in both cases.

Instead of turning to me, though, she turns to Amelia. "How could you have let this happen to your sister?"

"She was with *Guera*!" Amelia shoots back, stopping in her tracks and planting her hands on her hips. "Why don't you blame her?"

Amelia's right of course, and again, I wait for Alma to turn to me. She doesn't. Every bit of her fire stays on Amelia. "Her name is Faith and she is not responsible for Mari," she says in a low, angry voice. "You are. And Mari shouldn't have been at a party."

Amelia starts to protest, but Alma cuts her off. "You are grounded. Besides visiting your sister and going to work, you will not leave the house for a week."

Even Amelia knows enough to keep her mouth shut. She storms off to her truck, fuming, and drives away.

"I'm sorry," I say to Alma the second Amelia leaves. Those tears I'd been battling finally win the fight. "I should've…"

"*Mija*," she says in a strong voice that leaves no room for debate, "this is not your fault. You did everything you could. Now let me take you back to the college."

She drives Clem and me back to St. John's, windows rolled down to the cool night silence. Except for the occasional lowrider bouncing with a bass-line, the streets are deserted. The rule against tall buildings and bright lights keeps the sky huge and dark and pure. Gazing out at the star-filled quiet, loneliness swims through me, an isolated feeling of seven billion people occupying the same planet, each one alone. And yet, with Mari I felt a tear in that isolation. I stare into the night, thinking how I failed her. I could've watched her more closely and kept her from drinking. With Mom I was a kid. Her drugs and drinking were her deal, not mine. I get that now. Tonight was different. Mari was the kid.

I clench my fist around the Zippo and vow to find out what happened to my sister.

Thirteen

Loud pounding wakes me the next day. Sunday, thank God. It could be six a.m., could be noon. I have no idea. I stumble out of bed in a T-shirt and boxers, eyes crusted with sleep, hair matted to my face, and open the door.

"I called you three times, *Guera*." Amelia. Standing in the hall. Dressed head-to-toe in black, oversized silver rings adorning every finger of the hand raised to knock again. "Try leaving your phone on."

A jolt of panic erases what's left of sleep. "Is Mari okay? Did something happen?"

"Nothing else happened. I'm going to the hospital to see her." She takes a sharp breath, as if pained at having caught herself being nice, and says, "Gran made me bring you, but since your phone was off, I couldn't tell you." She rolls her eyes, making sure I'm clear that coming to get me is obligation, not kindness. "So? Coming or not?" This she says as if we had a plan, and I should've been ready.

"Give me five," I say, and slam the door. I throw on my favorite cuts-offs, black tee, and steel-toe, shit kickers—matching Amelia's attitudinal attire with my own—then step into the hall. "Let's go."

It's pouring again. By the time we race across the parking lot and fling ourselves into the truck, we're wet and miserable. Amelia starts the engine and turns on the windshield wipers. The blades make an angry screeching noise. She cuts the wheel hard as she pulls out of the campus parking lot. She swerves onto the main road and has to correct, sending us into the wrong lane and avoiding a collision only by the grace of chance that there are no other cars in our path. Driving while emotional. It's worse than texting. I raise my eyebrows and keep quiet. Without a bucket of water, the best way to fight fire is to let it smolder. Add nothing to spark its flames.

We make it to the hospital in one piece and find Mari in a private room on the third floor. Her eyes are closed, her black curls splayed-out on the pillow in a mat of uncombed tangles. Her lips are fissured and dry, the pale brown moons beneath her eyes swollen.

"Maybe we should come back," I whisper, but Amelia's already clomping across the floor.

"I'm not sleeping," Mari mumbles as Amelia reaches her side. "Just resting."

"Good, then sit up."

Slowly, and with some difficulty, Mari pulls herself upright. Amelia digs into her purse. She grabs a brush and starts to gently run it through Mari's hair. Mari's eyes droop shut.

I stand frozen at the door, feeling like an interloper, a stalker, an intruder on some private ceremony. Amelia knows exactly how to comfort Mari, and isn't it this knowledge, this shared experience, that makes people a family? You can't go to the store and buy history any more than you can buy love.

Amelia works the brush in slow, tender movements, and I get a glimpse beneath Operation Shock-and-Awe—the eff-you way she treats the world. Not that I can't relate to the whole pissed-off thing. I've spent most of my nearly seventeen years emitting an eff-off vibe, and for good reason. With a childhood cast of drug dealers, addicts, a sundry assortment of maternal boyfriends at various stages of drug-related decrepitude, and mostly apathetic school counselors, one can't blame a girl for a little eff-you action. Alvaro had a problem with drugs, and Mari said he liked to drink. I wonder if what fuels Amelia's desire to give the finger to the world stems from the same thing—being raised by an addict parent.

"You should just bring a clipper and chop it all off," Mari moans when Amelia hits a particularly difficult snarl.

"You always say that and you never mean it. Remember the time you got a wad of gum stuck in your hair and you begged Mom to shave your head? Then when she brought out the clippers you began to cry and begged her not to."

They both laugh. Even their small talk has history.

"So, what happened last night?" Amelia asks, changing the subject as she turns Mari's head and starts working the other side.

It's not relaxation this time that drives Mari's eyes to close. It's stress. I hear it in her voice. "I don't know. I can't remember anything."

"Not a thing?" Amelia stops brushing.

Mari sits motionless, her skinny arms sticking out of her nightgown, the oxygen tube coiling from nose to lap like a serpent. "I don't know. I was in the kitchen and the next thing I know I was outside." She opens her eyes. "I didn't take that drug! I swear to God!"

Amelia sets the brush on her lap and squeezes Mari's arm. "Try harder. What were you doing in the kitchen? Who was there with you?"

"I don't know."

It's Mari's tear-filled eyes that finally peel me away from the door. "Don't worry about it," I say, stepping into the room and intervening in Amelia's interrogation. "Your job is just to get better now. How are you feeling?"

"Okay, I guess, but they want to keep me here a few more days for observation." She yawns and lies back down.

"That's right. We can't let our favorite patient out too soon," I hear someone say. I hadn't heard anyone come in, but when I turn around a nurse is at the door, clipboard in hand. "But now Mari has to rest. She's had enough visitors already, and it isn't even noon."

"Enough?" I ask, surprised. "Who else was here?"

"Well, there was her grandmother. And the police with more questions. And then that young man. But she was sleeping when he came, and given her physical condition, the doctor told us not to let anyone wake her."

"Did you get his name?" I ask.

The nurse shoots me a look. "Sorry." She checks over Mari, asks a few questions, then leaves.

Amelia turns back to Mari once she's gone. In a soft, teasing voice, she says, "Do you have a boyfriend you haven't told me about?"

"I wish," Mari says, as her eyes droop close. Within moments her body is soft with sleep.

The second we're in the hall, Amelia turns to me. "What guy came to see my sister? The only guy friend she has is Abe Fong, and he lives in Dallas."

I stab the elevator button and let this information percolate as a theory slowly develops. Maybe Rudy, Pretty Boy, or Bulldog—whoever slipped her the drug—came to the hospital to intimidate Mari and make sure she didn't say anything that might implicate them. "I saw three guys giving her beer at the party," I tell Amelia.

I'm about to tell her the rest of my theory, but she stops walking and stares at me. "That was your idea of chaperoning?"

"If you hadn't brought her to the party there wouldn't have been a problem in the first place," I snap. "So get off your little righteous high horse. You're as much to blame for what happened as I am. As you know I wasn't there to chaperone!"

She attempts to kill me with her eyes. "Fine," she huffs. "We'll go talk to Rudy. He knows everyone. If someone gave my sister a drink and slipped her liquid gold, he'll know about it. And when I find out who it was, I'm going to kill the bastard."

I don't tell her that maybe the bastard she's going to want to kill is Rudy.

———

The rain has stopped when we leave the hospital. The air smells fresh enough to eat. We drive in silence, away from the city, until we reach the hills and bump along a teeth-rattling, pot-holed dirt road. Twenty minutes later, certain at least one of my internal organs has been knocked loose, Amelia stops in front of a doublewide trailer flanked by a graveyard of ancient cars.

The ground is muddy. I have to cross a set of tire tracks cut into the earth like ravines to get to the front door. Amelia opens the door without knocking. I follow her into a shadowy room with sheets covering the windows. The place smells of cat pee and cigarettes.

"Hello?" she calls into the silence.

No answer.

I follow her down a narrow windowless hall. She stops at the end of the hall and knocks on a door next to a bathroom.

Still no answer, so she pushes open the door and closes it behind us.

I'm guessing the room belongs to Rudy. It's what I'd expect from an eighteen-year-old dude living without parental supervision, except for the desk—a clean, well-organized work surface that contrasts with the dirty clothes on the floor, the unmade bed, the collection of empty beer bottles. A lone envelope lies in the middle of the desk. I pick it and see the name Holly Redding printed in black marker.

I'm about to sit down and look through the envelope when the door bangs opens and a scrawny white guy with a military flattop, plaid pajama pants, and a wife-beater tee is standing there, looking like he wants to kill us.

"For fuck's sake, what are you doing here, Mia?" the guy says, relaxing when he realizes he knows at least one of us.

"Hey, Charlie. Where's your roommate?" she says, instead of answering.

"I could ask you the same question," he retorts and slinks into the room. "That shithead woke me up in the middle of the night. He was out late. Then that chick showed up, then that truck."

"What truck?" I say, thinking of the tracks outside.

"What *chick*?" Amelia says.

"That chick who keeps calling." He flops onto the bed.

The answer breeds fire in Amelia's eyes. "*What* chick keeps calling?"

Charlie rakes his fingers through his hair. "The one who's always going off about all that stuff Rudy's into? You know, the chile lady?"

"Oh, you mean Holly." Amelia sounds relieved. "I thought he was screwing around."

Charlie lets out a hoarse laugh. "Not with that bitch. She was having a fit. I didn't see much, but I didn't have any trouble hearing."

"What were they talking about?" I ask, eyeing the envelope on the desk.

"Talking? Bitch, you're crazy if you think they were talking."

"My name's Faith, not 'Bitch,' thank you very much, and talking is a euphemism for whatever they were doing. Shouting. Whatever."

He stares at me, then turns to Amelia and laughs again. "Man, I like your friend. She's funny. That's some nice sounding talk. They were euphemizing about whatever that work is Rudy's doing with those chiles."

"Such as?"

"She was telling him he'd better watch his ass. I wouldn't let no bitch"—his eyes stray back to me—"*chick*…threaten me, but man, she was wild. I'd be scared, too, if I was Rudy."

"How was she threatening him?" I say, glancing at Amelia.

"Look, I ain't no FBI. I'm only saying what I heard."

"Which was?"

"She kept telling him to watch himself and that she wasn't afraid of Ernie and his guards and shit. Then she leaves."

"And that's it? That's all that happened?"

"Nah, man, there's more." He smirks, then laces his fingers behind his head and stretches out on the bed. He's playing with us now, fully aware that he has information we want, and he's going to enjoy stringing us along.

I don't know anything really about Holly or threats or guards, but I do know Charlie just said he was scared of her, and I use that to my advantage. I sit down next to him. "So, you're Rudy's roommate?"

He nods.

"Holly's pretty amped up about the chiles, huh?"

"Yeah, man. She's crazy."

"She'll probably be back to talk to him then. Since he's not here, I'm guessing she'll want to talk to you and see if you know where he is, and like you said, she's kind of crazy."

Charlie cuts his eyes at me, trying not to look scared, but I got his attention.

"So if you tell us what you know, maybe we can find Rudy and tell him to come back so you don't have to deal with Holly on your own."

"You really think she'd mess with me?" he asks, turning from trained fighting dog to milktooth puppy.

I shrug and act casual, like I couldn't care less.

"Okay, fine," he says, sitting up, eager now to talk. "So I'm going back to sleep, thinking I can finally get me some shuteye when I hear another car. And this one ain't Rudy's. Big-ass, eight-cylinder-sounding thing. Nothing like Rudy's girlie truck. And then someone starts pounding on the door, shouting Rudy's name, but Rudy don't answer, cause I'm guessing he took off after that Holly chick came around. I thought you were someone else coming around to mess with Rudy and keep me awake."

I don't comment on the fact it's one o'clock in the afternoon. "So do you have any idea where he went?"

"Nah, man. But if you find him, tell him to hurry up and get back," he says and then gets up and crosses the room. "Now I'm going to sleep."

"It sounds like Holly scared Rudy off," Amelia says when he's gone, sounding strangely happy with this theory. "He's probably hiding from her and will be back in a day or two. That woman's a freak."

"Maybe," I say, not convinced. If I connect the transaction at the Farmers' Market between Rudy and Bulldog with their little exchange at the party and the tire tracks outside—the kind of tracks made from a "big-ass, eight-cylinder thing" like the one Bulldog was driving— it seems more likely that Rudy's running away because he's a drug dealer and he ripped off his client, than he's running away from an environmentalist who's going to do what—throw compost in his face? And come to think of it, maybe it's not just pot he was selling to Bulldog. Rudy was one of the guys who gave Mari beer. Maybe he's the one dealing liquid gold. Maybe he's the one who slipped it into her beer. Maybe he ran away because he put his girlfriend's sister in the hospital.

"What's there to 'maybe' about?" Amelia snaps. "You heard Charlie. Holly was threatening Rudy. He probably ran off to get away from her. She's been on his case since he started working for Ernie and she found out about those genetically modified chiles. She won't shut up about it. She'll scream at anyone who'll listen. You'd think he was working on a nuke, not a piece of fruit."

She opens his closet door and peeks inside as if Rudy might be hiding in there. While her back is turned, I slip the envelope labeled "Holly" into my bag.

Fourteen

Jail Time for Radical Activist

Julia Martinez, *Santa Fe New Mexican*

April 10, 2009

The problems started with the proposed Santa Fe ski resort expansion, an expansion that would mean hacking into the untouched slopes of the Sangre de Cristo Mountains, habitat to black bears and mountain lions.

After an environmental-impact study was conducted and government agencies gave the green light to the project, things started to go wrong. Survey flags disappeared. Machinery was vandalized. When the first tractor was sabotaged and the driver nearly killed concerns got serious.

Holly Redding and her radical environmental group UpsideDown! claimed responsibility for the incidents, stating, "Our actions are in protest of the reckless destruction of the national forest, land that is protected for all species, not just for corporate profit." Ms. Redding was sentenced and served three months in jail.

"I remember when that happened," says Clem, the renegade rule-breaker who has been sitting next to me on my bed since Amelia dropped me off, the papers from the Holly envelope spread between us. "My mom used to give money to that group, but she stopped after that."

"So do you think Amelia could be right?" I stretch out on my stomach, chin in my hands. "Do you think Rudy could be running away from her?"

Clem folds his legs and leans back against the wall. "Your other idea sounds more likely. If he's dealing liquid gold he's got himself into some serious shit. Who knows what kind of people he's messed up with? That guy you call Bulldog might not be his only buyer."

He picks up another paper, this one a handwritten note.

Rudy, I'm watching you and I'm watching Ernie. There is no place for GMOs in New Mexico. We'll take action if we have to.

Holly Redding

Founder UpSideDown!

We look at each other. "Then again," Clem says. "That woman means business. Seems like Rudy was working up some kind of case against her."

I pull out a third paper from the envelope, this one a flyer with the UpsideDown! logo above the heading: NO GENETICALLY MODIFIED ORGANISMS IN NEW MEXICO! and the following bullet points:

- GMOs are unhealthy
- GMOs contaminate
- GMOs increase herbicide use

We sit silently, contemplating the information. The documents tell a story, but what story exactly? That Holly and Rudy are at odds, or is there something else? She was at Rudy's place last night when he went missing, and from what Charlie said she was pissed. Does Holly Redding have something to do with Rudy's disappearance? She's used radical tactics before, but never—what, kidnapping? Is Rudy really scared enough of her to run? Or did he take off because he's dealing liquid gold, and he knew his drugs sent Mari to the hospital?

A scratching sound in the hall interrupts my thoughts. At first I think some nocturnal rodent is on the prowl and I ignore it, but the sound gets louder, and I realize it's not a mouse on a mission. Someone's tapping on the door.

I turn frantically to Clem. "Get in the closet!"

He stares at me as if I've lost my mind.

"What if it's Guadalupe?" I say in a loud whisper. "You're not supposed to be in here."

"There's no closet," he says, without moving and seeming, if anything, amused. "And I don't think I'll fit in the dresser."

Normally I'm a rebel, an I-don't-give-a-shit-do-it-my-own-way girl, but Guadalupe's serious about the no opposite sex in the room—or sex in the room regardless of the gender coupling. I heard that Brian got a serious talking to, and Guadalupe threatened to send him home if she found him "cohabitating" with his boyfriend again.

There's another knock. Clem doesn't move, so I throw a blanket over him, then crack open the door and breathe a huge sigh of relief.

Dahlia, in a fluffy blue bathrobe and slippers, her hair a wild mass of red, is standing in the hall and grinning. "Hi! I saw the light on. I'm a night owl. I can never sleep before two."

I glance down the hall over her shoulder.

"Are you okay?" she asks, following my eyes with her gaze. "Can I come in?"

"I'm fine. Hi. Sorry. Come in." I move away from the door, so she can pass.

She slipper plods into the room and glances at the bed. "Oh, hey, Clem," she says to the human-shaped blanket. "You cold?"

"No. I'm hiding," says a flat, muffled voice. "Is it working?"

Dahlia raises her eyebrows and slowly nods. "Totally. If I were Guadalupe it would never have occurred to me that a boy was in here. I would've definitely thought Faith had gotten artsy and bought a sculpture she was protecting with the blanket."

"Yeah, this is Santa Fe, right?" Clem, still under the blanket, says. "People are artsy around here."

"Right. I mean who doesn't have a sculpture on their bed?"

"Marble's the new cool."

They joke and tease until they've used up all their oh-so-hilarious remarks and Clem takes off the blanket and Dahlia plops onto the bed. Her eyes dart from Clem to me and then they widen. "Am I...interrupting something?" she asks. "I mean you guys weren't..."

"No," I blurt, saving any embarrassing implications about our late night tryst. "We were just..." If Clem were naked under the blanket what we were doing would be easier to explain than the whole Rudy-Mari-liquid-gold-Holly-thing. "I'm working on a project about GMOs at my internship," I say.

"At one o'clock in the morning?" she asks, skeptically.

I hand her the flyer with the GMO bullet points as if to prove my case. "What do you think?" I ask, as much to get her opinion as to deflect our conversational trajectory.

"About what?"

"About genetically modified organisms. You work on an organic farm. You probably have an opinion."

"Well, I'm definitely on the side of natural. I mean if nature made it how bad could it be?"

"Nature made smallpox and Ebola," Clem chimes in. "I'd say they're pretty bad."

Not one to argue, Dahlia laughs and concedes that Clem has a point, but then she adds, "It just doesn't seem right to mix genes from different species. We're seriously messing with Mother Nature. Who knows what could happen? But I'll leave you guys to your...*research*." She gets up and goes to the door, but stops, and with a sly smile, says, "Remember, no glove no love!"

She darts out of the room before I can knock her out cold.

"So, that was awkward," I say, hoping that admitting the awkwardness will make it less so. Before I have a chance to figure out just how awkward Clem feels, my phone buzzes. I scoot over to the bed and grab it, knowing that Jesse's the only person who'd be Snapchatting me this late. I perch next to Clem, phone hugged to my chest, and tap open the red box on the screen to see a close-up of Jesse with a text bubble he's drawn in and the words: "Nothing Compares To You—Sinead O'Connor."

"That your boyfriend?" Clem asks.

I glance up as Jesse's image fades away. I don't say anything, but I guess my face reveals the answer. "How'd you know?"

He gives a shy smile and lowers his eyes. "Lucky guess or because you've resisted all my moves."

"What moves?" I ask, wondering if I'm romantically autistic and missed some amorous cue.

He looks up. "All those romantic cafeteria dinners?"

"I didn't realize baked macaroni was a move."

We both laugh, but for me the laugh and the teasing have nothing to do with being amused and everything to do with being uncomfortable. I seriously suck at this kind of conversation, and even if I were good at it, I don't have any answers. Liking Jesse plus liking Clem equals confusion with a coefficient of stupidity.

Clem rubs his bare foot along my bare leg, sending a bolt of lightning down my spine.

"So, you 'like me like me'?" I ask, ruining the moment and any possibility of romantic spontaneity.

"I'm not sure. How's that different from just liking you?"

"Like, more than friends?" I say, feeling my cheeks burn.

"Yeah."

"Why?" *Nice, Faith. Put him on the spot and then grill him. Way to win over a boy.*

"You really want me to explain?"

Now that the moment's already ruined, I realize that, yes. I do want to know. A boy like Clem, Mr. Equilibrium—everything in perfect balance, looks, manners, talent— could have any girl. So why me?

He looks uncomfortable as he rakes a hand through his hair. I consider telling him he doesn't have to explain, but then he begins. "When I saw you the first day here I could tell you were an outcast."

"Wow. Not the answer I was expecting. Thanks."

"No. Not in a bad way," he quickly adds.

"There's a good way to be an outcast?"

He looks even more uncomfortable than before, but at the same time, determined to get out the words. "You were sitting by yourself, and you looked so thoughtful and alone. Then I looked around at everyone else. All these smiling kids talking to each other so comfortably like they'd never felt out of place in their life. I've spent most of my life being in rooms where nobody looks like me. Orchestras. Summer music camps." He lowers his voice and fidgets with the papers. "Maybe it's weird, but I just got this feeling I could relate to you. I wanted to know what you were thinking. And then I found out and you're just so…yourself."

"And that's a good thing?"

"It's the only thing." Our eyes meet. We hold the contact for a minute, but it's hard to maintain that much honesty, and I look away. "But you said there's another guy…so I guess a 'thing' between us is out."

"YesNo," I blurt. The words come out so quickly they sound like sno. "I like you, too. You're…awesome." Okay *that* was dumb. "Really awesome," I add, as if that helps. "It's just… do we have to do anything about it right now? I mean I don't want to not do anything about it, but can we just like each other and see how that feels?"

"You mean be platonic girlfriend-boyfriend?" he asks, eyebrows raised.

I shrug and mumble yeah while I wait for him to laugh away the suggestion.

He smiles a little and then says, "Why not? I should go, though. We've gone far enough already. We should take things slowly. You already told me about your father and your family—that was like platonic first base or maybe even second. Platonic third base would be like…emotional stripping."

"Totally. I don't want to even think about a platonic home run."

He gets up to leave. As he crosses the room I think back to how the night started, the Holly papers and the reason I shared all this stuff with Clem in the first place. Not because of Rudy. Because of Mari. I have to find out who gave her the liquid gold.

"So, platonic boyfriend," I say, batting my eyelashes in mock flirtation. "I want to talk to that guy, Thomas, from the party after work tomorrow. Want to come with me?"

"I'll pick you up at work at five."

"Great," I say, and we hug, because even in platonic relationships, hugging is allowed.

Fifteen

My thoughts keep me tossing and turning all night, and at first light, I give up trying to sleep. I mope around my room for a while then head to work early. I'm thinking I'll be the first one there and need to use my key, but the door's already unlocked, the lab open. Esha's at her desk, messy-meet-chic ponytail—more messy than chic—some supersized Starbucks drink and a newspaper in front of her.

"You're early," she says.

"You too," I say, though I have no idea, maybe she always comes this early.

She stares off with an unfocused look in her eye like she's not seeing anything, tracing her fingers absently around the cup. "I have to run a meeting this morning. I needed some time to get prepared."

I nod, remembering the memo about a seven forty-five meeting, and head to my cubicle. As I pass by her desk, though, I notice the newspaper headline and stop: *Local Girl Dies of a Liquid Gold Overdose.*

"Oh my God!" I utter and grab the paper, thinking I'm not real family so nobody told me Mari died. I can hardly breathe as I read the first line, can hardly read the words blurred across the page. Then I see it: *Eslee Dominguez of Santa Ana Pueblo, age 17, died.*

I drop the paper, collapse into the closest chair, and cover my face with my hands. The overwhelming surge of relief that Mari's not dead mixes with the horrible news that someone else is. Someone died from a liquid gold overdose.

"Hey, you okay?" Esha asks.

I nod, but the truth of how I feel is anything but okay—Mom, drugs, death. In an upwelling of emotions the words come spilling out. I blurt out to Esha how I was at the party when the girl in the newspaper overdosed. I was at the hospital when they brought her in. I tell Esha about Mari and someone slipping her liquid gold, about the guys who could've slipped it to her.

As I tell her these things, my thoughts orbit around one person: Rudy. Again I wonder if he's the guy who slipped liquid gold to Mari. If so, did he slip it to Eslee too? And if not, did he sell it to her or whoever did? Then, something else occurs to me. Esha knows Rudy. Maybe she has an idea where he is.

I don't want to alarm her and let on to my suspicion that Rudy, the middleman for her chiles, might be a drug dealer. I can see she's upset—about Eslee's death, the party, the drugs, the meeting she has to run, or who knows what. I don't want to add to her burden, so I thank her for listening and tell her I feel better. "But there is one more thing, a coincidence," I say, keeping my tone light. "My half sister goes out with Rudy, the guy who works for Ernie and brings your chiles to the Farmers' Market. He was at the party, too. And then he kind of disappeared."

"Kind of?"

"Well, he hasn't called her in a few days, and she's worried about him. I know it's a weird question, but since you know the guy, I thought maybe you'd have some idea where he might be. I mean, who his friends are or something."

"Why would I know that?" she says, the sympathy in her voice replaced by something defensive.

"I don't know," I say, feeling stupid now. "I guess you wouldn't."

With Rudy on my mind, though, my thoughts go to Holly's visit to his trailer, to the envelope with the papers from her. I'm deciding if I should change direction and ask Esha about Holly when Jonah pokes his head into the lab.

"There you are," he says to Esha. "People are waiting upstairs for the meeting. You called it for seven forty-five. It's already eight o'clock."

"Crap. Sorry," she says, whirling around to the door. "I'll be right there."

I follow Jonah and Esha upstairs to the conference room where about twenty people are gathered. Dr. Richmond, I notice, isn't there.

Esha calls the meeting to a start. "Unfortunately, I have bad news," she says and glances around tiredly at the expectant faces. "The Oppenheim Foundation pulled out their funding for the final stages of field-testing on Sonya's GMO chile project. But I assure you," she quickly adds, "she's doing everything she can to secure more funding."

A stunned silence follows her proclamation. Glances are exchanged, papers rustle, bodies shift in chairs, then the questions begin.

"Does this mean there will be layoffs?" asks a woman with glasses and short dark hair who works in research and development.

"Does this have anything to do with UpsideDown!?" Henry, the skinny IT guy, asks.

A half dozen more questions follow, but there's something careful about the way the questions are asked, something cautious about the wording, as if what's being asked isn't what's meant. I get that there's something deeper that isn't being said.

When the meeting ends and people clear out, I lag behind. I'm still thinking about Rudy, and with Esha's talk of the chiles I get an idea. Maybe Ernie, the farmer he works for, has seen him. I wait for her to look up and notice me, but the tiny WiFi universe of her phone holds her attention. She's on a manic typing mission and doesn't look up. A lot of sighs and mad punching at the keyboard and it doesn't seem like she's going to notice me anytime soon, so I clear my throat and speak up. "I'd love to see the GMO chiles," I say. "Do you think I could go up to the farm where they're grown and visit the project?"

"Sonya goes up about once a week," Esha replies, attention still on her screen. "Let me check with her. It would be good for you to go."

"Hey, Esh," IT Henry says, coming into the room with a cup of coffee. "Thought you could use this."

"You're a god," she tells him, putting aside her phone.

With her back turned, I glance at her phone to see what's keeping her captive. The screen is open to a text of two words.

It's over

———

What's over? I wonder as I head down to the lab. *A relationship? Is that why she seems so exhausted and distracted? Not just because of funding. Because she's trying to dump some guy?* I open the lab door and tell myself to get a grip. Reading other people's texts? What's next? Joining the NSA? I turn on my computer and access the central server where SCPG does most of its big sequence analysis and continue my bioinformatics studies, but I find myself thinking about Eslee and the funding cut and Esha. I'm lost in these thoughts when a blast of music startles me.

"Esh took the rest of the morning off," Jonah tells me making the quintessential *mwa-ha-ha* villain laugh. "The music shall be mine!"

"Nice try," I say, going over to the mp3 player. "But it's my turn." I plug in my own device and change the tunes.

"Okay, but how about we don't slit our wrists today?" he says, teasing me about my playlist from last time when I accidentally put on my songs for mellow (i.e. depressed) moods with Radiohead leading the misery-fest.

"Fine," I say, and put on the best, hypnotic-groove reggae I can find. "Does this work?"

His answer is to bob his head to the beat.

We settle into our own musical universes, but I stay by Jonah's desk, wondering about his opinion of the meeting and that feeling I got that people weren't saying what was on their minds. "Bummer about the funding," I say at a song break, hoping to lure him into telling me what was really going on.

"Yeah. Huge bummer." He turns on his computer and waits for it to boot up. "Hang on, is this The Abyssinians?" he asks as the new song starts. "I love those blokes. Roots-reggae classic."

"Yeah, me too, but about that funding..." I say, coaxing him back onto the topic I want to talk about.

"Yeah. About that." He sighs and stares at the computer screen. "Sonya won't be able to come through another funding disaster after the *Brugmansia* catastrophe and the..."

"And the what?" I say when he leaves the thought unfinished.

"And the nothing," he says. "She'll have to find alternative income to keep SCPG running."

"Good thing about Esha's chiles then, right?"

Jonah looks away from the screen and folds his arms. "Esh needs to look good too. It was her idea."

"What was her idea?" I ask, surprised at how serious he's become.

"Sequencing *Brugmansia*."

"Did she come up with that when she was in South America?" I ask, remembering what Virg told me, that *Brugmansia* comes from a rare Peruvian plant.

"That's right. After her PhD and before she came here she studied ethnobotany in Peru. She spent three months in the Amazon with the Quechua people. One of the plants they use is *Brugmansia*, only they don't call it that. They call it *Toé*."

"What do they use it for?"

"I'm not an expert, but Esha was really into it. She said it had a variety of medicinal and ceremonial uses and that healers use it for visions."

"So, Esha learned about its compounds, had some new idea of how it could be used as an anti-seizure medicine, then she started to work here and brought the idea to Dr. Richmond?" I say, the story of Esha and her ties to *Brugmansia* taking shape.

"Something like that."

In the phrase "something like that" I get that there's something more he doesn't want to tell me, but now I'm curious about Dr. Richmond. "Was Dr. Richmond pissed when it didn't work out?"

"She doesn't blame Esha, but I think Esha feels responsible. She'd pushed the project pretty hard." He jerks his hands from the keyboard and swivels in his chair to look at me. "She won't admit it, but I'm guessing that's why she's putting in so much effort for the board dinner. She wants to impress the hell out of them. You have that on your calendar, right?"

"Yep," I say, but I'm not thinking about the dinner. I'm thinking about what it would be like to be in Esha's shoes. Adventures in the Amazon. Developing new medicines and cures and seeds. The innovation, the creativity, the freedom to dig into the unknown and see what you discover. Like being an artist with a blank canvas, only the canvas is the world.

The song changes to Peter Tosh. Jonah focuses back on his work, and I get that our conversation is over. I'm about to go back to my desk, but I think again about Esha and the text and the worry I read on her face. "It's none of my business," I say, "but Esha seemed kind of bummed out earlier. Do you think she broke up with her boyfriend or something?"

Jonah laughs. "No boyfriend."

"Why is that funny?"

"It's just kind of a joke between us. Esh doesn't always pick the best blokes."

I shrug and go back to my desk, but I can't concentrate. My thoughts won't settle. I can't sit still. I waste time Googling *Brugmansia* to learn about the plant Esha was studying. I'm just looking at the image of a white bell-shaped flower when my phone rings. I pick up and instantly panic. Alma.

"Is Mari okay?" I blurt, nervousness bubbling in my stomach. It's too much to hope that the news about Mari will be good, too much disappointment if it's not.

"The sexual assault nurse said there were no signs of trauma," Alma says. "She'll come home on Wednesday. The day after tomorrow."

I sigh and sink back down into my chair— the first good news I've had all morning.

Sixteen

At five o'clock, Clem's standing on a small patch of grass under a shade tree, waiting for me, as promised. I see him before he sees me, standing with his hands jammed in his pockets, looking sullen and far off in thought. I should ask him if he's okay, but with the good news of Mari and the bad news of Eslee, I tell him all that first.

"If that asshole Thomas had anything to do with giving liquid gold to those girls, I'm going to kick his ass," he says when I'm done talking.

"Leave that part to me," I say. "I doubt ass-kicking is one of your specialties."

"And it's one of yours?"

I shrug. "Kind of."

"You're kidding?" he says and laughs.

"Nope." Before I can think it through, I pull him toward me, place my hand on his back and hip-throw him to the ground. Even though I land him softly on the grass, I can't believe what I just did, and from the shocked expression on his face, neither can he.

He stands up slowly and brushes grass off his back and out of his hair. I wait for him to tell me I'm a freak and he'll never speak to me again. I wouldn't blame him. What kind of person uses judo and hip-throws a guy she likes to the ground? Instead of chewing me out, though, he starts to laugh, hysterical out-of-control snorts that rise from his belly and burst through his nose. I've never heard him laugh like this. I've never actually heard anyone laugh like this. Now I'm thinking maybe I shook something lose in his brain.

"Did I hurt you?" I ask nervously. "Do we need to go to the doctor?"

"I'm fine," he says when he catches his breath and can talk again. "Just surprised. I'm six feet. I've never had a girl manhandle me like that." He looks at me and shakes his head appreciatively. "I might not be able to walk for a month, but Faith Flores, you are a piece of work."

I take this as a compliment as I turn and get into his car.

———

We drive past the Masonic Temple, a huge pink castle of a building, out of place in this land of browns and beiges, then the mandatory Starbucks, and soon we turn into a neighborhood. He drives up a hill to a small mud-colored house with a one-car garage and a graveled front yard bordered by rows of purple bee-covered flowers.

Now that we're here, adrenaline fuels my central nervous system with anger-sparked jitters. If Pretty Boy laid one finger on Mari, a hip-throw will look like child's play.

Clem, having just experienced my moves, reads my thoughts or maybe my face because he nudges me as I ring the bell, and mutters, "Easy, Killer."

The house erupts with ear-piercing barking, and a nasally, not quite human voice, shouts: "Door-bell! Door-bell!" A second later, a freckled, sunburned girl with coltish legs and a parrot the size of a terrier perched on her shoulder comes to the door followed by two barking mops. One of the mops runs headfirst into the screen door; the other squats and pees.

"He-llo!" the bird caws.

"Uh, hi?" I say, not sure if I'm greeting the bird or the girl.

"He-llo!" the bird says again. "He-llo!"

"Mawmaw, that's enough," the girl scolds, then turns to the dog that just peed and exclaims, "Oh Diva, not again… THOMAS! Diva peed." She turns and disappears, but leaves the door open. I glance at Clem as we continue to stand there, waiting to see if, say, a monkey's coming next. A moment later the girl returns, birdless and dogless, though the barking continues from the back of the house.

"Hi," I say, having lost my earlier anger-fueled momentum to the menagerie. "I'm a friend of Thomas. Is he here?"

"Yeah," she says, blowing a wad of pink bubblegum in my face.

"Can I talk to him?"

"Wait a sec. THOMAS!" she shouts over her shoulder.

A second later Pretty Boy shows up. He's nothing like I remember. At the party he was decked out in low rider shorts, not quite butt crack material, but almost, a fitted tee to show off his pecs, and slicked-back hair. Now he's dressed in pale green scrubs, and his hair is combed flat and professional.

"Can I help you?" he says, picking fur off his shirt. Even his voice sounds more serious. No trace of the velvety smooth talker who offered Mari a beer.

"I met you at a party Saturday night," I begin, bracing for what's certain to be a fight.

He gives me a blank look. "Sorry…I don't remember. I was…" He looks over his shoulder and lowers his voice. "Kind of wasted."

"No shit. You offered my fourteen-year-old sister a beer, and then you were with her when I found her passed out in the rain? Ring any bells?"

The mountain of Pretty Boy steps out of the house. "Trina!" he calls, "I'll be outside. I have to talk to these people. And clean Mawmaw's cage while I'm out here!"

"'Kay!" comes the girl's voice from the back of the house. "But I'm not cleaning up after Diva! She just took a dookie in the living room."

With Pretty Boy's bulk lurking on his home turf, albeit the kind of nice suburban home turf where people don't jump each other in broad daylight, I pop my knuckles and prepare for him to kick the proverbial shit out of us.

"Holy crap," he says instead. "Is she okay?"

"Someone slipped her liquid gold," I say, watching closely for his reaction. "She ended up in the hospital, and it looks like the same person who slipped her the drug came to see her yesterday morning to make sure she didn't talk." I can't prove the connection, but he doesn't need to know that.

He looks taken aback, seriously hurt, like he's the damsel in distress and we're the aggressors, but then his pained expression changes to an incredulous, dropped-jaw stare. "Wait a minute, you don't think I did that to her?"

"No," Clem says, with exaggerated cheer. "We tracked you down because we're Scouts and we thought you might be worried."

"You were with her when she was passed out," I say, as a metallic green insect lands on my arm, its tiny claws gripping my skin. Thomas reaches over and delicately picks off the bug, releasing it onto one of the purple flowers. "Before that, you were offering her a drink," I go on, trying not to falter in my conviction: Just because he's not a bug smoosher doesn't mean he's the Dalai Lama. "So don't bullshit me. I want to know what happened. If you did anything to my sister, you're never going to be able to—"

Clem kicks me, and I refrain from enunciating the rest of my thought, which has to do with his future inability to procreate.

"Look," Pretty Boy says, "whatever happened to her, I didn't do it. I'm sorry for hitting on your sister and saying she wasn't hot. I was a dick."

"You don't see me arguing." I jam my hands in my pockets and lean against the porch rail.

Pretty Boy's steely gray eyes slide over me. "The other night at the party I saw her again a little while after you told me how old she was, and, man, was she out of it. Majorly shit-faced. But you weren't there, were you?" He glares at me, trying to shift the guilt from his to mine. "You didn't see how gone she was. You left her alone."

"I'm not the one on trial," I snap.

He runs a hand through his hair and puffs out his cheeks. "I saw her staggering around. I looked for you, but I didn't see you, so I followed her outside to make sure she was okay. I found her passed out. That's when you came out."

"I remember." I cross my arms and challenge him with my eyes. "It looked like you were running away."

"Yeah, well looks can be deceiving."

A phone rings inside the house, and the parrot shouts: "Tele-phone! Tele-phone!"

"So why didn't you stay and see how she was?" Clem asks, ignoring the screaming bird. "Why'd you take off?"

He answers Clem, but doesn't take his eyes off me. "Because I knew how it looked, and I didn't want to be in the exact position I'm in now."

I consider this possibility, but remind myself of the guy that came to see Mari in the hospital. "If you have nothing to hide, why'd you come to the hospital yesterday to see her?"

"I didn't. I was at work yesterday. I'm a vet tech. You can call if you want. Better yet, I can show you my time card. I just got paid." He pulls a piece of paper from his pocket and hands it to me. The hours. The days. The times. All generated by a computer. Sure enough he was working Sunday when whoever it was came to the hospital to see on Mari. "If you don't believe me, you can go over to the North Side Clinic and ask. I was working for Dr. Bloomberg. We had a cockapoo that was hit by a car. Poor little guy. I'm going back to check on him as soon as you leave."

"A cockapoo?"

"Yep. Cute little thing," he adds in a baby voice.

"You are *so* not what you seem," I say.

"People usually aren't. Now, if I were you and I wanted answers, I'd try to find out who else gave her a drink and could've slipped her the drugs. 'Cause it wasn't me."

"THOMAS!" Trina calls from inside the house. "Come quick! Devil just threw up!"

"I have to go. It looks like the guinea pig got into something. I'm sorry about your sister. When you find out what happened to her, I'd really like to know."

Seventeen

With Thomas ruled out, I should be thinking about the other two guys who could've come to see Mari—Rudy and Bulldog, but I can't stop thinking about how I'd felt earlier when Alma called and I thought she'd died. I realize I need to see her. I ask Clem if he can take me to the hospital. He agrees, but when we get in the car, he's quiet and I remember how he seemed before when he was waiting for me outside of SCPG, like something was on his mind.

We cruise up Alameda Street then turn onto St. Francis, the main drag through town, without talking. I look out the window as we tour the eclectic mishmash of Santa Fe—a river with no water, the upscale Whole Foods planted between a decrepit liquor store and a palm reader, a mural of corn and chile plants painted on a stucco wall in front of a tattoo parlor. Fifteen minutes later Clem pulls up in front of the hospital.

"So, you want to go to platonic third base?" he asks, as he cuts the engine.

I waggle my eyebrows, trying to get a smile out of him. "Sounds kinky."

"My dad's coming for my concert. I haven't told anyone,"

he says, not returning my smile. "My mom doesn't even know yet. He hasn't been here in two years."

"At least he's alive," I snap, irritated that he's pissed about having a father who cares enough about him in the first place to come visit. "People take things for granted."

Clem twists in his seat and his eyes drill into me. "Are you saying I take stuff for granted?"

"No. I'm saying *don't* take things for granted. If you're pissed, tell him. If you're glad he's coming, tell him that. I'm just saying don't wait to do the important shit. You might not get a chance."

He jiggles the keys and I think my little lecture has pissed him off more. Whatever. Let him be mad. Stress collides with lack of sleep and the weirdness today at SCPG and the result is internal combustion. I gear up to fight, but if I wanted a verbal sparring partner, I'm shit out of luck.

"Do you have regrets about your father?" he asks in a quiet, thoughtful voice.

I shrug, not ready to let go of my mood.

"What would you say to him if you could?" he presses.

"That he's a jerk."

"That's it?"

I feel him looking at me, waiting for my answer. "I'd ask him why he left my mom," I say, opening the door and getting out. "It doesn't matter, though, does it? He's dead. I'll never get to ask."

———

When the elevator releases us to Mari's floor, Clem waits in the hall as I go into her room. She's lying on her side, the TV on low, the small bundle of her body barely a lump under the covers.

"Hey," she murmurs, looking at me through tired, foggy eyes. Her curls lay listless around her shoulders like something dead. I have an irrational urge to shout at those formerly springy ringlets, to yell at them to bounce back to life.

Instead, I say the first stupid thing that pops into my mind. "You look great."

"Liar."

"Okay," I say, digging into my pocket for the lighter. "You look..." I don't know what to say, and finish with "tired," the only word that comes to mind.

"Yeah, well, I guess I am. That's not really news though, is it?"

The flatness of her voice together with her empty eyes and lifeless hair freaks me out—that and my little lecture to Clem about not taking things for granted. I fight off the lump in my throat.

"Did you hear about Eslee? The girl from the party?" she asks. I don't tell her that I already know what happened. I get that she wants to tell me herself. "I heard the nurses talking. They thought I was asleep." There's a tearful catch in her voice, and she wipes her nose on her arm. I listen through the shadows, through the beeping of machines, through the stale smell of sickness. "The same thing happened to her that happened to me. The paramedics brought her in with liquid gold in her system and then she died."

"That's terrible," I say, a calm so artificial it probably causes cancer. "But you're not going to die."

"I can't stop thinking about how that drug got into me," she goes on. "I keep going over that night and I just can't remember anything." Her voice rises with anxiety. She sits up and starts to cough.

"You don't have to remember anything," I say, upping the carcinogenic calm to keep her from getting more upset.

"You just have to get better." I sit on the bed with her for a few minutes until she falls asleep, then go back into the hall to get Clem.

I find him talking to one of the nurses whose back is to me. When she turns around, I'm surprised to see that it's his mom, Dolores. I'd forgotten she worked here.

She greets me with a warm hug like the one she gave me the first time we met. "Clem tells me Mari is your half sister," she says with a sympathetic smile. "She's such a sweetheart. I was here all weekend, so I was one of the nurses taking care of her."

"You were here on Sunday?" I blurt, brain tumbling back to Mari's anonymous visitor.

"All day," she says with a tired smile.

"A nurse said a boy came in to see Mari on Sunday," I explain, trying to keep the anxiousness from my voice. "But Mari was asleep. I wonder if you saw him or remember what he looked like?"

She steps back to let a man pushing a gurney pass. "It was busy Sunday," she says slowly. "But I remember a boy coming in and asking for Mari."

"What did he look like, Ma?" Clem asks.

She shakes her head. "I'm sorry, Sweetie. There were so many people here over the weekend. I just remember that he was a young man—a bit older than you. Oh, and he had a tattoo, but that's not saying much, is it? Every young person seems to be tattooed these days. It would be more of a statement to say he didn't have one." She gives Clem a stern look as if he's about to get inked.

I glance at the closed door of Mari's room, diving back into detective mode. "If you remember anything else will you let me know?"

She assures me she will and gives me her phone number in case I have more questions. "Do you need anything, Sweetheart? A nice home-cooked meal? Anything I can do for you?"

The offer of a home-cooked meal ignites a homesick yearning for Alma and her adobe house and the dogs and the cornflower blue kitchen—but how can you be homesick for a person you hardly know and a place that isn't yours? "I'll let you know," I say, then thank her, and we say good-bye.

"It sucks about your dad, and I'm really sorry," I say to Clem once we're outside, hoping this addendum to our earlier conversation substitutes as an apology. "Just don't neglect the mom factor, you know? She's really cool."

He squeezes my hand, a touch that tells me he accepts my apology, and says, "Noted. The mom factor will not be neglected."

We head toward Clem's car, and even though I'm all tingly from the amazing aftermath of his touch, I'm too consumed with the tattooed guy who came to see Mari to do anything about it. The description could belong to either Rudy or Bulldog— or, of course, someone else entirely—but the more I think about it, the more my thoughts ping on Rudy.

"Maybe Rudy thought it would be cute to get Mari high," I say, more to myself than to Clem, but of course he answers with a "huh?" because it's a hard to ignore such a non sequitur. "Or maybe he thought if she was out of it, Amelia could hang out at the party longer," I go on. "Or maybe"—now my temper flares— "he slipped her liquid gold because he wanted to hit on her. Then she ended up in the hospital and he panicked, so he came to see if she had any memory that the beer he gave her made her sick."

"That's a lot of maybes," Clem says.

"I know, but you have to start somewhere. You don't figure shit out by sitting around and contemplating your ass. I need to tell Amelia what we found out," I say as we reach his car. "She might hate me, but she is my sister and she should know what's going on. Can you drive me over there?" His stomach rumbles, and I quickly add, "I promise, we'll pig out as soon as we're done."

Despite our protesting bellies, he agrees and we set off for Alma's house. The drive is mostly a straight shot along a frontage road with the backdrop of pale desert to the west and mountains to the east. When we arrive, Clem says he'll hang outside with the dogs while I speak to Amelia. Nobody comes to the door when I ring, so I turn the knob. It's open. I go inside, leaving Clem with Biscochito and Sopapilla.

The first thing I hear when I step into the house is the sound of breaking glass followed by an elaborate string of expletives. I stroll cautiously to the kitchen where the dramatic soundtrack is playing out.

The word *tornado* comes to mind, the kind that sends trailer homes hurling through the air. Dishes, bowls, pots, and pans occupy every inch of counter space. Some of the kitchenware has migrated to the floor—a blender, cookbooks, baking trays. Flour coats all exposed surfaces. Eggshells drip the remains of their yolks. What appear to be dried cornhusks litter the floor. In the middle of it all stands Amelia, skinny legs sticking out of cut-off sweats, a blue bandanna tied over her hair, arms covered in flour.

"Everything okay here?" I ask from a safe distance at the doorway.

She whirls around and glares at me. "Does everything look okay?"

"What happened? Did the cookie monster break in?"

"Hilarious." She grabs a stainless steel mixing bowl and a wooden spoon and starts manically mixing some sort of pasty, yellowish gunk. "The stupid freaking masa isn't setting. Gran was supposed to buy masa *harina*. Not wheat flour! Not bread flour! *Corn* flour! You use *corn* flour to make tamales. And I thought we had two dozen corn husks, but we only had one dozen, and where the hell's the steamer, anyway?"

"Is someone having a birthday?" The only reason I ever knew anyone to make a special meal was if someone under ten was having a party, and even then, the meal usually came from a box.

"No! It's not a birthday!" Just then something on the stove releases a *sssss* sound and bubbles out of a pot. Amelia races to the stove, grabs the pot with bare hands, and promptly drops it.

I walk calmly to the stove and turn it off, then go to the freezer for ice. I hand her the ice wrapped in a dishtowel I find on the floor. "So, if it's not a birthday, then what?"

She presses the ice to her fingers and juts her chin toward the table without answering. I pick my way through the kitchen Armageddon and on the table find a letter to Amelia. "Dear Amelia," I read out loud. "You have been accepted as a contestant onto 'Teen Chef' with host, Andre Lamour, filming in Albuquerque on July 18th. You will be featured on the "Show Me How Spicy You Can Be" main course episode." I stop reading and look up. "This is great news. What's the problem?"

"No. It's not good news. Definitely not good news. It's bad news. Bad. Bad. Bad."

"Why?"

"Because I'll have to tell Mari I got accepted, and I'll have to tell Gran, and they'll make me do it, and I can't." Amelia tosses the ice into the sink and picks up the mixing bowl again. As she stirs, a blob of yellow batter flies out of the bowl and nails me in the face like a suicidal gnat.

I wipe away the blob and drop into a chair. "You don't have to tell anyone."

"What, and lie?" She glares at me as if I suggested Ramen noodles for dinner, PB and J on white bread, mac and cheese from a box.

"Not lie. Just don't tell." I start picking up dishes and carrying them to the sink.

"And then what? Just not do it?"

"I guess." I turn on the water and wait for it to get warm. "You just said you didn't want to."

Amelia slams the bowl on the counter. "I didn't say I didn't *want* to. I said I *can't*."

"Why? You have something to do on that day?"

Her answer is a glare.

I pour dish soap into the sink. As I watch bubbles form, I remember the first night I came here and what I heard Mari say about Amelia being on a cooking show. "Don't you get five thousand dollars if you win?"

She shrugs.

"And didn't you already beat out, what, twenty other people to make it onto the show?" I ask, turning off the water.

"Seventy-five."

"Right. So you must really suck."

"Whatever," she says, snatching up a dishtowel. "So I can cook, so can a lot of people."

"Yeah, but it's your dream. It doesn't matter about everyone else."

"Well, dreams are shit." She mops up egg yolk with the dry towel, creating an even bigger mess. "They never come true."

"That's optimistic."

"It's not optimism or pessimism. It's truth. Look around. The world's filled with people who had big dreams and thought they'd do something with their lives. It turns out that 'something' is a crap-ass job and a bunch of bratty kids."

"That's your truth, not mine," I challenge, refusing to give in to her lack of imagination.

"Okay Little Miss Orphan Annie. Let's play a game. What are your dreams?"

I don't have to play her little angst-filled game, but I answer despite myself. "To go to college and make something of myself."

"Just give in to the system, huh? Do what everyone expects?"

I take the bait, which I'm certain is what she wants. To fight. It's like cutting, a way of feeling something, a release. I shouldn't give her what she wants, any more than you should hand the cutter a knife, but I do. "No," I say. "To do what *nobody* expects. Nobody expects the offspring of a single mom heroin-addict to go to college. They expect me to screw up my life just like she did. So don't talk to me about sucking up to the system. And, by the way, you know what your problem is?"

She rolls her eyes. "Just one?"

"You think everyone else is to blame for your unhappiness. Well, you know what? That is one big pile of Sopapilla shit. If you want to blow off your talent as a chef to make a point to the world, be my guest, but news flash—if you don't give a crap, neither will anyone else. And by the way, in case you haven't noticed, your sister's in the hospital and she needs you."

"Thanks a lot for the info, Sis," she says sarcastically. "What would I have ever done without you?" She marches out of the room, leaving me alone.

As I let myself out, I realize I didn't even tell her about Rudy. Just as well, I decide. Amelia's an angry drama queen and a hopeless mess who will be absolutely no help in figuring out what happened to Mari or in finding Rudy. If I want to find him, I'll have to do it on my own. Good thing I have an idea for the next person to talk to: Holly Redding.

Eighteen

On the way back to the college I tell Clem my plan to visit Holly, and he agrees to drive me to the UpsideDown! office the next morning before he has to be at rehearsal and I have to be at work. When we arrive at St. John's, I ask if it's okay if he scrounges something to eat without me. He says yes, and I say good night and head back to the dorm by myself, shortcutting through a thicket of chamisa bushes. I'm starving, but more than that, desperate to be alone and think about everything that's happened today: Eslee's death, Esha and the funding cut, ruling out Pretty Boy as a suspect, Dolores' information about a tattooed guy, ruling in Rudy as suspect *numero uno*, Amelia and her pity party.

I'm lost in these thoughts when I notice a hummingbird. The creature makes me think of Mari and the calliope, and I stop for a closer look. That's when I realize it isn't a hummingbird, duh, because what kind of hummingbird flies at night? The bird, in fact, isn't even a bird. It's a moth, an amazing insect the size of my first. I watch the moth probe a white flower with its needle-like tongue. As I stand there communing with nature, I notice something about the flower looks familiar. And then I remember. It looks exactly like the flower I saw on the web today when I was researching *Brugmansia*. Virg said liquid gold comes from a rare Peruvian plant. What's it doing growing here? Then I remember something else.

I rush back to the dorm and stop in front of the O'Keeffe poster of the white flower that's hanging in the main entrance. The painting is of the same flower as the one growing outside. There's no mistaking the huge, white, tubular bloom. Does *Brugmansia* grow in Santa Fe as well as Peru? If anyone would know about O'Keeffe and her subject matter, it's Rejina. I ignore the time, go up to her room, and knock.

"It's open," Rejina calls.

I crack the door to the vague smell of pot, Jimi Hendrix music, a flickering candle instead of electric light (another no-no in the Guadalupe rule book, lest we burn down the college and the surrounding tinderbox of land). Bro Boy's stretched out on the bed in red sweats and a t-shirt. Rejina's sprawled out next to him, dressed, though barely, in a tank and tiny shorts.

"If I'm interrupting something I can come back."

"We're not holding a world summit," Rejina says sarcastically, though her Texas drawl makes the sarcasm sound sweet. "We're just hanging out." She changes position and rests her head on Bro Boy's lap, apparently not worried about any of Guadalupe's rules—candles, drugs, or boys. "So? You going to stand out there all night or come in?"

I slip into her room and close the door behind me.

"What's up? I never see you hanging out." She pats the bed. "Join us."

"I just wanted to ask you something," I say, in no way interested in a conversational ménage-a-trois. "It's about Georgia O'Keeffe."

"Well, if it's about Georgia…" Her face brightens and she sits up.

"Do you know anything about that white flower she painted? The one in the print downstairs when you come in?"

"Jimson weed? It grows all over the place around here. Georgia was known for her flower paintings. They made up a large percentage of her work. She painted enormous close-ups of flowers and transformed their contours into beautiful abstractions." Rejina's turned into some kind of art-curator-Georgia O'Keeffe-talking-head. I try to interrupt, but she's on a roll. "In the flowers she expressed what she felt, rather than what she had been taught." She smiles at me, as if waiting for an intellectually informed question from a curious art patron.

"Is it the same plant as *Brugmansia*?"

She lowers her eyebrows and looks stumped. "I have no idea."

"Why?" Bro Boy asks, his baked eyes coming to life. "You looking for some liquid gold? I can hook you up. But don't be messing with jimson weed on your own. You can get off on it, but it's wicked poisonous. Can kill you."

I shoot him a look. "I'm not trying to get liquid gold. I'm just curious." Before he can ask more questions, I thank Rejina for her time and scurry out of the room.

The second I'm in my own room, I turn on my computer and type in jimson weed. I read several pages of facts and learn that jimson weed, also called Datura, is in the family *Solanaceae*. All parts of the plant are toxic, with the alkaloids hyoscyamine, atropine, and scopolamine giving it its toxicity. There's a lot of variation in toxic levels among not just individual plants, but parts of the same plant. In Native American tribes of the Southwest, jimson weed was sometimes made into a tea by a Shaman or medicine man and used in rites of passage ceremonies to induce visions. It can result in agitation, uncoordination, hallucinations, and death.

When I'm finished researching jimson weed, I Google *Brugmansia* and learn that *Brugmansia* is also in the family *Solanaceae*; is also highly toxic, and has the same three alkaloids as jimson weed. All parts of the plant are poisonous. It's used in the Amazon for magical practices, visionary journeys, shape shifting, divination, clairvoyance, love magic, and as an aphrodisiac among other things, and if consumed carelessly, can cause serious mental and physical reactions, and death.

When I cross-check what I learned about each plant, I come up with the following: Both plants have the alkaloids hyoscyamine, atropine, and scopolamine. Both plants cause hallucination and death. Both plants are in the same family. The biggest difference? Jimson weed grows here.

Virg said liquid gold is coming in cheaper than before. Maybe the reason is someone's not making it from *Brugmansia*; they're making it from jimson weed. I look again at my notes. If the range of toxicity in jimson weed is unpredictable and varies between plants, and if that variation contributes to the possibility of overdose, that could be the reason Mari got so sick and Eslee died. If Rudy's dealing liquid gold, maybe he's harvesting the plant and maybe he's making it, too.

There's one person who might know enough about *Brugmansia* to tell me if my Rudy theory is possible: Esha. I decide to talk to her tomorrow—after I pay a visit to Holly. I check my phone calendar, which I've been keeping like a pro, to see what I've got down at work tomorrow. I don't see anything out of the ordinary. I'm about to close the calendar and turn off the lights when something totally different catches my eye. The date.

With everything else going on, I've managed to put out of my mind (okay, not deal with) the fact that this weekend is the Fourth of July, which means this weekend is Clem's concert *and* Jesse's visit. I've downplayed Jesse to Clem, and I haven't told Jesse about Clem. A bolt of high-octane, holy-shit shoots through me. I don't care that it's midnight. I jump out of bed and race down the hall to visit my friend, the night owl, hoping she'll know what to do.

Dahlia's sitting on her bed in Snoopy pajamas, eating potato chips, and playing Solitaire on her phone, when I barge into her room. "Hungry?" she says, holding out the chip bag and patting the mattress for me to join her.

"Starving." I collapse onto the bed and take a handful. "I'm glad you're up."

"I never go to bed before like two. I drive my parents crazy. They say I need to get more sleep, but I'm just a night person. What can I do?" She puts down her phone and stretches out, her head on the pillow. "What's your excuse?"

I shrug and lie down, sharing the pillow and inhaling potato chips. I feel stupid now coming to her for boy advice and I don't know how to bring up the topic, so instead of talking about me, I ask about her, hoping she'll telepathically get what I want to talk about. "Do you have a boyfriend?"

Her face goes crimson and she says, "I'll get back to you on that. Why, are you having boy problems?"

I cover my eyes with my arms and tell her about Jesse and Clem.

"I have a solution," she says when I'm done.

I roll onto my side and prop myself up with an elbow, eager for her advice.

"I'll take Clem. It's no problem. Send him over."

I flop onto my back and groan.

"Okay, how about this? Clem already knows about Jesse, right?"

"Yeah."

"But Jesse doesn't know about Clem."

"Right," I say, skeptical about where this is going.

"So don't tell him," she says, brightly. "You and Clem are platonic anyway, so what's the point in messing things up with Jesse when nothing's actually happened with Clem?"

My first reaction is that *everything's* happened with Clem—just not the physical part, and the physical part is just a manifestation of the chemistry, which is definitely there, but then again, she has a point.

"When exactly does Jesse get here?" she asks.

"Saturday morning."

"And Clem's concert's Friday night, so that means Friday is Clem's time. And you said his dad is coming, so he'll be busy with parental stuff after that anyway, so you have the rest of the weekend with Jesse." She gets up and turns off the light, then climbs back into bed. "I'm wicked tired now. Next time I can't sleep, I'll just make sure you're having boy problems."

I thank her and go back to my room, grateful I at least have one problem solved.

Nineteen

I haven't even gotten out of bed yet Tuesday morning when someone knocks. I sleepwalk to the door. Standing in the hall, looking like he hasn't slept, his hair a bed-head forest, is Clem.

"Cafeteria doesn't open for an hour," I say.

"I know, but I couldn't sleep and I thought maybe you'd be up. I should've known," he then rambles, more to himself than to me. "I shouldn't be surprised. I was stupid to even believe it."

"Stupid to believe what?"

He hands me his phone, open to an e-mail, instead of answering. I read:

Hi Buddy,

I won't be able to make it this weekend for the concert. Sorry. Derrick's got a big game. It's play-offs and you know how that is. Good luck. Sorry to miss it. I know you'll do great. Dad.

"Buddy?" is all I can say when I hand him back his phone. At least it's all I can say that doesn't involve a string of trash-talking four-letter words. Still, I can't resist a little dig. "Well, he's a dick. He has no idea what he's missing. I'll be there. So will Dahlia. We can't wait. So screw him." I get that Clem needs more cheering up, so I follow up with one my favorite mottos: when in doubt, eat, and say, "Let's get out of here and find some breakfast."

Fifteen minutes later, we're in Clem's favorite breakfast spot and he's speaking Spanish to the man who seats us. Not just the broken Spanglish any moron can speak, but the real deal. Full back-and-forth sentences that sound, well, like Spanish. As he speaks his mood brightens, the dad disappointment taking a backseat to the musicality of the language.

My mood, however, darkens. The more I listen, the more pissed off I get. I'm half Mexican, which I only found out about, so why should I actually be able to speak Spanish? Still, the idea of Mr. International Man with his one-fourth Hispanic blood being able to speak the language and me not being able to, gets me.

"So, another thing you're good at," I say, as if it's a crime.

"It's New Mexico," Clem says, shrugging. "My mom put me in a dual language program in kindergarten. I peed my pants on the first day of school because I didn't know how to ask where the bathroom was in Spanish and we weren't allowed to speak English." He chuckles, reminding me that humiliation plus distance equals humor. "I mostly learned how to speak it on the playground, though. When you're playing tag with kids who don't speak your language you kind of figure it out." He smiles and then says, "But Spanish is probably easy compared to Urdu. You said you spoke that by age three?"

"Two," I say, cracking a smile.

We turn our attention to the extensive menu. I know that whatever Clem orders I'll just end up coveting, so I decide to get what he gets. About twenty minutes later a plate of corn tortilla, topped with two eggs, chile, and cheese, served with a side of beans is set in front of me. Corn tortilla. Egg. Sauce. Cheese. What's not to like? I take a bite. And there we have it. I've found my food heaven.

By the time we're done stuffing our faces, it's almost eight o'clock, no time for post gastronomic napping before we go see Holly Redding. Clem drives us down Cerrillos Road, (pronounced like sopapilla with the *ee* sound—I've got that part of Spanish, at least) past the Indian School, the School for the Deaf, a bunch of tattoo and skate shops, and ten minutes later we're standing on a slab of broken and buckled concrete outside of UpsideDown!, a pinkish-beige building that's in, what I've come to recognize, a state of Santa Fe disrepair—stucco chipping, prickly things poking up through cracks in the asphalt, an optimistic tree plopped down in the middle of a barren dirt lot.

Clem knocks. Nobody answers, so he knocks again. I'm thinking we're too early and nobody's here when the door opens and there stands Holly, lead veggie from the Farmers' Market rally. I don't know if I was expecting her to still be dressed in costume or what, but I'm surprised at how unvegetable-like she is with her denim skirt, black tank top, and little round glasses.

"Can I help you?" she asks, looking surprised to see two teenagers loitering outside her office.

"My name's Faith and this is my friend, Clem," I say, realizing I hadn't thought this through. If I ask about Rudy she'll get defensive and I won't get any information. I fish in my sweatshirt pocket for the lighter and find the notepad I was taking notes on the other day when Esha taught me about bioinformatics. With the notebook comes a flash of inspiration: "I'm interested in what you do here. I was hoping I could ask you a few questions for my school paper. Summer school paper," I quickly add.

She looks skeptical, but agrees and ushers us into a bright, minimally furnished space with sun streaming through the east-facing windows and papers covering every surface. "Sorry about the mess," she says. "We have a lot going on right now, and we're short-staffed. We're a small nonprofit and it's grant writing season."

"It's neat compared to my room," Clem, ever the friend-maker, says, "Thanks for meeting with us."

"Yeah," I add, clumsily tagging onto Clem's thanks. I sit at the conference table and put my notebook on my lap. "So I wanted to know, I mean, for the paper...we wanted to know..." Clem nudges me. I clear my throat and start again. "I know you're an environmental group, but what exactly do you guys do here?"

Holly sits at the desk across from the table and stabs her glasses up her nose with a single finger. "Environmental activism. When the other groups fall short, we step in. We believe that traditional means of protest such as litigation and education take too long. So we're more direct in our methods. GMOs are our big thing right now."

"Why GMOs?" I ask, scribbling notes, maintaining my role as budding school journalist as I figure out a way to ask about Rudy.

"A lot of reasons. They hurt the environment for one. Do you know about the monarch butterfly?"

"I know they migrate to Mexico," I say, remembering some nature program Mom and I once watched with a serious-voiced male narrator and startling up-close footage of swarms of migrating monarchs filling the sky. "Oh, and they feed on milkweed."

"That's right, and their population is at an all-time low." She leans forward and knuckles her hands on her hips. "The monarch decline is directly linked to the increase in the planting of GMO crops engineered to tolerate huge amounts of corporate-produced herbicide." She accentuates the point with a pause while we take in the information and I scrawl more notes, then says. "There's been an explosion of genetically modified corn and soybeans engineered to tolerate herbicides, and this makes it possible for the big agricultural companies to dump millions of pounds of weed killer on fields and kill off the milkweed. No milkweed, no monarchs."

"No way," Clem says. "I love butterflies."

"Plus GMOs contaminate," Holly says, plowing on without acknowledging Mr. Nature Boy. "They can cross-pollinate, not to mention that by mixing genes from totally unrelated species, genetic engineering unleashes a host of unpredictable side effects that can result in new toxins, allergens, carcinogens, and nutritional deficiencies."

"But I also heard GMOs could help feed the world. I mean that's good, right?" I say. "Hungry people getting food? Innovations to save water and land?"

"GMOs have nothing to offer to the goals of reducing hunger and poverty," she says, a flurry of blond hair intensity. "They divert money and resources that would otherwise be spent on safer, more reliable and appropriate technologies."

I crack my knuckles and think about what she's saying about GMOs. It's the exact opposite of what Dr. Richmond said. How do you know what's true when people have such contrasting points of view? Dr. Richmond sounded right, but so does Holly. I realize Holly's looking at me. If I don't say something our little interview's going to be over, and I haven't even asked about Rudy. "So, is there a big GMO threat in New Mexico?" I blurt out, the first thing that comes to me.

"Huge," she says. "There are people right here in Santa Fe testing a GMO chile engineered to fight the beet leafhopper, an insect that feeds on weeds and certain crop plants such as chiles, and passes disease from weed to crop."

"But wouldn't you want scientists to solve that? If they had the technology wouldn't you want them to save the chile?" Clem asks.

"People brought the chile from Central Mexico up the Rio Grande to New Mexico a long time ago," she says, turning her attention to Clem. "You're not going to undo three billion years of evolution and think you're going to create something that can fool an insect. Then, of course, there's the issue with the scientist who's conducting the research."

"You mean Dr. Richmond?" I ask, forgetting that I'm not supposed to know anything about the project. "I heard her name somewhere," I swiftly add. "What issue does she have?"

Holly steeples her fingers in front of her lips and narrows her eyes as if deciding what to tell us. "She had a serious conflict of interest in a past research position at a company before she came to SCPG."

"What kind of conflict of interest?" I ask, remembering yesterday's meeting at work, the funding cut, the awkward between-the-line silences. Was this the thing everyone was tiptoeing around?

"Sonya Richmond owned over fifty thousand dollars in stock in the agrochemical company that sponsored her research on the herbicide they manufacture. She didn't disclose that information to anyone." We lapse into silence as she gets up, crosses the room, and pours herself a glass of water. I shift uncomfortably in my chair, corn tortillas and eggs curdling in my stomach, as I take this in. "And what do you think the results of her research were?" she asks, coming back to her seat and looking at me.

I pretend not to understand what she's getting at. "I have no idea."

"The results on the herbicide were glowing. Dr. Richmond,"—she air-quotes the word *doctor*—"looked at the soil microbiome and discovered no detrimental effects from the chemicals in the herbicide. I'd say the positive results were quite convenient coming from someone with so much to lose should the results be negative. When the general public discovered that she had such a stake in the company, her scientific reputation was quite tarnished." She crosses her legs, letting the top shoe dangle from her toes. "And now I hear SCPG just lost a major funder for the GMO chile project. She's going to be in a hurry to get those chiles to market. There are many corners one could cut when one's in a hurry." She stops just short of directly accusing Dr. Richmond of anything, but duh, you don't have to be a super brain to connect the dots: If Dr. Richmond lied before, or at least withheld the truth, why wouldn't she do it again? "Now," she says, getting up and starting toward the door, "I really do have to get to work."

Clem gets up, but I stay seated. "Actually, I have one more thing I'd like to ask."

She checks her watch with a pointed sigh. "Okay, but it'll have to be short."

"I'm looking for someone who's missing."

She laughs. "UpsideDown isn't in the business of locating missing persons. I'm not sure I can help you there."

"I'm looking for a guy named Rudy," I say, ignoring her. "He works for a farmer named Ernie Fuentes. I think you know him." Holly glances from Clem to me, raised eyebrows.

"I'm a friend of his girlfriend's. He disappeared. You were one of the last people to see him Saturday night, so I thought you might know something about where he is."

"I have no idea where he is," she says, folding her arms. "We had a business meeting the other night. What he did after that has nothing to do with me. Maybe he took a trip. I have no idea. Now, it's late. I really do have to get to work." This time she walks to the door and holds it open. As we're leaving, she gives a small, ironic smile and says, "Good luck with your school paper." I hear the quotations around "school paper" in her voice.

"What do you think?" Clem asks once she's closed the door and we're alone on the concrete.

"About Holly or about my boss?"

"Both."

"I think Holly knows something, and I think I have some investigating to do."

Twenty

When I get to work I hunt up Esha and find her armed with a stack of papers at the copy machine. I'm embarrassed about the personal info dump yesterday, but I still have the question about jimson weed. If I keep the question professional, about plants, I don't have to tell her my reason for asking.

"Hey, can I ask you a question?" I say. She nods, distracted by her copying task, which is perfect since maybe distraction means she won't wonder why I'm asking about liquid gold. "Jonah told me that you studied *Brugmansia*, and he told me about Dr. Richmond sequencing the plant, so I thought you might have an answer to something I've been wondering."

"I'll do my best." She puts a paper on the glass without looking at me. Her focus on this other task gives me confidence to go on.

"I found out about the plant jimson weed, and how it's really similar to *Brugmansia*, and that it grows all over the place here, so do you think someone could be using jimson weed to make liquid gold?" I hold my breath, hoping she won't ask why I want to know.

"Why do you want to know that?" she asks turning from the copier to me.

Crap. "The police officer I talked to the night Mari went to the hospital said that liquid gold is coming in cheaper now," I say with a sigh. "And they don't know why because it used to be so expensive and—"

"I can understand why you're worried about all of this with what happened to your sister," she interrupts. "But, Faith, this really isn't something for you to be involved with. This is a police matter."

"I know," I say quickly. "And I'll leave it for the police. I'm just really curious about this one thing and then I'll let it go. I promise."

Something flitters across her face, an emotion I can't read. Interest? Curiosity? Or maybe it's disgust. Maybe she knows I'm a junkie's kid—easy information to find out about me with everything that happened to my mom. Now I'm worried she thinks I'm doing drugs.

"It's possible," she says before I can assure her I'm not. She pushes the copy button and the machine whirs into action. "Like you said, the plants are very similar. They're both in the nightshade family, but they're in a different genus, so even though they both have toxic alkaloids, there'd be a lot of variation. Still, I wouldn't rule it out."

I quickly thank her, not wanting to prolong the topic, and am about to scurry off when she surprises me and says, "I was telling Sonya what a fast learner you are and how you'd like to go and see the GMO chiles, get a feel for the project. She's heading up there this afternoon. I think you're far enough ahead with lab work to spend a day in the field. It's a gorgeous day, too. What do you think?"

"Sure," I say, relieved at the change of topic and also eager to go up to Ernie's farm and see if I can find anything out about Rudy. Not just that, but Holly's perspective on GMOs gives me a few questions that I can ask Dr. Richmond while we're driving. The more I learn, the more confused I get. Every scientist has some angle, an interest or a starting point, so does that mean everyone brings a bias with them to whatever research they do? Is there even such a thing as unbiased truth in science? If there is, how do you know when you hear it unless you take the time to study and listen to both sides?

———

After lunch I slide into the passenger seat of Dr. Richmond's truck. With her strong hands and short hair tucked under a baseball cap, she has the vibe of a woman who could birth a baby in a barn, then leap up to split wood and milk the cows. She drives with aggressive confidence, not swearing or honking at the guy hogging two lanes as Mom would've done, or waiting patiently and turning on music to lower the stress level as Aunt T does, but weaving between lanes, slowing for nobody.

"So I have a question," I say, deciding not to waste any time and diving right into what Holly told me.

"I have an answer," Dr. Richmond answers lightly.

"I was talking to Holly Redding at UpsideDown! this morning." Dr. Richmond's gaze slides over to me when I mention Holly's name. "She told me that GMO corn and soybeans are directly responsible for the decline of monarch butterflies. I was wondering what you think."

"I'm not sure that Holly and I agree on this issue or any issues, for that matter, concerning GMOs," she replies, as she taps the blinker and cuts a quick left onto a smaller road. "Certainly monarchs are declining, and we need to find a solution. There's no debate about that, but their habitat is declining too, and the fact is their population has been going down for fifty years, since long before the introduction of GM crops. Farming is farming, and milkweed, unfortunately, is a weed. In traditional agriculture, herbicides have always been used and, quite honestly, the ones used before Glyphosate were a lot more toxic." She stops at a red light and taps a ragged fingernail on the steering wheel. "I think the solution to the monarch situation isn't to banish GMOs, as many would suggest, but to build corridors of milkweed and to conserve habitat."

"And what about the GMO chile?" I ask as the light changes and she starts up again. "Holly said you're not going to undo three billion years of evolution and think you're going to create something that can fool an insect."

"Holly might have a lot of opinions, but I've been studying this plant for a long time." She keeps the tone professional, but I hear the bite in her voice.

"So how does it work?" I ask, realizing that the inner-workings of the technology, the actual genetic basis of the engineering, are what fascinate me most.

"The chile is basically a chemical factory—the hot taste and the color are two molecules you're familiar with. Nowadays we can potentially trick the plant into making many different molecules."

"And that's what you've done?" I ask as we pass a sprawling casino set against red rock cliffs. "Trick the plant?"

"In terms of stopping the beet leafhopper, I believe so, yes. I found one biological pathway that was similar to a pathway that I knew about in another plant. I've spent the last two years working on the chile, adding a few biochemical steps, so I could get the plant to make a molecule that's similar to a known family of insecticides. The end product of that pathway stands a good chance of being a candidate to kill this nasty insect. The chiles have already passed approval from the EPA and USDA. We're in the final stages of FDA testing."

I think of Dr. Richmond losing funding and Holly's implications that she could cut corners. I shouldn't bring it up, but I do anyway. "I heard you lost some funding. Will that affect the project?"

"Of course!" she says sharply. "The timing is terrible. You have no idea how much the FDA testing cost us. But I'm not just a scientist, Faith. I'm a businesswoman. And businesswomen grow their businesses. SCPG is going to survive and I'm going to get this product to market. I'll work as hard as I need to and do whatever it takes. I won't let my people down." She swerves to miss an ambitious dog, whose chase-and-catch search instinct recognizes the moving vehicle as prey.

Red hills marked by mounds of piñon and juniper form a backdrop to the twisting road and towering cottonwood trees. I roll down the window and inhale the washed, clean scent of the air, the sweet scent of sage. We take a left onto a dirt road and drive down a long driveway bordered by irrigated fields. Green chiles dangle off rows of knee-high plants. A man wearing a blue baseball cap and jeans who's been kneeling in one of the rows stands up and waves.

Dr. Richmond returns the wave and pulls up in front of a small house on the far side of one of the fields. The blue-capped guy and a deliriously happy, oddly mismatched mutt—ears like a beagle, legs like a corgi (Borgi? Ceagle?)—come to the car to greet us.

I'd say hello, but I'm too busy noticing something else.

Two of the fields are separated from the rest by barbed wire, and standing at the edge of the barbed wire is a guy whose neck makes the cottonwood trunks look like twigs. Strapped around his woody torso is a gun.

Blue Cap follows my gaze. "Don't mind him," he tells me. "You can never be too careful." (Of what, he doesn't say.) And then, as if an armed man patrolling a chile field is as normal as a tractor in a sea of Midwestern wheat, he smiles and says, "I'm Ernie. Welcome to my farm."

Twenty-one

"So do all the farmers around here have guards or are you special?" I ask, safely hunkered in the truck while Dr. Richmond gets out.

Ernie takes off his cap and mops his brow with the back of his hand. "No," he says, with a little laugh. "I guess I'm special."

I don't find this answer exactly comforting. Who exactly is this Farmer Ernie guy, living miles from the nearest town with an armed guard patrolling his fields? Does he run some kind of survivalist cult? Is there a coven of women and children bunkered down somewhere, believing he's the messiah? Are they all going to drink the Kool-Aid?

I study the slump of Ernie's shoulders as he leans one hand on the truck and talks to Dr. Richmond. He doesn't look like the crazy cult type, but then again people never look crazy until after they do something crazy, like go on a shooting spree at a mall and we all say we should've known; he had that look. But this guy, he just looks old. Tired. Like he really loves his dog. I decide it's safe to untether myself from the truck.

I step outside and shield my eyes. There's a retina-burning brightness to the sun, a vapor-wicking quality to the air. I lick my lips, but the breeze quickly steals even this tiny bit of moisture, and almost instantly, I feel like a dried-out husk of some formerly juicy fruit. I mosey to the back of the truck where Dr. Richmond and Ernie, accompanied by Happy Mutt, are dragging out boots and boxes.

"Why don't you start off with Ernie?" she says to me, apparently used to the whole guard thing, as she slips off her sandals and sticks her bare feet into the rubber boots with a succulent slurping sound. "He'll give you a tour of the farm. I'll get started with my work in the field, and we can meet back here in a little while."

"Sure," I say, focusing back on my actual reason for coming—so I could talk to Ernie and see if he knows anything about Rudy.

As Dr. Richmond heads off to the fields, Ernie turns to me. "Sonya says you want to know about the chiles and her work up here," he says, that same singsong quality in his speech I've heard in locals since arriving in New Mexico, drawn-out vowels and a rise on last syllables as if every sentence is a question.

I shove my hands in my pockets. As I watch Dr. Richmond disappear into the field, I realize it's not only Rudy I want to know about. It's this whole GMO chile thing. Everywhere I turn, someone has something to say about it. I'll bet Ernie has an opinion, too. "So, how'd Dr. Richmond choose your farm for her project?"

"Nobody else wanted her," he says with a shrug and starts to walk. I follow him, along with Happy Mutt, who trots beside us with a dangling tongue and wagging tail.

"But you agreed? Why?" I ask as we pass an *acequia,* a narrow irrigation ditch, and I listen to birds arguing in a tree, the rumble of distant thunder. It's amazing what sky can do for land, changing the colors of the hills from pink to brown to orange with only the clouds as a filter.

"As a service to all the farmers around here. Everyone's worried. Farming isn't what it used to be." He keeps his eyes on the fields, but his gaze has a distant unfocused look. "It's not easy to make a living anymore, and we've been farming these chiles in my family for three generations." He stops in the shade of a cottonwood tree that shelters a small adobe house from the heat. I swat a fly from my arm. "Our relationship with food's important, no? It's our Earth. We have to treat it with respect. I want my workers to be treated with respect, too, but it's not that easy. I can't pay them good anymore. I don't like anybody to go home after working on a farm and not feed their family." He pauses and waves to a man out in the field dressed in a long-sleeved cotton shirt, jeans, and cowboy boots. The man waves back. They shout a few words in Spanish that make Ernie shake his head, then he starts talking to me again. "We used to have jobs for about two thousand people in this valley. Those numbers have dropped way down."

"What happened? Why'd those jobs disappear?" I ask as a herd of tiny insects gang up on my eyes.

"Lots of reasons. There's a virus that hurts the chile plants and brings down the yield. There's nematodes. Root borers. And the worst of all, the leafhoppers. They can destroy a harvest in a few days, and not even the chemicals will kill them anymore. These chiles, they taste good even to bugs."

"So Dr. Richmond came to you and you trusted her? It sounds like a lot of other people didn't," I say, and eradicate a colony of insects with a swat of my hand, hopefully the chile eating kind.

"I guess I'm not a lot of people, then, cause I figured I had to listen. What if she could save the chile? We could help families. Help the valley." He sighs and gazes out over his fields. "But not everyone sees it that way. They say I'm making a super chile. What do they call it, a frank chile?"

"Frankenfood chile." I hold out my arms straight and walk like the Frankenstein monster, which gets a laugh out of Ernie. "Who doesn't see it your way?"

He wipes his brow again, streaking dirt across his forehead. "Lots of people. Some farmers. Some people in town. They say GMOs are bad, but I'm not trying to get those big companies out here to do whatever they do with their corn and the soybeans. I'm just trying to save my farm, help the people, you know?" A trickle of sweat traces a line down Ernie's cheekbone. "We don't all have to agree. We had a meeting. I said 'Don't be afraid of science.' Some people could be reasoned with, others…" He stops talking and leans a hand against a tree.

"Others what?" I press.

"Others made threats." He looks toward the house. I follow his gaze. A curtain flutters in the breeze. For a second I think I see a face in the window, but I blink and whoever was there is gone.

"Who made the threats?" I say, keeping my eye on the house. "Other farmers?"

Ernie twists a red bandanna in his hands and he picks up the pace. "This woman, Holly."

"Holly Redding?" I blurt, looking away from the house and back at Ernie. "Were there threats against you?"

"She said she'd destroy our plants to get rid of our GMOs." He looks nervous, as if somebody's watching, listening in on what he says. "I told Doc about it, and she said we needed to keep our fields safe. She took the threats serious. Now she pays to have a guard here. I wasn't so sure at first. He makes some of the guys nervous, but her threats kept coming and I've gotta admit, I sleep better at night."

As we walk in Dr. Richmond's direction, my mind reels—Holly's threats, the guard, Rudy's disappearance, the possibility he's dealing liquid gold. Is there a connection between these things? I glance back at the house again and have the distinct feeling of being watched. Am I just paranoid, I wonder, picking up my pace, or is someone really there?

When we reach the gate of Dr. Richmond's test fields, Ernie stops. "Well," he says, "that's the tour. Would you like some lemonade?"

I'm parched enough to guzzle the Rio Grande, but before anything else distracts me from asking about Rudy, I tell Ernie I have a question. "It's about someone who works for you," I say. "His name is Rudy. He seems to have vanished. I know his girlfriend. She's worried sick. Have you seen him?"

"Haven't seen him for days," Ernie says, digging his toe into the dirt.

"Do you know where he might be?"

"No idea."

"Okay," I say, trying not to let it show how frustrated I am. "Did you know Holly came to his house and threatened him the night before he disappeared?"

Ernie looks up for a second, and then down again. "Nope."

He tosses out the cactus of answers, all thorns and needles, no trace of his earlier softness. I can practically pluck the prickles from his words. I ask another question about Rudy, but instead of answering, he says, "How about that lemonade now?"

He leads me through the gate and calls to the guard, a tall guy with pale-gray eyes, asking him to bring the drinks. The guard introduces himself as Tom and brings us each one of those giant Mickey Dees freebees with some Pixar character on it—cups that make him seem much less intimidating. We share the first lemonade, then another, and a third, all of which I gulp down.

"Hey, Lemonade Girl," he teases, as I chug a fourth cup. "Slow down. You'll burst."

When I'm done drinking, Ernie takes me to Dr. Richmond before going back to his own work. Dr. Richmond wastes no time in handing me a trowel, a bag of fertilizer, and giving me directions. "Work a little bit into the soil around each plant," she says, showing me how much each plant needs.

As I coax the fertilizer into the soil, the back of my neck moist with sweat, something about the chiles occurs to me. "So if red or green's the state question where are all the red chiles?"

"Color's just a matter of time," Dr. Richmond, who's on her knees a row away, answers. "They're all red if you let them mature."

We fertilize control Field A with the non-GMO chiles, then Field B, with her GMOs. When we finish the job, she shows me where Esha's extra-hot chiles grow, also in the guarded zone, and where her control chiles grow, in the non-guarded zone. The chiles in each field look exactly the same, no weird tentacles or strange appendages or glowing ooze that the Frankenfood reference might imply.

When the afternoon's work is finished, we say good-bye to Ernie, climb into the truck, and head back to town. The heat and sun have left me zapped. As we drive to Santa Fe, the lull of the road tugs at my consciousness and I nod off. My last thought before drifting away is that I'm no closer to finding Rudy.

I'm sleepy through the last hour of the day at the lab and

head out a few minutes before five to catch the bus back to the dorm, fantasizing about a pre-dinner nap. When I step outside into the bright late-day sun, at first I think I'm seeing things because why else would Amelia be parked in front of the building? But then, no, she honks, and I realize my half sister is no mirage.

"What are you doing here?" I ask through the open truck window.

"What do you think I'm doing here?" she says sarcastically, and then, with a huffy eye-roll, says, "I'm here to pick you up."

"And to what do I owe this chauffeuring occasion?" I say, just as huffy.

"I'm not a chauffer. It's not an occasion. I need your help." The request for help isn't asked. It's demanded.

I stick my hands on my hips, though I can't say I'm not intrigued. "Why on Earth do you need my help?"

"Because I asked around and got some information on the guy Rudy was selling chiles to at the Farmers' Market. His name is Cruz Sampson, and he was one of the last people to see Rudy. I got his address. I thought we could go and talk to him. See if he knows anything about where my asshole boyfriend's disappeared to."

"And I'm still waiting to hear why you need me?" I say, though secretly I'm pleased she does.

"Because he lives in Santa Cruz."

"California?"

"No, *Guera*. Santa Cruz, New Mexico. The heroin capital of the state. Also known for cocaine, crystal meth, and prescription painkiller abuse. And I'm not going up there by myself."

"So you're bringing me because I'm what, expendable? If some nasty drug dealer gets his panties in a bunch he can take it out on me?"

"No, I'm bringing you because you're…"

I get that she doesn't want to finish the thought, but I don't let her off the hook. "I'm what?"

She gives an exasperated sigh. "You're brave."

Though the compliment nearly gives me heart failure, I don't let on. Cool as ice itself, I shrug and say, "Okay, whatever," and climb into the truck.

We clank to the north end of town where the houses get bigger and the lots more spacious. She pulls into the parking lot of a burger place and cuts the engine. "I'm hungry," she says. "We'll eat, then go."

We're halfway across the lot when a group of rainbow-haired hipsters bubble out of a ruggedly fashionable vehicle in a fit of giggles. Amelia turns toward the laughter and freezes. I tug her arm, but when I notice her terrified expression, I let go.

"Let's get out of here," she whispers.

Before we can take a step, one of the hipsters, a girl with neon red hair who I recognize from the party the other night, steps out of formation. "Hey, Amelia," she calls in a snide voice, loud enough for all her minions to hear. "You know what the difference is between a smart Mexican and a unicorn?" She waits a beat, looking to her friends for approval, then answers her own dumb question with an even dumber answer. "Nothing. They're both fictional!"

The group bursts into a Greek chorus of hysterics as if cheap, racist jokes are the wittiest thing they've ever heard.

"WTF?" I mouth to Amelia with a nudge to her ribcage. I wait for her to sock Red in the nose and give her a face to match her hair, but she just stares at her feet without moving.

"I'm just glad your beaner father's six feet under where he belongs," Red goes on.

"Okay, you know what?" I say, unable to keep my mouth shut another second. I step in front of Amelia and square off with Red. "I have no idea who you are or what your problem is, but I don't care. You've made your loser point and we're out of here. Come on, Amelia." I grab her arm and give her a hard tug. The tug breaks her trance, and she takes a step to follow me.

"'Come on, Amelia,'" one of the toadies from the back of the crowd calls out in a high-pitched mocking voice. "Let your little half-breed bodyguard stand up for you."

It's not half-breed that gets me. I've been called worse. It's that the ass-hat who said it is cowering in the back behind some bigger kid, too scared to face me herself.

"You want to say that to my face?" I say, slowly turning back to the crowd.

Of course not.

Red, however, bolstered by numbers, resumes her crusade. "Your little friend Amelia's a Mexi-ho daughter of a job-stealing wetback." She spits, and a gob of saliva lands on the ground in front of Amelia's shoe.

"Hey, Red," I say, getting up in her pasty vampire face. "Your nose is bleeding."

She crosses her eyes, trying to get a look at the protuberance in the center of her face, and swipes a hand under her nostrils. "No, it's not."

I hit her with a right cross, the punch that starts with the rear foot, accelerates with a twist of the torso and launches from the shoulder. I slow it down at the last moment to avoid breaking bones, but the blow connects solidly, and I feel her nose spread out under my knuckles.

"It is now," I say, and grab Amelia's hand and make a run for it.

"What the hell was that about?" I blurt as we reach the truck and Amelia peels out of the parking lot, leaving the posse behind huddled in disbelief. "What's Red's problem?"

Amelia pulls off to the side of the road and stops the truck. "Nothing," she says, but I notice her hands are shaking.

"Nothing? Are you kidding me? I just stood off a gang of anti-Mexican, racist pigs and you're telling me it was nothing?"

I wait for the swearing and the lecture about how she didn't ask for my help—exactly what I myself would've said just months ago—but she surprises me. "That girl you called Red is Missy Erickson," she says, her hands shifting on the wheel and gripping harder. "Her dad was a foreman at the construction company where Dad worked, but he lost his job when he fell off a roof because he was so freaking drunk. Dad got promoted to his job. I guess her dad's been out of work ever since. And from what I've heard he's a total drunk." Amelia stares past me, her eyes distant. "Of course Missy doesn't say that. She says Mexicans are to blame for the lack of jobs because they'll work cheaper and Dad's to blame for her father losing his job because he's a Mexican."

"And she takes that out on you?"

Amelia gives a shrug that tries to say she doesn't care, but it's obvious she doesn't mean it. "She never liked me before, anyway. She was always going on about how Mexicans are illegals and that all we know how to do is sell drugs and mow lawns. Then when her dad lost his job, she and her posse got mean." She jerks open the glove box and grabs a tissue. She blows her nose hard and loud. "Missy and me and some of her gang were in a cooking class at school together in the spring," she goes on, tossing the tissue to the floor. "It was more than a class. It was an internship. We got to work with chefs from some of the big restaurants around town. Missy knew the class meant a lot to me. We had this big project. I made *mole*. I make the best freaking *mole*. Everyone knows that." I think back to the *mole* reference in the car the night of the party, Mari's comment that Amelia's *mole* is famous after what happened. "I know just how much cocoa powder and how many chiles to use, too much of either and you ruin the whole thing. But someone dumped like a whole bottle of extra-hot chile sauce into mine. The kind that comes with a skull and crossbones on the label. I had no idea what they'd done until Chef Anthony ate it and…" She's too upset to finish the thought. "That's why I can't be on that show. Everyone thinks I'm a screw-up. That my cooking's a joke. And if I by some miracle I did actually win, they'll just hate me even more."

"Or maybe everyone knows you were scammed. Maybe being on the show is a way of standing up to them," I say, handing her another tissue. "Dreams aren't all shit, you know. Sometimes they're the only things that keep you going."

Amelia chews her lip and twists an eyebrow ring. Our eyes meet, and for the first time the eye contact isn't poison. We sit silently after that. Amelia glances out the window, lost in thought, while I zone out and listen to a world of invisible insects whining in the early evening air. Somewhere I heard that cockroaches would be the only things to survive after a nuclear bomb. No idea why, but as I sit in the car with Amelia, I start thinking of giant cockroaches as world leaders and CEOs and teachers and artists and chefs, and I can't help it: I laugh.

"Something funny?" The words come with a glare.

"You ever think that humans won't be around forever?"

"That's what's funny?"

"Never mind," I say, embarrassed. "That was random."

"No," she says. "Well, I mean yeah, *Guera*, that was totally random, but I do think about stuff like that, I just thought I was the only one who had those weird thoughts." We hold each other's eyes for a second and then she says, "Sometimes when I'm so pissed off I can't stand it, I think about how all of our problems and issues seem so big, but really we're just a blip, and our problems, if you think about it, are an even smaller blip. Like a micro blip."

"A millimeter blip."

"A…" She stops.

"An Angstrom blip."

"A what?"

"Angstrom," I repeat. "It's ten million times smaller than a millimeter."

"Okay, you're not a *guera*," she says, rolling her eyes. "You're a nerd."

I ignore the friendly (I think?) dig, and go on. "And there's this one tree somewhere in California that's like five thousand years old. And then on the other end of the scale some insects only live a few minutes as adults. I guess time is a matter of perspective."

"Do you believe in God?"

"Wow," I say and laugh. "There's a question for you."

"Well? Do you?"

I pick at a loose thread on my shirt and stare out the windshield. "I don't know. Not really. I mean when my mom died I was like if there is a god, he-she-it sucks. And all the suffering in the world? Forget it. How do you reconcile *that* with God? What about you?"

"Totally," she says, shocking me with her spiritual certainty. "I figure if we don't know for sure, it feels better believing there is something out there, some power with a plan or whatever.

Some reason for all this." She swipes her hand in a gesture meant as a substitute for what words can't express. "Anyway, it's getting late. We should go." She pulls down the visor and checks her reflection in the mirror. Then she closes the visor and turns to me with a hint of a smile and says, "That bloody nose looked really good on Red."

Twenty-two

"Are we almost there?" I ask a half hour into the drive.

"How would I know? I've never been there," she snaps. "Calm your panties."

I tightly cross my legs. "My panties aren't the problem. I've gotta pee."

"Seriously? Can't you just squeeze or something?"

"I'm trying. It's not doing the trick. Pull over."

Amelia doesn't so much pull over as stop in the middle of the road, which I guess doesn't matter since the middle of the road is the middle of nowhere. I'm out the door and squatting before she's even come to a complete stop.

"Watch out for..." she starts.

"Ouch!"

"...cactus," she finishes.

The Faith Flores Guide Book for Desert Living, Rule One: Look before you squat. I waddle a few feet, pull out the spine, reposition myself, and this time manage to gush without piercing my other butt cheek and making symmetry of my ass.

Then I encounter the toilet paper problem.

"What's going on out there?" Amelia calls when I finish my business and don't come back to the car.

"Nothing. Just, uh…"

A wad of tissue flies out the door in my direction.

I wipe, climb back in the car, and balance on the seat on a lone butt cheek.

A few more minutes of teeth-chattering dirt road and we pass a mailbox at the top of a long, dirt driveway numbered 8005. "This is it," Amelia says. "Maybe we should park here and walk. I'm not sure driving into a stranger's place in the middle of nowhere right as it's getting dark is the best idea." She pulls to the side of the road and plucks the key from the ignition. "Be careful," she adds as we get out of the truck. "People around here like to keep pit bulls. And not as cuddly pets."

Rattlesnakes and pit bulls and cactus, oh my, I sing in my head as I try to see what's at the end of the driveway. Under a moonless sky, not a streetlight in forever, there's just one thing I can make out: *No Trespassing* posted in big, bright, orange letters.

"Couldn't we call first or something? Let him know we're coming?" I ask, as we approach the sign.

"I would've done that if I had a phone number for him, *Guera,*" she says with a glare. The glare quickly reconfigures into something less angry and more nervous. "Do you think we should turn back?"

"Probably," I say, and start down the driveway.

Amelia's arm brushes mine as we walk. I feel her unease in the graze of flesh, just as I feel mine, an unease both of us are either too proud or too stupid to admit.

We're about thirty feet down the driveway when I catch the metallic glint of a doublewide trailer and stop. The vibe of the place matches with what Amelia told me about this area being the heroin capital of New Mexico and it gives me the creeps. I doubt we'll be too welcome if we just go knock on the door, offering a cheery smile and a plate of cookies.

"Maybe you should wait here," I say to Amelia. "I'll go investigate."

Even in the dark I can feel the look she gives me. "Just because I said you're brave don't let it go to your head."

"I'm not being brave," I snap. "I just think we need to be cautious."

"Obviously," she says. Then, as if I'd asked to be put in charge, she adds, "What now?"

I think again about Amelia's declaration about the heroin and cocaine and crystal meth in this area, and then, of course, I think about Mom. The Philly drug dealers she got her junk from weren't exactly a friendly bunch. I have no idea who this Bulldog guy is. Maybe he's an organic farmer and loves puppies, but I don't want to chance it.

"Let's just check it out before we go knocking on the door," I say. We slip forward until we reach the trailer. I flatten myself against the metal siding and point to a window to the right of the front door. We crouch down and sidle along the edge of the trailer until we're under the dirty glass. A beam of fluorescence lights a single room.

I put my finger to my lips and motion her to stay low while I rise and peer inside into a small kitchen with blistered Formica counters and peeling yellow wallpaper. It's a kitchen shipwreck. Bulldog stands in the center of the flotsam and jetsam, deeply involved in some kitchen-related process.

"What's happening?" Amelia whispers and pops up next to me. I gesture for her to get down, but the girl and I are clearly related—she has a mind of her own and ignores me.

It's hard to see exactly what's going on through the cobwebs and dirt, but I see that Bulldog's wearing plastic gloves, the kind we wear in the SCPG lab when we're working with DNA samples and other sensitive materials. He works quickly, grinding something in a blender and then pouring the sludge into a pot. He pours steaming water from a kettle into the pot, then adds cooking oil and turns up the heat.

"What's he doing?" Amelia says in a not-so-quiet whisper.

Bulldog turns to the window, and we drop. My heart punches my chest as I wait to see if he heard us, if he's coming out to check on the sound. The desert isn't exactly filled with good places to hide. I glare at Amelia and this time slam my fingers to my lips. When Bulldog doesn't come out I decide it's safe to take another peek. Amelia stands up next to me.

Bulldog's still working. He starts sucking up the liquid with a turkey baster and straining the liquid through a coffee filter into a jar. Then he steps to the side, and I get a glimpse of what he's been working with: Chiles.

I don't get to see what comes next.

At that moment Amelia's phone rings. A full volume, mérengue ringtone.

"Are you kidding?" I hiss. "You didn't think to turn that thing off when we went creeping away from the car in the dark?"

She doesn't get to answer because right then all hell breaks loose.

Twenty-three

"What the...?" Bulldog shouts as the trailer door bangs open with a thud.

Before I can grab for her, Amelia's up and running. We race away from the trailer, doing our best to avoid prairie dog holes and cactus. Bulldog's somewhere behind us, shouting about trespassing and guns and the right to protect his property. I have no idea if he actually has a gun, but I'm glad we have a head start. I don't want to stick around to find out. We're running up the driveway, barely maintaining our lead, when my toe catches in a hole. I stumble and come down hard on a rock. Blood pours from my knee. I try to stand, knowing every second lost means a gain for Bulldog.

"Come on!" hisses Amelia, who's turned into some kind of Olympic sprinter. She grabs my arm and yanks me to my feet, but the best I can do is hobble. "For fuck's sake, *Guera*," she cries and pulls me against her hip. I lean my weight on her body, and we do an awkward three-legged stumble to the truck.

Amelia starts the engine before I even close my door. A second later she's making the world's most pathetic getaway. She attempts to gun it down the road, but the truck will have nothing to do with speed. I glance over my shoulder.

No headlights from other cars. No streetlights or well-lit homes interrupting the dark. Just earth and sky and an ocean of tumbleweed, chamisa, and rock formations changed into monsters by the dark.

"He's not following," I say, as I catch my breath and blot at my knee with one of the dirty tissues.

She nervously eyes the rearview mirror, accelerating at exactly the wrong time, and as we speed around a corner there's a spray of dirt and stones as the tires glance off the embankment. I'm thinking we survived Bulldog's wrath, but we might not survive Amelia's driving.

My stomach roils with nausea. I roll down the window and squeeze my eyes shut, hoping not to blow chunks all over Amelia's truck. When the tires find purchase, Amelia slows to a non-lethal speed, and I'm certain I can speak without turning into Mt. Saint Vomitus. I open my eyes, take a breath, and think back to the trailer.

"You're a chef," I say slowly, going over the scene in Bulldog's kitchen. "Have you ever seen someone cook chiles like that? It didn't look like Bulldog was making stew for his grannie."

"For once you're right," she says. "So what are you thinking?"

"I don't know, but there was something weird about those chiles."

"Weird chiles, huh?" Amelia says. Maybe it's exhaustion or stress, but she giggles, a vocalization I wouldn't have thought her capable of. It's like hearing a cat bark or a dog meow. "Sounds serious." She widens her eyes and makes the universal *oooohhh* creepy-ghost sound. "What's next, evil corn?"

Whatever symptoms are making her loopy I have them, too. "I don't know," I say, with a snort of laughter. "Wanker watermelon?"

"Asshole apples."

We go off on a fruit and veggie alliteration trip, killing ourselves with delirious hysterics as we try to coin a nefarious adjective to match a fruit or vegetable for every letter of the alphabet.

When we exhaust our imaginations and creativity at H (hickey honeydews), Amelia sighs and says, "I'm starving. We never got to eat before."

Without waiting to see if I'm hungry too, she jerks the truck into the left lane and makes a hard turn into a massive stucco compound. Neon lights of an enormous sign glare against the desert dark, telling us where we are: Camel Rock Casino.

Amelia, catching my confused expression, says, "Don't worry, *Guera*, we're not here to gamble. It's Santa Fe, home of nothing open past nine. The casino has a snack bar that stays open late."

We cross the parking lot, enter a side door far away from the valet-guarded front entrance, and descend the escalator into the bowels of the building where the gambling takes place—a subterranean gaming hell. Disney-gone-bad on uppers. The strangling stink of cigarettes assaults my nose and mixes with the overly lit, flashing colors, ping of machines, and piped-in music. I'm wondering if anyone ever died of sensory overload as we skirt the edge of the room and go into the snack bar. Amelia buys a sandwich, chips, and a large, slushy, pink drink that looks like Smurf puke. I tell her my stomach is off and don't feel like eating, and we take a seat at one of the three plastic tables in the back of the room.

"Here," she says, pushing the Smurf puke toward me. "Try some. It'll help your stomach."

I handle the drink like it's toxic waste, which judging from the color, it might well be. "What is it?"

"It won't kill you, if that's what you're asking," she says. "Drink."

I take a tentative sip, and she's right. Crushed ice laced with some kind of artificial flavor relieves the bile taste in my mouth. She looks at me with a sigh as I drink and says, "Well, operation Cruz was a total bust. We didn't even get to talk to him."

"Yeah, and unless we get his number, we're not going to."

"What's next? Any ideas?"

"Not really," I say. "But give me time and I'll think of something."

She's about to respond when her phone rings with the same mérengue ring tone as before. I see the face on the screen as she goes to answer: Mari.

"Don't tell her where we were," I mouth, not wanting to add to Mari's worries.

"Sorry I didn't answer before," I hear Amelia say, then— "I was just out with Faith." Then— "Getting something to eat. You can say hi to her yourself." Amelia puts the phone on speaker.

"Hey," comes Mari's voice a second later. "You guys bonding?"

"Yep, total bondage," Amelia answers dryly for me.

"I think you mean bonding," I say, but she ignores me.

"We're best friends now," Amelia goes on in a voice I can't interpret.

"Well, that's good because I come home tomorrow and I want you both to be there. You'll come over, Faith?"

"Of course," I say, glancing at Amelia whose expression reveals nothing. "You staying out of trouble?"

"All I do is lie around and watch TV. Today on "The Price is Right" this lady won a washing machine and a new car.

That was the highlight of my day. Or maybe it was "General Hospital" when the hot bisexual doctor found out the secretary from the insurance company is pregnant with his son." She sighs. "I know, pathetic, right?"

"No," Amelia answers. "Not pathetic. Normal. See you tomorrow."

"'Kay," she says. "Just don't kill each other, 'best friends.'"

As Mari hangs up, a woman plunks down into a chair at the next table and slumps over a drink, muttering to herself about the slots. With the reminder of slot machines and gambling I recall the fact that we're in a casino. Not just any casino, a casino in the middle of the New Mexico desert. Six months ago if someone told me I'd be sitting in a snack bar in a casino in New Mexico with my half sister, talking on the phone to my other half sister, I'd have asked them what they were on.

"You never know," I sigh, more to myself than to Amelia, but she responds.

"Never know what?"

"How things are going to go."

It's a random comment, and I expect her to roll her eyes. Instead she gives a knowing nod, bringing her own meaning to the statement. "I guess you don't," she says. "Expect the worse. That's my philosophy." With that bit of anti-wisdom, she grabs the food she hasn't finished and we leave, no plan about our next step in finding Rudy and no idea what Bulldog was doing in the trailer.

———

Clem, Dahlia, Rejina, Brian, Bro Boy, and a few other interns are hanging out in the common room when I get back to the dorm. Clem wears earbuds. Dahlia's lounging on her stomach on the couch, reading, and Rejina and Bro Boy are curled up together on another couch, an entanglement of arms and hips and shoulders like they've morphed into some new GMO—Brejina or Roboy. I pause for a second, deciding if I should go in and say hi, but the whole exhaustion thing makes my decision for me. I'm heading for the stairs when Dahlia looks up, waves, and mouths the words "come over here."

"Yikes," she says when I go in and reach her side. "You look horrible. What happened?"

"Thanks, and long story."

She puts down her novel and flips onto her side. "I have all night."

Before I can answer, Clem takes out his earbuds and looks up at me from his seat across from Dahlia. "Hey," he says, "you look terrible."

"Thanks a lot, guys," I tease, knowing full well how awful I must look. "You're great for a girl's ego."

Dahlia starts apologizing and Clem turns red and starts explaining what he meant by terrible. He touches my wrist as he stutters out his apology. His fingers on my flesh make me forget how I look. Make me forget Bulldog. Make me forget my name. Those fingers, they should be in a museum, have their own song, their own country, their own...

"What happened to your knee?" Dahlia asks, intruding on my finger lust.

Clem withdraws his fingers (bye, oh beautiful digits) and glances down at my knee. I have no interest in discussing my bloodstained limb, but with the fresh feel of Clem's fingers on my flesh, I think I should at least tell him about the trailer, especially since he knows everything so far. When I look at him, though, I see his tired eyes and remember his ass-wipe father who bailed on coming here, the concert in three days, the Paganini piece. I don't want to add to his stress, so I lie.

"I fell down. I'm a klutz. What can I say?" I can't tell if they believe me, but I tell them I'm exhausted, promise we'll talk in the morning, and say good night.

My phone buzzes with a text as I'm heading upstairs. I check the screen: Jesse asking for a Skype. We haven't talked in a few days. I'm hit with a fresh wave of dread. I still haven't told Jesse anything about Clem. A big fat *nada* on the communication front. If I try to play it cool and act like nothing's up, he'll know I'm bullshitting. Jesse has a serious bullshit detector. I think of texting back and telling him I'm too tired to Skype, but even that he won't buy, so I do the only thing I can think of: ignore the message and promise myself to respond in the morning.

Twenty-four

I wake up early Wednesday and bound out of bed like a kid on Christmas morning. At first I have no idea what's causing such a manic response to sunrise. Usually I'm late to bed, late to rise, but as I smile into the new day, I remember. Mari. She gets out of the hospital today. Screw Amelia and whether or not she wants me to show up for homecoming festivities with Mari and Alma. Screw it if I'm just a fifty percent member of the Flores clan. I'm going over to celebrate.

As I get dressed I notice my phone on the dresser staring at me despondently, reminding me that I owe Jesse a call. I contemplate calling now, a quick what's up/I'm fine/you? But I still have to get dressed and eat breakfast and there's no such thing as quick in Jesse-speak. Even though it's only six-thirty, I decide I don't have time. I'll call him after work, before I go see Mari.

In the cafeteria, Clem is thankfully too distracted to ask me more about my previous night's escapades and Dahlia isn't there. I attempt to engage him in conversation, check in on how he's doing, but he's in a pensive mood, and doesn't say much. We pound coffee and gorge on carbs, able to be silent in each other's company. With Jesse, it's a full-throttle kind of thing—always something to talk about, to debate, to get into, a song to hear, a movie to watch. There's an exciting on-the-go vibe with him that definitely fuels a part of me. Silence, though, I'm starting to understand, is its own kind of pleasure, and the wisdom of not speaking fuels me, too.

I sigh and stuff down more jam on toast. Having two boys fuel two very different aspects of myself should be something to celebrate, but I'm not throwing any parties. They'll both be here in three days, and I can't be lighting my fire with two guys. I'll have to choose. Again, the two-boy-love-triangle dilemma—and my love life has become a cliché—a cliché I'm not interested in thinking about right now. I get up, say good-bye to Clem, and head out to work where I can lose myself in data.

"SCPG will stand behind the genetically modified chile!" I hear Dr. Richmond say, okay, more like yell, when I get to work and pass by her office. "Your threats won't work."

"We won't stand for it!" the now familiar voice of Holly Redding replies in the same heated tone. "We'll do whatever it takes to stop you."

I pause by the water cooler outside Dr. Richmond's door and take my time pulling the cup from the dispenser... dropped that one...have to get a new one...oops...that one looks dirty. Can never be too careful with germs.

"Don't be silly," Dr. Richmond fires back. "We're already in the field stage. We're growing the chiles, Holly. Those chiles are the future of the industry, whether you like it or not. We've passed EPA and USDA requirements. FDA is the last testing to pass. The regulations are stringent. We wouldn't have gotten this far if there was a problem."

"*If* there was a problem?" Holly barks. "There *is* a problem. It's called seed contamination. It's called heirloom varieties. It's called Mother Nature knows best. It's called we won't stand for this!"

"And what are you going to do? Sabotage our fields? Like you did at the ski resort? Holly, be reasonable."

"There are many environmental groups in town who *do* reasonable. If you want to talk to them, fine. But you're talking to me. Upside Down! is about action. We'll do whatever it takes to stop you. You can count on that. Now, if you'll excuse me."

Holly steps out of the office and brushes past me. I can't tell if she sees me, and if she does, if she connects me with the teen journalist visiting her office yesterday. I quickly turn to the water cooler and put my cup under the spout as Dr. Richmond steps into the hall.

"Need some help with that?" she asks, turning over my cup, which I realize is upside down, water spilling all over the floor.

"Uh, yeah. I have a drinking problem," I say, laughing at my lame joke.

She doesn't smile. *Right then.* I chug the water to keep myself from saying anything else stupid.

"I assume you heard that discussion just now in my office, and I apologize," Dr. Richmond says, her eyes directed down the hall where Holly disappeared. "Ms. Redding barged in here and insisted on talking to me, if talking is what you call what we were doing. She said we had a meeting scheduled. That I'd asked her to come." From the look on Dr. Richmond's face I'm thinking there was no meeting. "She's on the fringe of reason, and we need to be very careful with our product around her."

"How so?" I ask, though I suspect she's referring to the newspaper article: "Jail Time for Radical Activist."

"She's used radical tactics before. I prefer not to think about what she could do to our chiles given the chance. But that's why we have a guard at the production site. We have to be especially careful with the board dinner coming up next week." She smiles and composes herself, as if a twist of the lips and a smoothing of her shirt can reverse the effects of what just happened. "I hope you're looking forward to that event. I know it will be grand." With that parting bit of inspiration, she returns to her office.

—————

"I know it will be grand," Esha repeats five minutes later when I'm in the lab recounting my conversation with Dr. Richmond. "How can it be grand when the caterer just backed out? Now it's just going to be nothing. I'm a scientist, not an event coordinator. She wants grand she should hire Martha Stewart." Esha collapses into her desk chair and drops her face into her hands, repeating the words: "I know it will be grand," sounding more and more unhinged with each repetition. "One week to go, and we're without a caterer. All the boardmembers coming. But no food! What am I supposed to do? Make mac and cheese for thirty because that's about the best I got."

"That's not true. You make excellent Ramen," Jonah teases. "And your peanut butter and jelly." He makes his fingers and thumb into a tripod and kisses them into the air. "The best."

"I have an idea," I say to Esha who doesn't seem amused by Jonah's joking. "You and Dr. Richmond are growing chiles, right?"

"Faith, please. I can't discuss the chiles right now."

"I don't want to discuss them. I want to eat them." This statement catches her attention, and she looks up at me.

"What if we wow the guests at the board meeting with the best chile everything…chile *rellenos* and *mole*?" I say, the only two chile dishes I know. "We'll have a whole meal featuring chiles. Since Dr. Richmond's chiles aren't on the market yet, we can use yours."

Jonah nods, his eyes on Esha, our fearless leader, to see what she'll think.

"Mine?" she repeats.

"Yeah. Red-hot chiles. The best and the spiciest. The boardmembers will love it."

She nods and twists her necklace, looking skeptical about the idea. "I guess I could find time to go up to the farm and get a few for you. And who are we going to hire to cater this 'grand' chile meal on such short notice?"

"I know a great chef," I say, the idea forming as it leaves my lips. "She's not very well known, and she's kind of young, but she's good."

Esha sighs and slumps back down. "Is she expensive? We don't have a big budget. We need hors d'oeuvres and a three-course meal for fifteen. The people at Sophia's Catering were giving us a deal and—"

"I have a connection," I interrupt, sickened by the idea even as I'm proposing it. "Let me see what I can do.

Esha agrees, but I can tell she's nervous. I think about what Jonah told me, how she feels responsible for what happened with *Brugmansia*, and how much she wants to impress the board. That means I have to make this happen. I can't let her down. While she and Jonah go back to work, I sit at my desk, computer on, and pretend to work, but instead of getting into data, I Google chile recipes. As I scroll through a mountain of recipes, my stomach twists. *What was I thinking? How will I ever get Amelia to agree to do this? If she says no*

I'm screwed. What am I going to do? Order Taco Bell? I'm lost in worrying mode when I feel a shadow looming over me. I look up and see Esha.

"How's work going?" she asks as I quickly minimize the window on my screen. "Everything okay? I didn't ask before. I was too preoccupied."

"Great, everything's great!" I sound psychotically enthusiastic even to my own ears. As I glance at Esha, something occurs to me: Bulldog distributes her chiles. She knows him. She knows chiles. It's an a + b = c kind of thing. Maybe she has an idea about what he was doing in his trailer. "But something weird did happen last night," I say, and tell the story.

She stares at me, looking horrified as I talk. "You shouldn't be snooping around in the dark where there's a no trespassing sign," she says sharply. Not the answer I was expecting. "That sort of thing could get you killed, Faith. You have to think. I have no idea what Cruz was doing with chiles in his trailer and, frankly, I have no idea why you should care either. Maybe he was doing a science project. I have no idea. He's my distributor. That's it. You need to focus on your work. I hired you because you're smart. So start acting like it."

"Fine," I say and fold my arms. About a dozen things line up to lash off my tongue, easy venomous retorts, but before I can unleash the Faith Flores viper, I stop myself and breathe. (Thank you, Aunt T, for that lesson on anger management.) Telling off Esha will only end one way: Getting fired. "You're right," I say. "I don't know—"

"No," she interrupts with a long sigh and a twist of her necklace. "I'm sorry. I was harsh. I just know that area, Faith. The places you're sneaking around. There are a lot of drugs up there, dangerous people. I don't want you to get hurt."

Alma picks me up after work, repeating the same routine from the first time she took me home to meet Mari and Amelia. That day feels like a decade ago, I think, remembering how nervous I was.

Mari flings open the door and jumps out of the truck before Alma cuts the engine. "I'm going home," she sings with unabashed enthusiasm, then hugs me. With her thin arms circling my torso and her hair tickling my cheeks, I'm plunged into total time-warp mode. We've only known each other for a week, but it feels like forever.

We finish our embrace and squeeze into the front of the truck, next to Alma. Her hair is loose and long around her shoulders, her eyes clear and bright. "*Miijas,*" she says with a fiercely protective smile, "let's go home."

When we get to Alma's, Biscochito and Sopapilla are waiting outside. At the sight of Mari, they bark and wag and whine with seismic enthusiasm, then Sopapilla shoots off to find a ball and Biscochito flops over for tummy rubs. As I watch Biscochito belly up, paws skyward, head askew, tail wagging, it hits me how most people (present company included) could learn a thing or two about love and loyalty—and especially about being in the present—from a canine.

Alma disappears into the house and soon we follow. Smell like memory hits me the second we open the door. Aunt T's house has the stale mustiness of the herb section in the health food store. Places with Mom always smelled old and dirty, the need for laundry and dishwashing. The smell that I already recognize as that of Alma, Mari, and Amelia is this: a savory concoction of garlic, onion, and chile.

"Where's Amelia?" I ask, realizing that more than anyone I associate these smells with her.

"At the store. Needed a few things. She'll be home soon," Alma tells me. "She made Mari a welcome home meal and wanted it to be perfect. Let's go outside. It's a beautiful evening."

We go out a side door to a flagstone patio set amid a profusion of flowering plants—*Monet on drugs*, I think remembering the junior high trip to the Philly art museum and the impressionist paintings we saw there.

"Do you like it, *Mija?*" Alma asks, eyes folding into weathered creases of sun and smiles.

"Gran did this all herself," Mari says before I can answer. "You should've seen it when she bought the place, right Gran?" She twinkles up at Alma. "All dirt and weeds and rocks."

"Just needed some loving hands," Alma says proudly. "Come, I'll show you around." She leads me to a coyote fence, another New Mexico concept I've gleaned, putting me one step closer to the local category. The earth in front of the fence bursts with white flowers.

"I know this one, jimson weed, right?" I say, recognizing what I get now is a total New Mexican classic. I don't say it's possibly the liquid gold plant, but in case they wonder how I know what it is, I quickly add, "Georgia O'Keeffe painted it. I've seen the posters."

"That's right, and this one over here's *Eragrostis trichodes,*" Alma says, citing the Latin name as she slips her hand into mine. "The common name's sand love grass. I planted it as much for the name as for anything else. And this one's *Philadelphus microphyllus*, mock orange. The butterflies love it. Here's *Ribes cereum*, wax currant, great for the robins, and here's *Mahonia haematocarpa*, red barberry desert holly—another snack for the birds. Of course there's *Allium sativum*—garlic, and these are the *Agastaches*. Great for hummingbirds."

"Man," I say when she pauses for breath. "You're like a total botanical dictionary."

She laughs. "I took a few courses at the community college, that's all."

"She's being modest," Mari chimes in. "She didn't just take the courses. She taught them. She's a master gardener. I swear Gran knows everything there is to know about native plants of New Mexico. People are always calling for her advice. Garden hysteria. It could be midnight and people are like 'oh my God! I have yellow spots on my roses!'"

Alma laughs and waves away the compliment. "I always wanted to go to university and be a botanist, but my family was too poor when I was growing up in Mexico and once I came to the United States I had to start working. So university was just a dream."

"You still could go," I say.

"At my age?" She laughs again, holding her hand to her chest. "No, *Mija*. I don't think so, but I think I passed on those scientist genes to you. Science must be in our shared genetic code, no?"

Something jumps in my chest when she says this. The idea that my love of science, my wonder for the world and all the things we don't know about it, could be inherited from a grandmother I just met congeals the connection, the sense that maybe I really do belong with these people.

We walk the perimeter of the yard and end up next to a low, south-facing adobe wall bordered by flowering shrubs. Beneath the shrubs I see two rocks, each one painted with an intricately detailed hummingbird. I bend down and pick one up. "What are these?"

"Mari painted them. There's one for Alvaro. One for

Mary—their mother. Alvaro's is a calliope and Mary's is a rufous. Isn't that right, *Mija?*" she asks, glancing at Mari.

Mari just nods and I notice the twinkle in her eyes is gone, like her spirit's been severed from her body. "I'm tired," is all she says, and now I notice the shadows beneath her eyes, the lingering effect of the hospital and the liquid gold and the loss of both parents. "I'm going to go take a nap."

I swallow back a lump. I love you seems too forward and, anyways, the words stick in my throat. "Okay," I say, lamely. "Have a good rest."

Alma squeezes my hand and silently we go back inside. She sits on the couch and pats the seat for me to join her. I expect her to say something about Mari. Instead she says, "Want to see some pictures of Alvaro?"

The question catches me by surprise. I've seen exactly two pictures of my father, and I'm not sure I want to see more, to immerse myself in the man who sired three kids, one of whom he ditched, but when I open my mouth to say no, the word *yes* comes out instead. Yes. I do want to see the photos. Yes, I do want to know more about The Jerk. The Sperm Donor. Daddy Dearest. Because Mari loved him and maybe that means he wasn't all bad.

Alma lumbers over to a chest beneath the front window and opens the lid. She bends over and digs around for a moment, then slowly straightens. "They're not here," she says, turning to face me. "Amelia must have them. She's been possessive of the pictures lately. Could you go get them for me, *Mija?* They're in a blue photo album. She probably has them in her closet."

"Of course," I say. I realize I've never been in Amelia's room. I go in expecting some black hole, soul-sucking décor, but what I find is a total surprise. Lavender walls with white trim. White bedspread atop of a neatly made bed. A bulletin board with professional photos of artsy looking foods. A neatly stacked pile of *Cook's Illustrated* magazine. It's like looking inside someone's diary.

Even though I'm completely curious about the mismatch of the room with the girl I know, I'm overtaken by a strong sense that I shouldn't be here. I go to her closet and focus on finding the photo album. I'm looking through a pile of sweatshirts and tees when I see not the photo album Alma asked for, but something else. A shoebox with blue duct tape. The box Rudy gave Amelia at the Farmers' Market. I pick it up and am contemplating how to remove the tape without Amelia knowing when I hear a voice behind me.

"What the hell are you doing, *Guera?*"

I spin around.

"I didn't hear you come in," I say to Amelia, a stupid and obvious statement, and also not a response to her question, so I add, "Alma asked me to come in and get a photo album."

"Well, that's not it, is it?" she snaps, but beneath the bravado, she looks terrified. She snatches the box from my hands, puts it back in the closet, then turns back to me and hands me a photo album. "Here. This is what Gran wanted you to get."

I start to leave, but when I pass the stack of cooking magazines, I stop. Cooking takes me to catering, which takes me to Esha, which takes me to the board meeting and the fact I said I had a chef. I volunteered Amelia. And I didn't just volunteer her. I billed her as a pro. Esha's counting on me to come through. What was I thinking? Amelia will never do it. *How am I ever going to get her to say yes?*

"Something else?" Amelia asks when I don't leave.

"Actually, I have something to ask you."

"Okay, then ask."

"It's a favor really."

"Fine. A favor. What?"

I bite my lip, ready to fight, bribe, barter, and beg. "So, there's this big-deal, boardmember dinner meeting at SCPG next week. My boss is presenting her research." I pause and reach for the lighter. "There'll be about fifteen people there, and the caterer backed out. They're thinking of featuring various chile dishes. I thought maybe you could…" I pause again. "Maybe be the chef?"

She shrugs. "Okay, sure."

"Okay, sure?" I repeat, thinking total earwax situation, and I heard wrong.

"Yeah, Why not? Sounds fun."

I look around for a flying pig. All I see is an enthusiastic robin singing in a tree outside the window. "Okay, then… really?"

"Yes, *Guera*. Really, but we'll need to plan the menu," she tells me as if her agreeing to do this is no big deal. "But I can't do it now. I have to finish Mari's dinner."

"Yeah, sure," I say and back out of the room before she can change her mind.

As Amelia finishes getting dinner ready, I sit on the couch with Alma and she shows me a half dozen photos of my father, all when he was about my age. I'm struck again not just by how handsome he is with his dark skin and eyes, but by how normal he looks, just some kid. Alma tells me a little bit about him—mundane everyday facts— that he played soccer and loved horses and had a dog named Cairo. A bubble of anger rises up in me, but almost as soon as if forms, it pops. I'm with Alma now, and Mari, and yes, (big sigh) even Amelia. I might have gotten my genes from Alvaro, but the truth is, it feels like the whole Dad-DNA thing skipped a generation—went straight from Alma to me.

Alma and I sit together until Amelia calls us to the table and Mari emerges from her room. After last week's dinner here, a meal in which Amelia stormed away and refused to speak to me, I have no idea what to expect. But Amelia is civil, decent even. We talk, share food and stories and laughter. Sitting here in a "How was your day?" and "Please pass the salt" kind of normalness, I get that normal isn't nothing—it's everything. The shallowest of trivial banter has never felt so deep.

Twenty-five

I manage not to contact Jesse for the rest of the workweek, and by the time Friday arrives I figure it's just twenty-four hours until I see him. I can make up for blowing him off then. I already told Clem I'd be busy this weekend, but tonight, the night of his orchestral debut with the Dallas Symphony, is all about my platonic boyfriend—well, my platonic boyfriend and Dahlia.

Dahlia's convinced me to go the plaza for a live Latin band before we head to the Lensic. I agreed—on one condition: I don't dance. To this she responded with a mysterious and unsettling, "We'll see about that." You'd think, though, instead of heading to the central square in Santa Fe, we were heading to fashion week in Paris. She's having some kind of mental fashion breakdown, laying waste to her closet in manic what-to-wear frenzy. Worse: she wants my opinion.

"What about this one?" she asks, spinning around in what must be the tenth outfit.

"It's great," I say, as enthusiastically as I responded to the other nine.

"That's what you said about the last one and the one before that," she protests, ripping off the shirt and standing in front of me, all hands-on-hips exasperation in her bra and underwear.

"Sorry, I guess I just think you look good in all of them."

"But one has to be better than the other," she insists.

I slap my hands on my thighs, determined to actually leave the dorm before tomorrow. "Okay, the green thing," I say decisively.

"What green thing?"

"That one." I point to a wad of silky green fabric now balled up on the floor.

"You mean the tunic?" She picks up the fabric and dangles it between two fingers as if it's a rat carcass. I nod, and she shakes her head and makes a disgusted sound in her throat. "That one's horrible!"

I groan and fall back onto the bed.

She finally decides on a blue thing—I mean tunic—which to me looks a lot like the green thing, but whatever, nobody ever named me fashion editor of *Vogue*. She pulls on black leggings and silver flats, pins her hair back, rolls on lipstick, and changes the rubber bands of her braces to match the blue tunic. Matching rubber bands? Lipstick? Okay, now I'm worried. Why my farm girl friend, Dahlia, who in the three weeks I've known her wears the same thing three days in a row and often forgets to brush her hair, has gone all runway-queen-from-hell is one mystery I can't solve.

When we get downtown, though, the reason becomes clear. She drags me to the Häagen-Dazs on the edge of the plaza, but we don't go inside. We stand on the sidewalk amid flocks of tourists, while Dahlia checks her phone every five seconds to see if anyone's texted. I'm about to break rank and head for a scoop of double chocolate when a ponytailed guy with a tie-dye shirt and a Jesus beard comes toward us. Dahlia's face lights up.

"Hey," Jesus says to Dahlia.

"Hey," she says back.

They stand there all oversized grins and self-conscious hands with the awkwardness of two people who like each other, but haven't committed to the liking, and want to touch, but haven't committed to the touching. After several minutes of witnessing Dahlia and Jesus making lovey eyes at each other, I clear my throat.

"Oh, sorry!" Dahlia turns bright red and spins around to me. "Faith," she says, pushing me forward so I nearly fall and take out Jesus. "This is Marcus. Marcus this is—"

"Faith," he says with a bright smile. "I got it."

"Marcus works on the farm," she says to me, but her eyes are glued to her guy. As we order ice cream, Jesus/Marcus tells me that he's really into organic goat-farming (hence Dahlia's goat cheese) and I'm thinking these two are a match made in the pasture. The talk of farming also reminds me of my trip to Ernie's, of Rudy's absence, that I still need to come up with a plan for finding him. But that, I decide, is for tomorrow. Right now is for ice cream.

When we finish our ice cream, we wander to the plaza; the center of downtown activity, with a stage at one end where a band called *El Corazón* is playing upbeat Latin sounding stuff. Grass and trees border the concrete square in front of the stage where serious dancers who know the moves congregate up close to the band, and the less serious ones who don't, but try anyway, teem in the back. A girl in a sparkly tube top executes improbable tricks with a hula hoop; another blows giant soap bubbles. There's a guy talking to himself and a guy talking to anyone who'll listen. There's a bald guy making balloon animals, a shirtless hacky sack guy, a bunch of stoners, vendors selling popcorn and drinks and fajitas and green chile burgers, and families with dogs and kids playing in the grass. Jesus/Marcus and Dahlia join the dancers, but I stay safely on the edge, sticking with one fact I know to be true. I can't dance.

I'm happily planted in my non-dancing bubble when someone gropes my shoulder. I whirl around, fist cocked, ready to punch the lights out of whoever's assaulted my personal space.

"Surprise!" the blue-eyed phantom standing in front of me says. I go mute, a speechless cross between mortification and delight. "Nice to see you, too," Jesse says when I continue not to speak.

"You're a day early," is what finally comes out of my mouth. "What are you doing here?"

"Dancing. Obviously." He circles his hips in a way that reminds me of a squid or some other soft-bodied invertebrate. "And you're my partner." He takes my hands in his and starts to move his feet.

"No way," I say, trying to pull away.

Jesse, not one to give up, places his hands on my hips, places mine on his shoulders, and moves his feet in a simple motion—back-front-side-side—simple, that is, if there weren't a hundred people bumping into us and if the foot pattern didn't also require synchronized hip movement. We haven't even said hello or established why he's here early, but this is so Jesse. Just jump into it, whatever "it" is. I thaw the tiniest bit.

"Where'd you learn to dance?" I ask as I step on his toe.

"Rebecca Romero's bat mitzvah. She's Cuban and Jewish, and cute as hell. I took three weeks of salsa lessons before the big day, so I could impress her."

"And did you?" I ask as he twirls me under his arm.

"Totally," Jesse, ever so modest, says. " She was hot for me after she saw my moves. After the first song we went straight to the janitor's closet to make out. When she was supposed to be blessing the bread and nobody knew where she was, the rabbi came looking for us. I'll never forget his face when he opened the closet door."

The tale of swapping spit with Rebecca Romero distracts me, and before I know it, I'm doing something that could—if you're being generous or you're from another planet where everyone has two left feet— be called dancing. The craziest thing of all, though, is it's fun. Jesse spins me under the other armpit, turns me back to face him, and miraculously, we continue the step without missing a beat.

"I had no idea you could dance!" I call out over the music. It seems like an impossibly ridiculous thing to say with him showing up out of nowhere and everything else there is to ask about and explain, but somehow it's the only thing to say.

"I had no idea you could either!" he shouts back.

"I can't. You're doing it for me. I'd fall down if you weren't guiding me."

The song goes from whatever rhythm this one was into a new one. I'm certain Jesse can't possibly know the moves to this new beat, but there he is, the king of Latin grooves, shaking it down.

Dahlia dances over to me and takes my hand, stealing me from Jesse. "Who's your friend?" she asks as she tries to get my feet to follow a new sequence of steps.

"Jesse," I say, and stumble into a blue-haired guy who's making up his own moves that have little in common with the beat.

"Jesse!" she blurts. Apparently the arrival of Jesse negates her need to dance. She pulls me through the crowd to the side of the dance floor, all wide eyes and flushed cheeks. "He's supposed to come tomorrow *after* the concert," she hisses as if I orchestrated his arrival a night early on purpose. *"After* you devout your attention to Clem!" She throws him a look. I've never seen Dahlia throw anybody a look before. It's quite impressive. "What are we going to do?"

"About what?" Jesse, who's been dancing with Jesus/ Marcus, says, coming up behind me.

"About the fact you're a day early and we have tickets for a concert," Dahlia, whose "we" isn't lost on me, says, coming to my rescue and answering for me.

For one relief of a second I think she's solved the problem. We have plans that can't be changed. This isn't a lie. I'll catch up with Jesse tomorrow.

I'm just about to tell Jesse this, when Jesus/Marcus says, "No worries, bro, I have an extra ticket. We can all sit together."

Twenty-six

I sit erect in my plush, red, third row, center seat of the Lensic, feeling lobotomized, because if I had a brain I'd claim swine flu or cowpox and slink back to the dorm, crawl into bed, and avoid both Jesse and Clem forever. It's to late to fake catastrophic, contagious disease, though. The orchestra's already on stage, a cacophony of sound as the various instruments tune. Jesse smiles at me and says something. I return the smile, but not the conversation. I'm too busy managing the twist of guilt knifing my gut. The lights go down. Jesse takes my hand, and I let him, but my hand in his feels abstract, formless, disconnected from my body. Then Clem walks onto stage, and my breath catches.

I've never been around a guy in a suit before. Suits are for corporate, talking-head types. But Clem in a suit is something completely different. Clem in a suit is the Aurora Borealis. Niagara Falls. The Sistine Chapel. The person on stage is both Clem and not Clem. It's like he just walked into himself, like everything else was practice. Then the conductor lifts his baton. The string section starts soft and light, the woodwinds join in, then the brass. Finally, Clem lifts his bow and starts to play.

The sound of his violin makes a beeline for my heart. I want to eat the notes, inhale them, turn them into color and paint my room with them. The music is Clem and Clem is the music. It's so beautiful and perfect and flawless that for ten minutes or two hours or however long he plays, I don't move. I'm not even sure I breathe. It's not until the lights go up for intermission that I notice Jesse's hand is no longer holding mine. I mumble a word to him about having to pee and avoid his eye as I make for the bathroom. Dahlia follows me out of the theater, down the outside corridor where we manage to score a second-place position in the already forming line.

"Wow, Clem's amazing!" Dahlia says, as she heads into a stall.

"Yeah, he's all unfair talent quotient, huh?" I say, having no idea how to express my true feelings and making a joke instead. I don't actually have to pee, so I stand outside her stall and talk through the door as a parade of women filter in and out of the bathroom. "I wonder if his getting so much talent means someone else got less," I go on, as Dahlia comes out of the stall and washes her hands. "Like there's only a certain amount of talent in the world and if one person got more, then another person got less, and—"

"Yep. I got it," she says, turning off the water. "And you're rambling. Rambling is a bad sign. You're in deep." She pulls her lips back, leans forward, and checks her braces in the mirror. When she's satisfied with her dental appearance, she turns to me. "And Jesse's pretty darned cute, too. What are you going to do?"

What I'm going to do, I think as we leave the bathroom, is change the subject, so I do and say, "Can your boyfriend walk on water?"

Dahlia stops and turns to me. She looks confused, but then her eyes crinkle into a smile and she laughs. "Oh! You mean because of his hair and beard! I never asked, but I'll bet he can turn water into wine."

When we return to our seats, Jesse and Jesus/Marcus are engaged in a lively conversation about the logistics of green manure (Jesse never met a conversational topic he didn't like), which means I'm off the hook for talking. I study the program and see that Clem's nemesis is up next: Paganini. I think of the last few weeks of his panicked rehearsals, his insistence that he can't play the piece, and suddenly I'm nervous for him. What if he really does blow it? I glance over my shoulder. From what I can tell there isn't an empty seat. The whole place is waiting to hear Clem and the Dallas Symphony bust out *Caprice No. 1*. If I were the one up there, there'd be shit stains all over the floor.

The lights dim. The orchestra starts back up. And Paganini is flawless. All Clem's worry for *nada*. No need to pull the fire alarm or set off the patriotic fireworks. Clem out-Paganinis Paganini. And I'm not the only one who thinks so. He finishes the piece to a standing ovation and bows to the cheers of hundreds of people.

"I didn't know you liked classical," Jesse says when the concert's over and we're in the lobby with the last of the stragglers, waiting for Dahlia and Jesus/Marcus, who are talking to someone Dahlia knows.

"Yeah, well," I say, hoping my cheeks aren't as red as they feel. "Paganini rocks."

Jesse stares at me with raised eyebrows over such long-lashed perfectly blue eyes. He considers what I said for a second and then says, "Who's the guy?"

"What guy?"

"On the violin? The one you couldn't stop looking at. The one playing Paganini."

"Oh!" I say with a little laugh. "That guy? That's Clem." Round of applause for Captain Obvious. I'm officially the world's biggest loser. Jesse came all the way to Santa Fe from Philly to see me, and all I can say is "that's Clem," like his name wasn't even in the program? It's not just the cliché of liking two boys, it's that I didn't say anything to Jesse. I forced him into this situation because I didn't have the guts to tell him what was going on. "He's…" I begin, but before I can get any further than my monosyllabic mumble Dahlia and Jesus/ Marcus are back, and now they're holding hands.

"Okey dokey!" Dahlia says in a voice so flooded with puppy love, she doesn't notice the solid wall of tension dividing Jesse and me. "What do you guys want to do?"

I told Clem I'd meet him at the stage door, but I don't want to bring Jesse with me, and I don't want to ditch him, either. Turns out the decision is made for me because before anyone can answer Dahlia's question, Clem emerges from the theater, arm extended in a wave. He races across the lobby, largely empty of concertgoers now, the most beautiful smile swimming around in his coffee eyes. He goes for a hug, but panic leaps around inside me like a trapped animal and at the moment of bodily contact I go stiff. Clem's arms drop. He looks at me, then at Jesse. The smile falls out of his eyes and off his face.

"Jesse," I say, clearing my throat and manhandling the lighter. "Meet Clem. Clem, meet Jesse." My introduction is followed by the world's most awkward silence. Jesse looks at Clem. Clem looks at me. Jesus/Marcus looks at Dahlia, Dahlia looks at Jesus/Marcus. I look at the floor.

Jesse breaks the silence first. I lift my eyes to see him offer his hand to Clem. "You were awesome, man," he says. "First class talent." He's so decent and civilized and cool that I want to cry. He turns to me, but I can't meet his eye. "I'm beat. Long day traveling. I'll text you in the morning, Faith."

I open my mouth to respond, but no sound comes out as he disappears out of the theater.

A lot of foot fidgeting follows Jesse's departure. I can tell that Dahlia and Jesus/Marcus want to leave, too, either because they want to be alone or they think I need to be alone with Clem, so I force myself to speak. I turn to Dahlia, and in a false joking manner, say, "You kids have fun. I can get back to the dorm on my own."

Dahlia squeezes my hand, but I'm too embarrassed to look at her. I resume my study of the floor as she and Jesus/Marcus take off. It's just Clem and me and the last of the stragglers in the lobby.

"You were really good," I tell him, as two ushers come by and congratulate him on his performance. "You nailed Paganini. I never knew you could play like that. You were so amazing. I can't imagine why you were worried. I saw your mom, too. She looked so proud." The armor of my silence has cracked, and now I can't stop talking. I would keep going, but Clem interrupts.

"So, that's Jesse, huh?" he says, shifting his violin case under his right arm. "Well, I can't say you didn't tell me you were dating someone. The only thing I don't get is why you didn't tell me he was coming?" I try to speak, since now that I started I want to keep going, but he turns to look at me and our eyes don't so much as meet as collide. "Why did you have to bring him here tonight, Faith?" he asks quietly. "To my concert?"

"I'm really sorry," I blurt before he can cut me off. "He showed up a day early. I wasn't expecting him and then Jesus invited him—"

"Who?"

"Never mind." I bury my face in my hands, imagining how sabotaged Clem must feel. First his dad bails and then I show up with Jesse. And then how Jesse must feel. I don't call him for a week and then I don't tell him about Clem and bring him here? "We could still celebrate?" I suggest, but it's more of a question.

The look he gives me magnifies how lame I already feel. "I don't think so," he says. "I'm going to go meet up with my mom and some of the people from the orchestra. I'll see you around tomorrow."

He walks away, and I'm left in the stony silence of his departure. I look around the empty lobby, thinking no place has ever seemed so sad.

Twenty-seven

I knock on Clem's door and call his name the second I wake up the next morning at the crack of ten. He doesn't answer. I don't know if it's because he isn't there or because he doesn't want to see me. I feel horrible, an emotional hangover that makes me want to crawl back into bed for the rest of the day. I plod back to my room and am just pulling the covers over my head when my phone dings with a text. I lunge for the device, thinking Jesse or Clem.

Neither. It's Amelia with an order: **Meet in an hour on the plaza to talk about the menu.**

I groan. I have no interest in talking about menus today, but with Clem AWOL and who knows if Jesse's talking to me, the topic is a welcome distraction. I text back and tell her I'll be there.

Of course I could text Jesse or Clem and ruin my perfectly good record of horrible communication and hurting people I care about, but since the lobe of my brain that deals with self-expression, apologies, and word formation seems to have been deleted, the phone remains in my hand with a blank screen.

I'm going about my business of getting dressed, pulling on my favorite comfort clothes—cut-off jeans, faded blue tank top, and Converses, when the phone dings again. I expect it's Amelia needing something else, but this time when I check the screen, it's Jesse.

> My hotel is five minutes from the plaza. Meet there at eleven?

Yes, I immediately reply, disregarding the fact I'll have to introduce him to Amelia.

———

But at eleven sharp, when I find Jesse on the grass of the plaza playing hackey sack with a trio of local dudes wearing leather jackets despite the climbing temperature, I start worrying about last night. Instead of going over to him, I hide behind a tree and watch the game. Every time the little cloth ball gets kicked to Jesse he misses, but he makes a joke with each miss and the other guys don't seem to mind. I should stop hiding and go over and say hi, but every time I'm about to step out from behind the tree and announce myself, I lose my courage. *What's he going to say about last night? Did he ask me to meet him so he could tell me I'm a disloyal coward and he wants nothing more to do with me?* I'm attempting to become one with the tree when a mother sitting on the grass by the tree with her young daughter gives me a funny look.

"Hey," I say with a little laugh. "Tree-hugger, you know?" I flash a smile and toss a peace sign, channeling my inner hippie, but I guess I seem like a scary teen on drugs because the woman stands, grabs her daughter's hand, and leads her away.

I sigh, step out into the open, and call Jesse's name. Just as the word leaves my lips, I see Amelia heading my way. The timing is a relief. Maybe Jesse won't say anything about last night if someone else is there

"Hey," I say, nervously to Jesse, who abandons the game when he sees me, then to Amelia, who reaches my side.

They each say hey, but Amelia's peering at Jesse and, without taking out her earbuds, asks, "Who's the guy?"

"Jesse," I answer, as if his name explains everything.

"Faith's boyfriend," he adds, and I wonder if there isn't a twinge of sarcasm in his voice. "I'm here for the weekend. Just came in from Philly. Who are you?"

"Amelia," she says, narrowing her eyes and checking him out, an obvious head-to-toe appraisal. "Boyfriend, huh?" She folds her arms and pulls out her earbuds. "You're not one of those white guys who only go for brown girls because they're exotic, are you?"

"I thought I wasn't brown," I interject. "I thought I was a *guera*."

She ignores me.

"Nah," Jesse says, pushing at a strand of hair, which he's wearing clipped back in barrettes. "I'm one of those white boys who go for girls I like, regardless of their color. I dated a purple girl once. She was hot. She turned fuchsia in the sun. What about you? Are you one of those tough girls who only goes for bad boys?"

"Nah, I'm one of those tough girls who goes for boys, no matter what they are."

This gets a laugh out of Jesse. One thing about Jesse is that when he laughs, you can't help but join in, and Amelia's no exception. The laughter is like an octopus with its ink, changing the atmosphere into something totally new.

"What's up with your hair, anyway?" she asks Jesse—a critical question with a playful vibe. "Why the girlie clips?"

"Barrettes are the new masculine. What's up with your eyebrows? Why the minefield for a metal detector?"

"It's supposed to be intimidating," Amelia says, turning her expression into a mockery of her own scowl. "Does it work?"

"Totally. I'm terrified. Good thing I'm armed."

"What, you carrying Mace, tough guy?"

"Nope." He reaches into his pocket and pulls out a rumpled bag of candy. "But I have Skittles." He throws one at her and pings it off her arm. "Candy warfare. One of these could take out an eye. Want some?" Amelia accepts, and it's then that Jesse hones in on the earbuds draped around her neck, the faint trace of music still playing. "What are you listening to?"

"You wouldn't know them," Amelia says, slipping the earbuds into her pocket as if to protect her music from Jesse's prying.

He challenges her with folded arms and a stare. "Try me."

"The Metallic Mister Rogers," she says, with a smirk.

"Three guys from Louisiana. Electric guitar, bass, and drums. All have the last name Rogers. They perform in red cardigans. Formed in 1984, broke up and came back for a live concert in 2010? You mean *that* Metallic Mister Rogers?"

For the first time since I've known Amelia, she's speechless—but not for long. For the next ten minutes, she and Jesse partake in a discussion of music. Although I could participate in some of the sub-categories (classics, indie-rock, reggae), I keep my mouth shut and listen, using my silence as an opportunity to learn a thing or two about my half sister. I learn that, like Jesse, she's a vacuole of random facts, hers pertaining to the genre of "scientifically improvable musical information." For example: Termites eat wood twice as fast when listening to heavy metal. Or: Flowers grow faster when listening to music. And: Loud music makes a person drink more in less time. But also: A song that gets stuck in your ear is called an earworm. To top if off, I learn that Amelia likes Broadway show tunes, can name six different jazz saxophonists, and played percussion in sixth-grade band.

When they finish their musical bondage, that endearing misuse of the word attributed to my dear half sister, Amelia turns back to me. "So, *Guera*, your boyfriend's not bad," she says as if Jesse's not standing there, then she changes the subject. "Now let's talk about the event."

"I was thinking," I begin, but before I can get any further she whips out a notebook and starts firing off questions. "What are the facilities like for cooking?"

"Um, I don't think there are much for facilities. I think you have to cook at home," I say, digging my toe into the dirt. I hadn't actually considered the logistics of the meal besides that there'd be food.

"Fine. I can handle that. What about plates and utensils, glasses, tableware?"

I feel my eyes widen. "I guess you have to provide that stuff," I say nervously, waiting for her to throw the notebook at me, tell me she's a chef not a catering company, and quit. "The meal's in the boardroom. There's not much of a kitchen. But there is a microwave!" I add as an afterthought.

"Great," she says sarcastically. "I'll bring some Jiffy Pop."

As she chews her pencil, lost in thought, I'm thinking, *that's it. She's going to bail. No kitchen. No plates. She's one person, not a catering company.* I'm working myself into a mental sweat, when she nods and says, "Okay. Fine. I did the math. You said fifteen people. Gran has enough plates and utensils at home. We'll borrow what she has. And for the meal? You said they're thinking of featuring various chile dishes?"

"Actually, that was my idea," I say hesitantly, unsure if she'll like it. Before she can give me her opinion, I tell her about Esha's extra-hot chiles that I want to showcase.

"And how do we get those extra-hot chiles?"

Esha said she'd go up to Ernie's farm and get them for me, but as Amelia asks the question I realize I could save her the stress of the trip and get them myself. "I have to go up to Ernie's farm and get them," I say.

Again, I expect her to protest, to tell me we can't plan a meal around something we don't even have yet. Again, she surprises me. "Fine. We'll go Monday. I'll pick you up after work. " She twists an eyebrow ring and her eyes narrow into slits. "Maybe Ernie will have an idea what happened to my asshole boyfriend."

"Good idea," I say, but I avoid telling her that I already asked Ernie about Rudy. I don't want to send her off on an anger tirade and have her impulsively quit the catering job. More than that, though, I don't say anything about Rudy or Mari or who drugged her because not knowing what the next step is in my investigation stresses me out, and with Jesse and last night lurking in the background, I have all the stress I can handle right now.

After Amelia leaves, Jesse informs me that he's hungry, and we wander the perimeter of the plaza, checking out food options. Unable to decide on just one thing, he settles for a fajita, roasted corn on the cob, and frozen lemonade. Where that beanpole puts the amount of food he inhales is one of the mysteries of the world. I, on the other hand, am too anxious to eat as I anticipate a conversation about last night, (i.e., What's my problem?), so we sit in the shade, the powder-blue New Mexico sky peeking through the leaves, and I watch Beanpole Boy enjoy his meal.

For a few minutes the only sounds coming from Jesse are orgasmic moans of digestive delight. He uses his shirt as a napkin as he eats, leaving several stains, but he doesn't seem to mind that the more he wipes, the more derelict his appearance.

By the end of the frozen lemonade, his white tee is tie-dyed with food. Between that, his torn jeans, and the hole in his right sneaker, he's doing a good impression of a homeless kid.

When he's finished the last bite, he lies back on the grass in a post food-orgy coma. I, on the other hand, am too antsy to stay seated. "Let's walk," I say.

He agrees, and we wander off the plaza toward the Plaza of the Governors, a really old building where Native American people gather under the front portal to sell silver jewelry to hordes of tourists.

"Your half sister's cool," he says as we pass a woman with piles of blond hair who's speaking to a native guy as if he doesn't understand English.

I resist the urge to tell the woman that the native guy was in this country long before she was, and I'm quite sure he has a firm grasp on the language, and instead say to Jesse, "I wasn't sure you guys would hit it off."

"Why not?"

I shrug. "You're just really different."

"So? People can be different and get along. How's the whole new fam thing going, anyways? I wouldn't know because let's see, I called you and texted you five, no I think, seven times, this week and you didn't return any of my messages." We walk by an art gallery with two life-sized metal statues of mountain lions guarding the door. A mom and dad have their kid posed in front of one of the lions for a photo. Jesse steps around them and stops walking. In the pause that follows I brace myself for what's coming next. "What's going on with Clem? It was obvious last night that you're totally into him."

And here we are, at the part of the program I've been dreading. I drag the toe of my sneaker along the sidewalk, staring at a cigarette butt someone's mashed into a crack in the concrete.

"That's nice, honey, now smile!" the father of the posed child says.

I look at the bright smile of the little girl, and for one anger-driven moment I want to rip it off her face, mash it into the ground with the chewing gum and cigarette butts. I quickly recover from this sadistic desire, but something sad and heavy swarms in to take its place. It's so easy to trust when you're little and then you get older and it all goes to shit.

Then again, maybe there's not some cosmic truth about growing up and the "it" of existence turning to excrement. Maybe the real problem is that with my mom's arsenal of drugs, bad relationships, and booze, she imprisoned me behind a fortress of distrust. I'm almost seventeen, though. I don't want to live behind that wall. I don't want her story to be my story, to define who I am.

The family leaves and Jesse moves into the shade of the awning and sits on a bench next to the lion. I sit next to him and take a deep breath, trying to collect enough momentum to start jackhammering those walls.

"I'm sorry," I say, then go silent and stare at my thighs. I study a small scab on my left leg, knowing I owe Jesse more than one stale word and silence. Didn't he once say that what he liked best about me was that I was real? Even if I don't have all the answers, I can at least tell him the questions. I can try being honest. I knot my hands tightly in my lap and clear my throat. "Meeting Clem opened my eyes to something. You and me, Jesse, we got together at a really hard time in my life with my mom's murder, and we've been together since that all went down." I give a small laugh. "I mean, duh, that's obvious. It's just I never had a boyfriend before you. It's like getting married to the only person you ever had sex with."

"But we haven't had sex."

"Okay, bad analogy. I'm just saying maybe I don't know how having a boyfriend's supposed to feel or what I'm supposed to do or what I want if I've only ever been with one person. Or maybe," I add more quietly, "I just can't do commitment."

"That's an excuse and you know it. It's not what's in your brain, Faith." He swings around on the bench to face me and reaches out his hand and softly touches my chest over my heart. "It's what's here." Before I know what's happening he leans over and suddenly we're a tangle of knees and faces and noses and tongues, and, oh mercy, his lips are soft.

Someone whistles from across the street, and I pull away, flushed and weak and embarrassed and wanting more and wanting to run. Jesse reaches for me again, but a woman in clattering heels and serious lipstick comes out of the gallery and gives us a look that says we are not welcome to suck face in the entrance to her shop.

"Come on," I say. I take his hand and we get up and start to walk up the wrong side of a one-way street across from a bus station and next to an alley. "I'm really glad you came, Jesse. And I am sorry. I know it's just a word, but I am." A car honks and the bus rattles into the station. "Maybe we don't have to decide anything right now and we can see what happens when I get home? We still have senior year together." I'm about to say more, but something catches my eye and I stop. Across the street, parked in the alley, is a big silver truck with jacked-up tires and a Broncos plate.

Bulldog's truck.

"What's wrong?" Jesse asks when I don't move.

"Nothing," I mutter.

"When you say 'nothing' with that voice it definitely means something."

"Stay here," I say, rather than responding.

"Where are you going?"

I dash across the street without answering, but Jesse's not a dog. He doesn't stay where I told him. I go to the truck and peer into the window, Jesse crowding up behind me.

"Why do I get the feeling you're about to do something stupid?"

"I have no idea. Just keep guard and tell me if anyone's coming." I try the door, but it's locked. The window's partly down, but not enough to get my hand in. I scurry around to the back of the truck. The latch on the cab is broken.

"Faith," Jesse protests, but I'm already crawling in.

There's not much to see in the back, except for a pair of smelly shoes and a bunch of dirt. A small window leads from the cab to the front of the truck. Before I can work out if I'll fit, I have my shoulders wedged through the opening. I hear Jesse protesting, but I ignore him and focus on making myself small. I wiggle my torso, trying to yank through the half of me still stuck in the hinterlands, but my lower parts won't fit through this damned birth canal of a window. I twist and squirm without result.

"Someone's coming!" Jesse shout-whispers.

A whiplash of panic sends my hands flying for the steering wheel. I grab and pull as hard as I can. My hips and legs cheesegrate against the glass, and I scrape through the opening and tumble into the front seat.

"Come on, let's go!" Jesse hisses.

I glance out the window. The people coming are holding hands. They have no idea this isn't my truck, so I sit in the driver's seat and act like I belong here until they pass. The second they're out of sight, I jerk open the glove box and tear through the contents: a registration to Cruz Sampson, tissues, sunglasses, maps.

"Hurry up," Jesse urges again.

I scan the front seat, but I don't see anything that can give me information on Bulldog. I'm about to get out when something shiny catches my eye. I ram my hand into the gap between the driver's seat and center console and fish out a pendant with the same design and hanging on the same beaded chain as the one Esha wears. What's Esha's necklace doing in Bulldog's truck?

"Come on, Faith. This isn't funny. A guy's coming."

I look out the window. At the end of the alley, heading rapidly in this direction, is Bulldog.

I look around wildly for an out. It's too hard to fit back through the window, and if I open the door and get out he'll see me. I crouch down in the seat, hoping in the next five seconds I'll come up with a plan.

Bulldog's maybe two yards from the truck now. Any minute he'll get in and find me. It's then I hear Jesse, in a loud, put-on drunk slur, say, "Hey, man, got a cig I could bum?"

"No, man, now move out of my way. That's my truck."

"Ah, shit, I don't feel too good," Jesse says in response to this.

I glance over my shoulder. Bulldog's feet from the door, but Jesse's grabbed onto his shirt, and he's making a gagging sound like he's going to hurl. Bulldog's attention is on the vagabond kid about to puke on his nice clothes.

I use the distraction to open the passenger door and creep out of the truck.

"Get off me!" Bulldog shouts, and I hear what sounds like someone getting punched. I turn back and when I do, I catch Jesse's eye. Even though he's holding half his face and he's obviously in pain, he shakes his head and mouths, "Run."

I follow Jesse's advice and sprint, fearing if Bulldog sees me and matches my face with the person who was sneaking around his trailer the other night, I'm dead. I stop running only when I'm out of sight and hear the rev of an engine. I wait for Jesse by a dumpster at the back door of some restaurant with the cardboard boxes and recycling bins and trash. He shows up a few minutes later, cupping a hand over one eye, looking at me furiously with the other.

"What the hell, Faith?" he exclaims the second he sees me. "Who was that monster?"

"Bulldog," I say, trembling with adrenaline.

"Bulldog. Great. You couldn't have picked some guy called Poodle to mess with?"

"Let me see your eye."

He mutters something and moves his hand to reveal his eye, which is red and pinched and angry-looking.

"We need to get some ice," I say, and start to walk, but when I notice he's not coming, I turn.

He's planted by the dumpster, hand protectively cupped around his eye again. "I'm not moving until you tell me who the hell Bulldog is, why you were in his truck, and why I just got my face punched on your behalf."

The back door to the shop opens and a guy speaking Spanish slings out a bag of trash to the dumpster, narrowly missing Jesse in the process. The guy pauses when he sees us and says something in Spanish that I don't understand, but I intuit that it has something to do with our loitering by the restaurant.

For the second time I start to leave the alley and the organic rot smell emanating from the dumpster. Jesse, however, still doesn't move. If I want to take care of his eye, I'd better start talking. I'm about to fill him on the details of the other night at Bulldog's trailer, but my mind leads me back to last year, to Jesse and me in a North Philly methadone clinic, to gunfire and our narrow escape—all my fault. I'm not putting him in danger again. This is my bad guy and my mess. "He's my boss's boyfriend, and he's been missing," I say juxtaposing Amelia and Rudy's story onto Esha. "She's been worried, and—"

"Faith," Jesse interrupts. "I know you're lying." I try to chime in, but he holds up a hand. "If we're going to be together, you have to be straight with me, not just about Clem, but about everything, about Bulldog and what you're doing."

I look at the ground. Is it a lie if you're telling it to protect someone? I should be honest, but I look up and say, "You need some ice."

Jesse looks at me for a minute, then shakes his head. "Come on. Let's go."

We don't talk as we head back to his hotel where we go straight through the pastel-colored lobby with a Southwest-on-steroids motif and head to the ice machine. A bag of ice in hand, we go to his room while I gingerly tend to his wound.

"Okay, I have an idea," he finally says. I'm wishing he didn't have an idea because having an idea is the exact opposite of having spontaneity, which means he's not about to kiss me. "I'm going to leave a day early. You're going to go back to your dorm and sort out whatever this Bulldog thing is." I try to protest against him leaving early, but he waves me off and keeps talking. "You have another month here. You have this new family to figure out, you have some guy named Bulldog to deal with, and you have Clem. Not to mention the actual work you came to do. When you come back we'll figure out what we're doing. I'll wait for you. Just do me one favor?"

"What?" I ask, fighting the lump in my throat.

"Don't get yourself killed."

Twenty-eight

It drizzles all day Sunday. I lie in bed and peer through the window at the arroyos and hills, the rivulets forming on hard earth, the channels being cut through soft sand. It's a good day for rain—weather to match my mood. I pass the morning in bed, missing Jesse, missing Clem, wondering where they both are, feeling more and more mortified about showing up with Jesse at Clem's concert the other night, not to mention worrying about finding Rudy and finding an answer to who drugged Mari.

By evening I need distraction from worrying about Jesse and Clem and Bulldog and Rudy and liquid gold and Mari and Holly and GMOs, so I stalk Dahlia's room, then pretend I hadn't been stalking when she gets back from an all-day date with Jesus/Marcus. Finally, after hearing the details of her burgeoning love, I call it an early night.

Clem's not at breakfast on Monday, and Dahlia informs me he's staying with his mom for a few days. He needed some space is how she puts it. I don't ask space from what, though I suspect it has something to do with me. I promise myself I'll text him later today, and head to work.

Esha's not in the lab yet when I arrive, so I turn on my computer to work on read alignments, but I can't focus. I get up and wander over to Jonah's desk. "You seen Esha?" I ask.

"She wasn't feeling well. Took the day off. She'll be calling me later to check in, so if you need anything I can pass it on."

"Could you just tell her that I'm going up to Ernie's farm tonight and I can get some of her chiles for the board dinner myself?" I say. "Save her the trip."

Jonah nods and goes back to work, but I don't leave because standing there, a new thought occurs to me. "You're still here," he says without looking up. "And I can't work with you standing there."

"You said she has bad choices in guys."

He sighs, pushes back from his desk and this time looks all the way up at me. "I shouldn't have said anything about that. Forget it. That's personal stuff. I don't know why you're so interested."

"Was Cruz Sampson one of those guys?"

Jonah's mouth opens and closes again as he studies me. "How do you know about that?"

I didn't, I think, *you just told me*. I don't say this though. Instead, I shrug and vaguely say, "I just had a feeling." My real feelings, though, are far more complex, like why did Esha tell me she hardly knew Cruz? "When were they together?"

"A while ago," Jonah says. "Before she went to Peru, a little bit after."

"And how bad was it?" I know I'm pushing my luck, but now I'm wondering if they hooked up again. Maybe the other day when her text said, "It's over" it was Cruz she was texting. Maybe he had given her the necklace and she gave it back to him as a breakup move.

"He was into drugs," Jonah finally says. "It was a bad scene. Now look, that's all I'm going to—"

"What kind of drugs?"

"Faith." The way he says my name should make me shut up, but of course I don't.

"Liquid gold?"

The look on his face tells me this is the answer.

I spend the rest of the day comparing performances of short read algorithms and looking at alignments for the cabbage genome, which I've been studying in my continuing bioinformatics education. I manage to lose myself in the data, and soon I've forgotten my other worries and concerns. As I work, I think about how we're all united by these four chemical letters. There's no black or white or brown A, T, C, or G. No gay or straight or bi A, T, C, or G. No Muslim or Christian or Jewish or Hindu A, T, C or G. No snow leopard or mountain gorilla or humpback whale A, T, C, or G. It's all the same four letters, and when we kill each other or die, all those letters decompose into exactly the same thing.

Strings of letters, sheets of data, and soon it's five o'clock. As promised, Amelia's waiting out front to take us up to Ernie's farm. We take off, or at least we try to. Amelia's truck is threatening the last of its vehicular existence. After ten minutes of turning the key and checking the oil and turning the key some more, the faithful dinosaur kicks into action. The good news is that we manage to sputter along all the way to Ernie's. The bad news is the truck dies at the top of his driveway.

"Well, it was bound to happen sometime," I say, getting out of the truck. "How many miles does that thing have?"

"Three hundred thousand," she responds. "But that has nothing to do with why we ran out of gas."

The same happy mutt that followed Ernie and me through the fields the other day greets us as we walk toward his house. The dog wags his tail ferociously and does a terrible job of being a guard. Immediately Amelia's slapping her knees, talking baby talk to the dog. "Come here, puppy wuppy. Cutie-kins. Oh, you're so cute. You're such a good dog. Yes. You're a good dog, aren't you? Good dog. Yes. What's your name? Huh? Come on. Tell me. What's your name?"

I stare at Amelia as if she's lost her mind, but when she keeps up the baby talk, insisting the dog tells her its name, I bend down and join the love fest. We're crouched over the dog, united in unadulterated canine bliss, so it's no surprise that neither of us notice the burly guy towering above us until he says, "Take your hands off the dog and tell me what you're doing here and who you are."

The dog, confused by the change of tone, whimpers and his tail goes down. I leap up. Amelia, on the other hand, too smitten with the dog to notice the guy, continues stroking her new friend.

I clear my throat and tap her shoulder. She looks up, noticing for the first time that in fact a none-too-friendly man is standing there, and, in fact, now is not the time for dog baby talk. She releases her hold on the dog and backs up behind me. The dog follows.

"Sorry," I say, forcing myself to convey every bit of confidence I can muster. It's then I realize I recognize him. "Tom, right?" I blurt. "I met you when I was here a few days ago with Dr. Richmond. My name's Faith. Ernie was giving me a tour of the farm? He said if I needed anything I could come back. I was hoping to see him again." I wait anxiously for his response.

Tom doesn't move. He stands in front of us with a bone-crushing expression. I see the cogs of his memory working, and I can only hope he has good facial recognition, and if not, that Amelia's right and there is a God.

Finally, he relaxes. "I remember. Lemonade Girl, right?"

"Right," I say, nearly collapsing with relief. "Lemonade Girl."

Amelia lets out a breath and starts petting the dog again.

"That there's Buck," Tom says, pointing at the dog. "Ernie found him wandering down Cerrillos Road about three years ago. Half starved, poor fellow. Ernie rescued him and now he's the friendliest dog around."

Tom's whole demeanor changes as he speaks about Buck. He seems a lot less like a thunderstorm and more like a sun shower. The dog brings out a sparkle in his eye, a smile to his voice. Funny how even the toughest people can go soft in the face of an animal. I go off on a mental vacation, fantasizing about how we should drop dogs and cats and bunnies and guinea pigs into war zones. *Hamsters for Iraq! Pets for peace!*

"... and that's his story. Anyway, I'm sorry for the unfriendly greeting," Tom finishes. I realize I hadn't been listening and quickly snap back into the conversation. "We're being extra careful around here. We've had more threats about those chiles. It's gotten bad. Come on, I'll tell Ernie you're here."

Tom leads the way down the driveway, followed by Amelia and her new best friend, Buck. Ernie steps out onto the porch as we approach and calls out hello. I look up and wave, surprised to see how bad he looks, like he hasn't slept since I saw him three days ago. Also like he hasn't changed his clothes. And possibly hasn't bathed.

"Wasn't expecting you back so soon," he says, his bowlegged limp leading him across the porch.

"If it's a bad time we can come back," I say, gently urging Buck up the porch steps ahead of me.

Ernie sinks into a rocking chair and reaches for Buck who curls up at his feet. "Now's as a good a time as any."

I introduce Amelia, but before she can ask about Rudy, I speak. "Tom said you had more threats?"

Ernie picks at his teeth with a toothpick. He gazes out across his fields and doesn't respond.

"What happened?" I ask, gently pushing.

"I have something to give to Dr. Richmond," he says, instead of answering. "I wanted to give it to her in person, but I need to stay here with Tom and help him watch the place."

I glance at Amelia to see if she's following. She just shakes her head and shrugs.

"You'll see her tomorrow?" he asks. I assure him I will, and he says, "Then could you please bring something to her? I already told the police." He nods to Tom, who goes into the house and comes back a minute later carrying a slip of paper.

Ernie opens the paper, slides a pair of reading glasses from his pocket, and begins to read the letter to us. "Ernie. We are not playing around anymore. The GMO chile is a serious compromise to the safety of our traditional crop, to our ecosystem, and to our heritage. We will not stand for it. Consider yourself warned. If you do not pull the GMO chile from your field immediately, we will take action. We are not afraid of playing with fire."

"Can I see it?" I ask when he's done reading. He sighs and hands me the paper. I scan it and see the UpsideDown! logo printed at the top of the letter. "What did the police say when you told them?"

He takes off his glasses and rubs his eyes. "They said they talked to Holly, but she says she didn't write it."

"Yeah, well, the logo would be a clue that she did," I say, handing back the note.

A yellow butterfly the size of my hand wafts past my shoulder. As I watch its effortless flight, my mind drifts to Holly and her little visit to SCPG last Wednesday, the day she barged in and said she had a meeting. Was this the threat Dr. Richmond was talking about?

We listen as the cottonwood leaves rustle in a faint breeze. Ernie reaches down to Buck—snoring now, paws twitching—and strokes his head. I gaze out toward the near field, where a small falcon, a kestrel probably (a name I learned from my junkie-naturalist mom, go figure), hovers.

As I watch the bird, I remember the time in fifth grade when my teacher packed up the class and bussed us out of north Philly to a nature preserve, a tiny dot of undeveloped wetlands. Although we were just outside the city, we might as well have been transported to Mars, our closest experience with nature having been flushing spiders down the toilet and stomping on cockroaches.

A guide led us through the preserve, pointing out various plants and animal tracks. At the end of the field trip, she gathered the rambunctious group of ten- and eleven-year-olds into a circle, pulled a journal from her backpack, and read the words: "When we try to pick out anything by itself, we find it hitched to everything else in the Universe."

I was too young to take in the quote and understand what she was trying to tell us, but the words stuck. Sitting here now on Ernie's farm, watching the graceful hunter, the quote comes back to me, and I understand. Our actions matter. Kill that kestrel (spider-cockroach-mouse-snake-species of choice) and set off a chain of events, events we humans with our narrow vision might never understand. Then, an even more startling thought jumps into my head: *Food.* Not because I'm hungry and want some munchies (although there is that), but because suddenly I get what Holly and Esha and Dr. Richmond and Ernie have all been saying in their own way: What we eat has everything to do with how we take care of this little round planet orbiting the sun, this little cosmic speck we call home. *GMOs. Pesticides. Overpopulation. Fast food. Organic. Local. Sustainable. Plastic bag munchies. Environmental degradation. DQ-TacoBell-MickeyDs....* Shit. The gastronomic choices make my head hurt. And all I want is a snack. Are we really what we eat? Am I really one big French fry?

Buck barks at something known only to him, startling me off my contemplation, and I remember my reason for being here. "I came up to get a few of Esha's chiles for a special event we're planning," I say to Ernie.

"Sure," he says. "But first come inside. I've been rude. You're my guests. My wife, Edith, is rolling over in her grave right now. Come in and I'll get you something to drink."

I trail Ernie, Amelia, and Buck into the house and down a narrow hall with a scuffed wood floor, low beamed ceilings, and walls crammed with black-and-white photographs of brides and grooms, babies, and children. We duck into a small, homey kitchen and gather around a large wooden table that takes up most of the space. Ernie's just set down three glasses when there's a loud shattering noise in the next room.

Buck bolts on the kind of mental barking mission that makes you think the world's come to an end. The three of us clamber after him into a dusky room, the blinds closed against the evening sun, where a clay pot lies shattered on the tiled floor. A figure wrapped in a colorful Mexican blanket kneels beside the pot, picking up the pieces.

The figure looks up and freezes when we come in.

Amelia screams, then races across the floor and socks Rudy in the nose.

Twenty-nine

"Where'd you learn to punch like that?" Rudy asks once Ernie has him settled in a chair back in the kitchen, an ice pack covering half his face.

"From Faith," she says, tossing a nod in my direction. "You're lucky I didn't break it. Now start talking. And this had better be good."

"I'm sorry," he begins. "I—"

"Sorry, my ass!" Amelia cuts in.

Rudy tries again, the ice pack and swollen nose giving his speech a pinched, nasally quality. "It started after the party that night—"

"When you disappeared?" she interrupts again.

I turn to Amelia. With her spiky hair, cut-off jeans, and piercings, she's a warrior badass not to be messed with, but if she doesn't shut up we'll never get Rudy's story. "Maybe you should let him explain," I whisper.

She crosses her arms. "Fine. Go ahead." He opens his mouth to speak, but before he can get out a single word, she says, "I can't wait to hear this."

Rudy sighs and slumps into his chair. I notice for the first time that he looks like crap. His clothes—*rumpled* would be a nice way of putting it. Hair—*dirty* would be generous. Eyes—*stoned* or *sleepless*, take your pick.

"That Saturday night after the party Holly came by my house and made all sorts of threats against me and Ernie," he says, taking the ice pack from his nose and setting it on the table. "She said she wasn't afraid of taking radical action to stop the GMO chiles. She said she'd do what it took. I was scared she'd hurt Ernie, so I drove up to his place to warn him. I've been hiding here since then. Just now when I heard voices I came downstairs to see who was here. It was dark. I bumped into the pot, and that's when you all came in."

"Are you serious?" Amelia says with a sharp laugh. "There are enough holes in that story to sink the *Titanic*. Start telling me the truth or you're looking at a broken nose for real."

I stroll casually to Rudy's side and put a hand on his shoulder. "So, about that whole 'breaking your nose' thing." I jut my chin at Xena, Warrior Princess, across the table. "I think she's serious. If I were you, I'd start talking."

Rudy picks up the ice pack and places it back on his nose with a dramatic sigh, as if to remind us of his terrible agony.

"Now," I say.

"Fine. You want the story? Here it is. That day when Cruz came to the Farmers' Market to pick up those expensive chiles he buys from Esha I started thinking about the whole deal. Looks like he's paying a pretty fee for them, which means he must be selling them for a butt load, so I borrowed a few to see what the big deal was."

"Borrowed?" Amelia scoffs. "You mean stole."

"Okay, so you were delivering the extra-hot chiles. Fine," I say, trying to move us forward and actually learn something from Rudy. "You steal a few from Bulldog—I mean Cruz, and then what?"

"Then he shows up at the party and starts getting all in my face about these chiles I owe him. What's the big deal? They're freaking chiles, man. Not diamonds! But *pinche* gringo doesn't see it that way. He goes all sicko and starts threatening me and shit."

He stops talking and gives Amelia a pleading look. She narrows her eyes. "Then what?"

"I took off from the party and drove around a while so I could be sure he wasn't following me, then I went home." He keeps his gaze on Amelia as if he can get her to forgive him with the desperation in his eyes. "I was about to call you, Babe, but Holly showed up. I already told you how *that* went. I started getting nervous about Ernie, so, like I said; I drove up here to warn him that Holly was on the warpath. He said not to worry because of the guard. He said Doctor Richmond wouldn't let anything happen to the fields, but I thought, yeah, she'll protect her fields, but what about protecting us? So I decided to hide out here. I went upstairs and that's when it happened."

"When *what* happened?" I ask, in no mood for his dramatic flair.

"I smoked a little weed to relax, you know? Then I tasted the chile, just to see how hot it was. And man, I can't remember anything after that. That chile, it did something to me. That's why I didn't call. I wasn't right, man. All week. Like the chile drugged me, and this week, I've been laying low, getting better."

"Gee. That's logical," Amelia snorts. "It was the chile that drugged you, not the shwagg. Nobody ever laces pot with anything, like say PCP, but they go around lacing chiles all the time."

"It wasn't the pot! I'd smoked the same batch before. It was the chiles!" Rudy insists.

Ernie, who I hadn't realized was standing behind me, kicks a chair. I jerk around and see his pinched, angry mouth. "That's what he keeps saying! 'The chile made me sick! The chile made me sick!'" He throws up his hands. "But how could a chile make you that sick? I've seen it before."

"Seen what?" I ask, gently.

"The heroin."

"The heroin?" I repeat, not because I didn't hear, but because I'm so surprised it's the only thing that comes out.

"You know how many kids around here screw up their lives with that junk? How many make the deal with the devil? I've seen those kids on heroin before. Same as Rudy was. The confusion. The hard time breathing. The blue around his mouth. I knew that boy did pot, but I never thought he'd do heroin, especially not here." Ernie's eyes flash. "I don't have money to take him to the hospital. Insurance. Doctors. And I was scared, too. And mad! Someone does heroin in my house? And I think to myself, Ernie, don't you take that boy to the hospital. Let him get over this on his own. Teach him a lesson. See if he ever does heroin again! That's why I didn't want anybody knowing he was here. I didn't want anyone knowing about the drugs."

"It wasn't heroin!" Rudy shouts. He jumps up from his chair and for a minute I think he's going to take a swing at Ernie, but he just stands there looking lost and then slumps back down. "I think Cruz put drugs in the chiles. I was hallucinating and out of it and half dead." He pauses, then says, "I think it was liquid gold."

"Liquid gold in the chiles!" It's Ernie's turn to shout. "How could there be liquid gold in the chiles?"

"I don't know!"

I take the seat across from Rudy and lean forward, elbows on the table. His talk of liquid gold in the chiles brings me back to my suspicion that Rudy's the one who slipped Mari the drug. "Are you sure the chiles you delivered to Cruz weren't a cover up for what you were really selling? Liquid gold, maybe?"

"You think I'm dealing liquid gold? Man, I'm not that stupid!"

A point to be debated, but before I can say anything else, Amelia bursts out, "Wait a minute! Was that you? Did you give my sister liquid gold and then come to the hospital to see if she had any memory that the beer you gave her made her sick?"

Rudy looks confused, and I realize that if he's telling the truth he was holed up here the whole time Mari was in the hospital and has no idea what happened. Amelia looks like she wants to kill him. Before she can throttle her boyfriend I fill him in on the details. He looks completely surprised by the story. He's either a freaking brilliant actor or he truly has nothing to do with what happened. I close my eyes, thinking of what to do next. Then it comes to me: Dolores said the guy who came to the hospital had a tattoo.

"I have an idea," I say. "Give me a second." I find Dolores' number and dial, maintaining the peace by holding everyone's curiosity as I wait for her to answer.

Someone picks up and says hello on the first ring, but it's not Dolores. It's Clem.

My first panicked reaction upon hearing Clem's voice for the first time in three days is to hang up, but with everyone watching me, I offer a shaky hello and then, not knowing what else to say, add, "I was calling your mom."

"She's in the shower. I answered for her." He pauses, a long silence into which I read about eight million different things. "Funny that you'd call my mom and not me."

"I know, right. Ha ha?" I glance at the people in the room who are waiting to hear the brilliant idea I have that will shed light on Mari's hospital visitor. I hold up my finger, indicating I need a second, and turn my back. "I'm not alone right now, but I really want to see you. Dahlia said you needed space and I thought you didn't want to talk to me, so I didn't call, but now I'm talking to you and..." Dahlia's right. I do ramble. "When are you coming back?"

"Tomorrow evening. I'll be there for dinner," he says. "Hang on, my mom's out of the shower."

"Baked macaroni tomorrow night at six?" I quickly say before he can hand over the phone.

I think I can hear a smile in his voice when he agrees. "Okay. Baked macaroni. I'll come by your room tomorrow. Here's my mom."

I say hello to Dolores, ask how she is, and get to the business of the call. "I'd asked you about a guy who came to see Mari in the hospital. You told me he had a tattoo. I wonder if you remember anything about the tattoo like which arm it was on, or what it was of?"

"I can't tell you which arm," she says, "but I remember it was of some kind of animal. An eagle maybe, or was it a bear? It was one of those big tattoos, meant to look scary. Your sister Mari's a sweetheart. I hope that helps with whatever you're trying to find out."

"It helps a lot. Thanks." I hang up, then turn to Rudy. "Roll up your sleeves."

"Why?" he says, scooting his chair back.

"Because I said so." I shoot him a look. He glances at Amelia who gives him the same look. He sighs and caves.

I hold up Rudy's tattooed arm, then tell Amelia what Dolores told me. Amelia and I stare at the small red Zia Sun symbol, like the one on the New Mexico flag, tattooed onto his arm. No bear. No eagle.

"Looks like it wasn't Rudy who came to the hospital," I say.

Amelia, apparently not yet willing to accept Rudy's story and the nine-day disappearance of her boyfriend, stomps out of the kitchen. Ernie and Buck follow. I go to the window and look out over the chile fields, at the orange streaked sky and cottonwood branches thrashing in the wind. There's one way to know for sure if what Rudy's saying is true.

I turn back to him and say, "You have any more of those chiles you stole from Cruz?"

Thirty

While Rudy tracks down Amelia to make nice or to have it out or whatever, I sit on a couch in a small out-of-the-way room at the back of the house. It'll be a while before the anti-lovebirds make up (if they do) and then there's the whole no-gas situation Amelia has to deal with, so I have some time before we go.

I pick up the chile Rudy claims was laced with liquid gold and turn it over in my fingers, studying the green color, feeling the smooth texture. Virg said they don't know where liquid gold is coming from. Maybe this is the answer. Maybe Bulldog's buying the chiles from Esha and spiking them, and that's what he was doing in his trailer. Maybe he's using jimson weed, the local plant, to make the drug. But if Bulldog *is* lacing them, I think, sitting up and looking again at the chile, wouldn't he do that after he buys them? Rudy stole them before Bulldog got his hands on them. Then again, who knows what else Bulldog could've done or if Rudy's even telling the truth?

I stare at the chile for a long time, debating what I'm about to do. Being an addict's daughter I've never been tempted to test fate and experiment with drugs or alcohol. So what if the chile *is* spiked and I eat some and develop a taste for liquid gold? I get that addiction isn't a single gene, *but still*, I think, blinking on an image of Mom high and passed out in some shithole apartment where we lived, her clothes dirty and smelling of cigarettes and puke—*drugs suck.*

Forget it. There has to be another way.

I turn on the TV and sink back into the sofa. Instead of staring at the problem of Rudy's story and the chile head on, I zone out and loosen my mind, let my brain recalibrate and see what comes to me. I lounge through two sitcoms, no idea what they're about—both because they're not about anything and because there's something about the chile lingering in the back of my mind just out of reach. When the second show ends, no idea what time it is, still no sign of Rudy and Amelia, I turn off the TV, close my eyes, and try to catch that nagging thought.

And then it comes to me in one synaptic blast. How could I not have seen this before? Rudy wasn't the only one who tasted one of Bulldog's chiles. Mari cooked one into the stew she brought to the party. Worse, Mari wasn't the only one who ate the stew.

I get up and pace, heart thundering, an adrenaline tremble in my hands as I take myself back to the night of the party: *Mari, Clem, and I are standing together outside the kitchen when two girls come by. One of them is saying how good the chile stew is. Mari's stew. The one she made with the chile she took from Rudy.* My breath quickens. That girl was Eslee. The one who died of a liquid gold overdose.

I race through the house, looking for Amelia to tell her this news. Rudy was telling the truth. Liquid gold wasn't slipped into Mari's beer. She accidentally ate it in the stew she cooked. Virg said it's hard to regulate the dosage of the drug. Mari used the whole chile. There was too much liquid gold in the stew. That's why Eslee died.

I'm too amped up to think straight or work though the details of how this happened. I just know I need to find Amelia. I call her name, but she doesn't answer. I prowl the house looking for her, tapping open doors as I go, but I can't find her or Rudy anywhere. When I crack one door, I find Ernie asleep, Buck at his feet. I check my phone—nine-thirty. I don't care how late it is. We have to get back to Santa Fe and tell Virg about Bulldog and the chiles.

I run outside and stumble up the driveway in the dark, calling for Amelia. Her truck is gone, and she's nowhere in sight. Did she and Rudy ditch me? Did they go off on some little jaunt to make up or more likely to kill each other? I'm seeing metaphorical angry red, as I realize Amelia left me here for her guy. That's when I notice something stinging my eyes. More than that, it's hard to breathe. I think it's my sympathetic nervous system pumping out stress, making me wheeze, and I turn back to the house. That's when I see it.

It's not my nervous system messing with me.

Ernie's chile fields are on fire.

I don't think. I run. Down the driveway. Huffing toward the fields through a disorienting haze of heat and smoke. My eyes burn. Smoke chokes my lungs. Through the smoke I see a figure, a flash of blond, at least I think I do. I scream for help, but no answer. I quickly push the apparition from my mind for more urgent matters. The wind is fanning the fire, pushing the flames toward Ernie's house. He and Buck are inside.

I tear off to the house and burst through the door, shouting Ernie's name.

Buck barrels out of the bedroom, barking. Ernie's a step behind in his pajamas. I don't have to say anything. The fire speaks for itself.

"Is anyone else in the house?" I shout.

"I don't know," Ernie says, standing there in bare feet. "I don't think so...I..."

"Go check!" I order, taking control. Buck, second in command, continues to bark until Ernie shakes himself from his shock and turns back to look.

The second he turns, I yank my phone from my pocket to call 911.

———

I stand at a safe distance at the top of the driveway as firefighters combat the blaze. Hot orange flames shoot up against a black sky, hiss through swirls of smoke. My lungs and eyes burn as I listen to shouts and sirens, worrying the fire will take Ernie's house. But the firefighters manage to keep the land from igniting and by midnight they have the blaze contained, smoldering down to sparks and ash. The fields are charred, but the house is safe and nobody is hurt.

I'm exhausted and dirty and parched, and all I want to do is collapse and sleep for two years, but I was the one who made the call and the cops want to speak to me. I cooperate the best I can, but my memory of the events is shaky. All I recall is that it was around nine-thirty when I discovered the fire and I'd been outside looking for Amelia. As I tell the cops this part, I remember something else. The reason I was looking for Amelia was because I wanted to tell her about Bulldog and the chiles. I wanted to get back to Santa Fe and talk to Virg. When the fire happened, I never made the call.

It's one in the morning, but the second I finish my interview I dial Virg's number. He doesn't answer—big surprise, given the hour—so I leave a message and tell him my theory about Bulldog, liquid gold, and the chiles. When I hang up, I go back to the house and find Amelia standing at the door, waiting for me.

"Where were you?" I ask as I climb over a soot-stained step and collapse onto the porch.

"Rudy and I went for a drive so we could talk."

"I thought you were out of gas," I snap, still irritated that she left.

"He filled the tank. I'm really sorry for disappearing," she says, and for once sounds contrite and not angry.

Her eyes are red—from smoke or exhaustion or tears I have no idea and I'm too tired to ask, also too tired to keep being pissed. "I think Rudy's telling the truth about the chiles," I say, then realize Amelia never knew about the chile Mari stole from Rudy at the Farmers' Market. I break the news to her as gently as I can, explaining that Mari used one of the drugged chiles to make the stew.

I don't need to see her face to feel her reaction. "So Bulldog laced the chile that almost killed my sister and killed Eslee," she says when I finish. "I'm going to kill him."

"I already called Officer Virgil, the cop who interviewed us the night of the party," I assure her. "I told him what I think. Let's not go killing anyone. Let's sleep and start fresh in a few hours."

Amelia agrees and we go inside. She and Rudy curl up on the couch like puppies. I fall asleep in a recliner chair, but my dreams are restless, my sleep filled with combat and questions, and at first light I'm up. I steal into the kitchen and find Ernie sitting at the table, a piece of paper next to him, staring out over his burned fields.

I sit next to him and see the paper is the note from UpsideDown! The note sparks something I'd forgotten—the flash of a person through the flames. I can't believe I forgot that. Holly with her blond hair and radical tactics. Was she the one who burned the fields?

I finger my phone and think of calling Virg again, but his focus needs to be on Bulldog. The fire is a totally different thing. I could call the local cops, but they'll think I'm making it up if I go to them now and tell them that I saw someone last night. I take my hand off my phone and, as I do, realize the real reason I don't want to go to the cops about this. If I tell them about Holly I'll never get a chance to talk to her—procedures, due process, whatever. But I've already spoken to Holly Redding about GMOs, and not just about any GMOs, about the GMO chile my boss engineered. This fire is personal. I want to talk to her myself.

I tiptoe into the sitting room where Amelia and Rudy are still sleeping and quietly pick up her purse. I'm digging through the pockets for her keys, trying not to make a sound, when I feel a hand on my shoulder and jump. Amelia's eyes are open, and she's looking at me.

"What're you doing, *Guera?*" she whispers into the shadows.

"Going to talk to Holly," I sigh, too tired to lie.

She slips out from under Rudy's arm and sits up. "You can't do that. She's crazy. She could be dangerous." She keeps her voice low, careful not to wake her snoring boyfriend. "What if she has a gun or something?"

I don't think Holly's that kind of crazy, but then again, I have no idea what kind of crazy she is. It's too late to back down, though. I have a plan and I'm sticking with it. "The world's full of what ifs," I say firmly. "I'm going."

"Fine, then I'm coming with you."

"No way. You just said she could be dangerous."

"And you just said the world's full of what ifs."

"No," I say again.

She reaches into her pocket and dangles her keys. I lunge for them, but she snatches them away. "You want to go, I'm your ride."

At seven-thirty Amelia and I reach the address that she Googled for Holly Redding. We walk up a graveled path bordered by a nicely maintained garden and approach the turquoise blue front door. I knock. Nobody answers. I glance at Amelia and knock again.

Two more knocks, and finally the door cracks open. Holly stands cautiously in the opening. "Can I help you?"

"I met you the other day," I say, before she can decide we're selling magazines or religion and slam the door. "I came to UpsideDown! I'm Faith Flores. This is Amelia."

She nods at Amelia, then gives me a wary look. "I remember. What are you doing at my house?"

"I wanted to talk to you about Ernie's chile fields."

"I already spoke to the cops about the note."

She starts to shut the door, but Amelia shoots out a hand and blocks it from closing. "And what about the fire?" she says.

Holly looks surprised. "What fire?"

"Oh, come on," I say, riled, but what was I expecting? That she'd just admit to being an arsonist? "Someone burned the GMO chiles last night."

Now she really looks surprised, scared, too. "You can talk to my attorney," she says, and starts to close the door for a second time.

"Should I also talk to your attorney about the fact you barged into SCPG last week and made threats against Dr. Richmond's genetically modified chiles?"

She doesn't open the door any wider, but she doesn't shut it, either. "Okay, no more games. Who exactly are you?"

"I'm an intern at SCPG." I feel Amelia's eyes on me as I squint against the sun peeking up over the house. "I saw you there last week. I heard you talking to Dr. Richmond. Why did you barge in?"

"*Barge* in?" She scoffs and jerks open the door wider. I get a flash of pretty ochre-colored walls behind her, but then she's up close and in my face and all I see is eyes, nose, and hair. "I didn't *barge* in. Esha Margolis invited me. She e-mailed me and asked me to come. She said that her boss wanted to talk to me."

"Esha e-mailed you?" I say, confused by this version of events, but I stick to my story and keep on the questions. "I heard you say that you'd do whatever it takes to stop her, and then the chiles went up in flames."

"I know what I said," she shoots back. "Haven't you ever said something out of anger when you were provoked?" She glances at Amelia, who's letting me take the lead, then back at me. "Look, Faith. UpsideDown! will take action, but the radical tactics are the past."

"You told me you weren't mainstream," I persist. "You said that UpsideDown! does what other environmental groups won't."

"Right, and we're *not* mainstream. What I meant is street theater. Costumes. Marches. Not arson."

"And what about the note you wrote to Ernie?" Amelia says. "It was from UpsideDown! You said you weren't afraid of playing with fire."

She gives a sharp laugh. "Do you really think if I was going to burn down someone's fields I'd write them a note first and tell them I was going to do it? Please. Look. I'm not perfect, okay? My tactics might be unusual. That doesn't mean I'd set fire to someone's fields. Besides," she adds, "I was working late last night. There were two people with me. I'm glad to give you their numbers and you can check for yourself, if that will satisfy you and get you to leave me alone."

"Well, if you didn't do it," I say, taking this in, "who did?"

She holds my eye without flinching. "I'd say someone with something to hide. Now, if you'll excuse me." This time she does close the door.

"What do you think?" Amelia asks as we walk away. "Who do you think burned the fields?"

"I don't know," I admit as we climb into her truck and her phone rings—two lines of "Under Pressure," David Bowie and Freddie Mercury.

"Hey, Babe," she says a second later. With the abducted, alien-girl lilt to her voice, I'm guessing she and Rudy made up.

I stare out the window as they talk. As she tells her boyfriend my idea about how the drugged chile killed Eslee and hurt Mari, I wonder what clue I'm missing. Who burned the fields and why?

Amelia hangs up and starts the truck, but before she puts it in drive she says, "There's something I don't get. If Bulldog laced the chiles, how did liquid gold get into the chile Mari took before he got hold of it?"

Although I've been wondering the same thing without coming up with an answer, her question sparks something new in my brain, something I learned in chemistry class: solvent partitioning. How certain chemicals dissolve in certain substances. In his trailer, it looked like Bulldog was making a paste with the chile on the counter and then adding oil to the paste. He sucked off the oil layer with that turkey baster, and what did he have? An oily, gold-colored substance that could be slipped into a drink: in other words, a liquid gold.

"What if liquid gold isn't added *after* the chile is harvested?" I say, turning to face her. "What if it's added *before* it's harvested? Before it's even grown. When it's a seed."

"What do you mean?"

"What if it's being genetically engineered? What if liquid gold is being grown inside the chile as a way to sell a drug that nobody can detect?"

"Are you serious?" she asks, eyes widening.

"Totally."

"But who—?"

"I don't know," I interrupt, unwilling to speculate further until I have more time to think and investigate. "I have to get to work. I'll do some research and call you as soon as I have an answer."

Thirty-one

When Amelia drops me off at SCPG, everyone already knows about the fire. Dr. Richmond and Esha are on their way to speak with the police. I want to get to Esha before she leaves and tell her what I know, but as I approach her, my momentum tanks. I can't say why exactly, but I decide it's best for now to keep my thoughts to myself.

"You okay?" she asks when I come to a halt several inches from where she's standing.

"No, I mean, yeah. I'm fine. This is just so awful."

"I know, but we're not letting Holly Redding's tactics stop us. The board meeting is this Friday and we're going ahead with it." Despite how fatigued she looks, she speaks with conviction, and I can't say I'm not the tiniest bit impressed. "The fire is a setback, but it won't stop us."

I consider asking about what Holly told me—how Esha had invited her in to talk to Dr. Richmond, saying Dr. Richmond had called the meeting, but my phone rings. I check the screen and see it's Virg. I tell Esha I'll see her later and step into the hall to take the call.

"Hey," I say, once I'm alone. "What's up? Did you get my message? Did you find Bulldog—I mean Cruz?"

"Yes. I got your message. I just called to say that we're following up on your information," he says—cop talk for I ain't telling you nothing.

———

What if it's added before it's harvested, when it's still a seed? I think as I stare at my computer screen late that afternoon back in the dorm, the question a singularity in my consciousness. If liquid gold was added to the chile as a seed, it was genetically engineered that way and there are only two people who could've done such a thing: Esha and Dr. Richmond.

Dr. Richmond's the one who sequenced *Brugmansia*. She's the one, according to Holly, with the unethical past and the conflict of interest, the one trying to keep the company from tanking. So what if she's the one engineering a liquid gold chile for a profit? I Google her name and consult the oracle of information to see what more I can learn.

Fifteen minutes later, I know the following: Dr. Richmond did own over fifty thousand dollars in stock in the agrochemical company that sponsored her research on the herbicide they manufactured as Holly had said. No, she didn't disclose that information to anyone, and yes, the results of her research were glowing. However, what I also find out, and what Holly failed to tell me, is that Dr. Richmond paid to have her research independently verified, and not just that, she divested all her assets in the company and publically apologized for not disclosing the information. So, if anything, her reputation wasn't tarnished. It was varnished. She came out glowing. The independent research confirmed her findings. She gave back the money. She wasn't just clean; she was antiseptic.

And Esha? The oracle tells me little about her that I don't already know.

I turn away from the computer, the late afternoon sun slanting through my window, and let my thoughts wander to everything I've learned about Esha over the past few weeks—Peru, dating Bulldog, the fact that she feels like *Brugmansia* and the financial fiasco was her fault, how Jonah said she wants to make it up to Dr. Richmond.

As music drifts in from the hall, some morose-sounding indie thing, I hypothesize the following: Jonah said Esha and Bulldog were a thing, so maybe he was the boyfriend who gave her the necklace. Jonah also said Bulldog had a taste for liquid gold. He also said there'd been a bad scene with Bulldog and Esha. What if the bad scene was about drugs?

My heart bashes my ribs as this idea moves into my mind. What if the reason Esha wanted Dr. Richmond to sequence *Brugmansia* was because she and Bulldog were using liquid gold and Esha wanted to have the sequence so she could engineer the drug herself?

I can't stay seated as the pieces fall together. I pace and think. Esha studied in Peru and learned about *Brugmansia*. She came back and got Dr. Richmond to sequence the plant. She accessed the sequence, modified her own chile, and voila! She and her guy had their own personal drug. I kick clothes and shoes out of my way as I stride from one wall to the other, hard thwaks against the floor. Did she want liquid gold for personal use and then she started selling it at a profit—income she could use to pay back SCPG and show her worth?

The story is a great theory, but without evidence, it's just that—a theory. Dizzy with disgust, I stop pacing and close my eyes. If I were evidence, what would I be? Back in Philly the evidence of the clinical trial was as simple as medical records. What's simple here—a note or some kind of data? Then it comes to me. Rudy's chile. I still have it.

I open my eyes and race to my dresser. I open the top drawer and take out the plastic container with the chile. I could sequence this; see what's hidden in the genetic code. But no. That would take too long to learn and be too obvious. I need to look at something that's already been sequenced. I put the container with the chile on my desk. As I put it down, I know just what to do.

Data. Esha had her chile sequenced at SCPG. I enter the bar code for that sample.

I'm so busy developing a plan to get into the lab so I can look at Esha's chile data, I almost miss the knock-turned-pounding on my door until I hear Clem in the hall shouting: "Baked macaroni's getting cold!"

Thirty-two

I open the door, set eyes on Clem, and my brain turns off.

In a gush of hormones and libido, my arms are around him. He's totally surprised, but then his arms are around me, too. Not just arms. Lips. Oh, lips. That very soft, very warm, very wet point of contact. Somehow we end up in my room, door closed, pressed against each other, fumbling and embracing, and then he stops.

"Not exactly platonic," he says.

I've never been more out of words. It's like someone hit my verbal off switch. I perch on the edge of my bed and take another deep breath, my lips still tingling from the kiss.

"What do you think?" Clem asks in a soft voice, almost a whisper in my ear.

My body/brain goes geographic, with my brain in the North Pole, saying no, and my body in the South Pole, saying yes. The South Pole wins. "Try again?"

An answer to which he heeds. He sits down next to me, and this time the kiss is slow, not desperate. His heart ticks against mine. His hand is on my back, under my shirt, but it's not just my back that feels the touch. Who knew toes and earlobes and thighs and hair follicles had so many nerve endings? The kiss is its own language; our lips utter the last syllable, and it's done. We're quiet for a few minutes, a thing without name radiating between us.

"So, what's next?" I finally ask, as much to myself as to him, because for once I have no answer.

"I don't know," he says with a sheepish shrug. "Dinner?"

———

We sit in the back of the cafeteria, our usual spot by the bathrooms. Not because we enjoy the odor of toilets, but because it's the most private place in the very unprivate setting. It's impossible to eat baked macaroni after that kiss and my food languishes on my tray, getting cold.

"So," Clem says, the "so" filling in for about seven thousand things we could/should/need to say. "We don't need to decide anything. I'm not pressuring you. I mean we don't have to…"

My phone rings, giving him an excuse to stop fumbling for words. I don't pick up, though. I let it go to voice mail. His fumbling interrupted, it's my turn to try. "You're right. We…I mean…I— Can we just…?"

It rings again. I'm about to turn off the ringer, but Clem says, "Answer it. Someone really wants to talk to you. We can talk…or whatever…later."

I check and see that it's Amelia calling again and tell Clem who it is in case he thinks it's Jesse. "It's kind of private," I add, thinking she wants information about the chiles and not wanting to talk about it in front of Clem. "Do you mind?"

He says he doesn't mind. We lock eyes for a second as if unsure whether our parting should now include a kiss. I guess we haven't reached the kissing in public stage because as I get up to go, he gives my hand a quick squeeze and tells me he'll see me later.

"So if the liquid gold was put into the chiles when it was a seed, how would you find out?" Amelia says when I answer, as if we'd been in the middle of a conservation.

"Hold on." I take my tray to the kitchen and leave the cafeteria for some privacy. "I was thinking about that before, too," I say once I'm alone in the hall. "I need to go to SCPG and look at some data."

"When?" she asks. "Tonight?"

"Tonight? No way," is my immediate response, but then I pause and think, why not? Nobody will be there, and it'll be impossible to go through Esha's data when everyone's around. "Actually, yeah," I correct. "Tonight."

"Perfect, I'll pick you up."

"Wait," I blurt before she can hang up. "What I'm going to do might not technically be legal."

"Illegal activities?" she says. "I'll be there in ten."

When we go inside SCPG it's dark in that horror-movie kind of way just before the deranged killer enters the house. Even though I have a key and I'm not breaking and entering, snooping through someone's data, as I'm about to do, isn't just unethical, it's possibly illegal, so I don't turn on a light. We feel our way down the stairs and into the lab in the dark.

"We don't have a lot of time and this could take a while. We need to connect to the server, but that's simple," I say, as we reach my desk and my Nerd Girl alter ego springs to life. When my home screen comes up, I access the program Esha showed me how to connect to the central server where SCPG stores results from its big sequence analysis jobs.

"What exactly is it we're doing?" Amelia asks, sidling up to me, two butts sharing my chair.

"Esha had her extra-hot chile sequenced. If she's growing a liquid gold GMO, she'd need to sequence it to make sure the changes in the DNA are there and to find out how many copies of the new genes there are and which chromosomes they're on. That sort of thing." I can tell from her silence that "that sort of thing" means nothing to Amelia, but I keep going. "What I have to do is look at her sequence and compare it to a normal chile genome and see what I find. If what I said before about there being liquid gold produced in her chiles is true, the answer's hidden in plain sight. It's that simple."

"How exactly is that simple?"

"Dr. Richmond's already sequenced a normal chile genome, so we have a reference to compare our data to. It's what I've been learning. It's called bioinformatics. All we have to do is take little short DNA reads that came off the sequencer and find out where they line up to the reference. Then we can see how Esha's chile differs from a normal chile."

I glance at Amelia to see if she's following. Her expression tells me she's not.

"Okay, how about this?" I say. "Imagine you have a long sentence, plus a bag of words. The sentence is the reference and the words are your sequence reads from Esha's chile. You take the words and find their matches in the sentence. That way you can find missing letters and spelling mistakes. You might even have extra words that aren't in the sentence."

Amelia twists an eyebrow ring. "But why would she leave all the data on the computer?"

"Like I said, it's hidden in plain sight. The people in the lab sequence DNA for hundreds of sources. That's their job. To sequence, not to interpret. Nobody ever actually examines the data. It would be like a postman reading your mail."

"And I'm guessing going into someone else's data is a violation of privacy that could get us both into a ton of trouble?"

"Kind of," I say, wondering if she's getting cold feet.

She smiles. "Cool. What are we waiting for?"

With Amelia at my side, I browse through computer folders and files, looking for Esha's data. That's when the first problem occurs. The dreaded password. Esha told me big data systems usually have shared areas, no password needed. But no. When I find Esha's folders on the server, I need her password. All my Nerd-Girl sparkle extinguishes and dies.

"What's wrong?" Amelia asks.

"I need Esha's password."

"Then let's go find it. People usually keep passwords written down somewhere."

I'm going on three hours sleep and this could take hours, but if we want answers, what choice do we have? "Okay, let's try her desk." I lead Amelia to Esha's cubicle and flip on a small light.

I'm on my knees, digging through papers in the bottom drawer for anything that could be related to a password, when I find something that makes me freeze.

"Found it?" Amelia asks.

"Nope, but I found something really interesting." I lay a single sheet of paper on Esha's desk. "Why do you think Esha has a paper with the UpsideDown! logo in her drawer?"

"It's easy to copy a logo and type a letter," Amelia says, letting out a soft whistle. "Could Esha be the one who wrote the threat letters to Ernie?"

The fire and the events leading up to it stagger through my mind as she says this. Esha invited Holly to SPCG. She said it was Dr. Richmond who wanted to talk to her. What if Esha wanted Holly to create a scene and make her look like a whack job capable of arson. What if she was already planning the fire, but when she found out I'd gone up to Ernie's to harvest the chiles for the board meeting, she had to act quickly.

"What if Holly is telling the truth and she didn't set the fire?" I say. "What if Esha burned them so there'd be no more evidence of her liquid gold chiles?"

"Oh, man," Amelia says, the words filling in for the hugeness of the possibility.

I slip the paper back into the drawer for police evidence, should we get that far, and continue to search. Thirty minutes later the clock's ticking, and we've totally struck out. Operation Failure. No password. No database. I slump back onto my hands, defeated and pissed—and no way giving up.

Amelia sits in Esha's chair, elbows on the desk, checking out the photos. "Who's that?" she says, glancing at the monkey.

"Waldo," I say, feeling totally dejected. "Wait...work mascot... people always use their pet names as passwords." I race back over to my desk and type in Waldo. Nothing happens. I try again, this time with a capital W. Still nothing. I sit in frustrated silence and try Esha, then Esha Waldo. *Nada.* I try about twenty different words I associate with Esha— Peru. Plants. Botany. All are strikes.

"Can I try?" Amelia eventually asks.

"Be my guest." I back away and hold my hands up, certain there's no way Amelia's going to crack Esha's password.

Amelia sits down and types with me peering over her shoulder. A second later the screen opens and just like that, I assume Esha's identity. Her own personal corner of the system is suddenly available.

"How the hell did you do that?" I say, astonished that she did; annoyed that I didn't.

She shrugs and gets up, so I can resume prime computer position. "I figured the photo was a clue. The monkey with the band name? If she didn't write down her password, she kept it in her mind that way. WaldoU2. Simple."

"Simple, right," I mutter and lean back in my chair. "First thing is to see if Esha's aligned her chile genome reads to the reference yet. If she has, that will save us hours," I say, thinking through all the bioinformatics Esha's been teaching me the last few days, the practice drills I've been doing. After a few minutes of searching her files, I strike gold—a folder called genome_chile_alignments. Together we look at the folder, containing a series of files, each named similarly: some number followed by ".bam."

"Any idea what this stuff means?" Amelia asks.

"I think it's sets of read-alignment data that corresponds to each chile chromosome."

"And that would mean?"

"If her extra-hot chile contains some foreign genes, then there'll be reads that don't match the reference. There's software to find these reads. Esha showed me how to use it. It shouldn't take that long."

We don't talk as I anxiously check the size of the output files every few minutes and see that they're still growing. After about a half hour of nervous silence, I have a file containing all of the extra-hot chile sequences that don't match the reference.

"Look," I say, the thump of my heart matching the excitement of the discovery. "The extra-hot chile isn't the same as the reference chile. So we have to figure out what the reads mean." I remember something I heard about back in Philly when I was trying to find out what happened to my mom. "There's a public database called GenBank. It's a huge collection of genetic data containing almost everything ever sequenced. We can search it to see if we find any genes that match our mystery reads. It's public access. I just need to figure out how to use it."

"Meaning we need caffeine and junk food?"

While Amelia goes on a phone flashlight adventure and sniffs out the place for sugar and caffeine, I study the how-to tutorials on the GenBank website until I have enough of an idea how to get started. I paste in our mystery reads, choose some default options among the confusing set of choices, and kick the process into action, hoping I've done this correctly. And, hello, ladies and gents! The machine whirs into action. Although there are hundreds of reads in our set from the extra-hot chile, GenBank must have some seriously powerful computers paid for by our tax dollars because the answers come back in a few seconds.

Amelia marches back in with enough vending machine junk food to fuel my entire senior class through first period.

"Get this," I say, reaching for a half-eaten bar of chocolate she must've scrounged from someone's stash. "The extra-hot chile has at least five genes that code for enzymes that aren't in the normal chile."

"It's late, and I slept through bio," she says. "Meaning?"

"Meaning that the cells in the extra-hot chile are doing something a normal chile doesn't do, and I don't think it's an accident." I put down the chocolate, too excited to eat. "My guess is those genes are giving Esha's chile some new ability. But a guess isn't evidence. I need to find out what the output product is of the enzymes."

Again, Amelia wants to know how, and again, I tell her I have to figure it out. I consult my friend, Google, and discover a database of biological pathways called MetaCyc. It's public access. After I watch the tutorial, I learn that MetaCyc is a database of metabolic pathways from all domains of life containing more than 2,000 pathways from more than 2,500 different organisms.

I search the database with the enzyme names from Esha's chiles.

Each search comes up with a hit that describes the reaction done by the enzyme. When I put all the chemical reactions together, I have an answer. I sit back and take my fingers from the keyboard. "Looks like the enzymes create the pathway for making liquid gold," I say, letting out the breath I've been holding for what feels like all night. "And they all come from the plant *Brugmansia.*"

Amelia stares at me with a cautiously guarded expression, one that echoes how I'm feeling. For the first time since we've met, it's like looking in the mirror. "Does that mean we have proof?" she whispers, as if she's afraid the proof will disappear if she speaks any louder.

I nod. "We nailed her."

She keeps staring. "I know that look. You have a plan."

"Yep," I say, elusively.

"You going to tell me—or don't you trust me?"

I consider this question as I look at her angry face, then speak for several minutes.

"You sure about this?" she asks when I'm done.

I turn the question of trust back on her. "You'll just have to have faith."

Thirty-three

I have Friday off to prepare for the board meeting, and at nine a.m., after an evening with Clem in which we kissed twice more and still managed not to define what we're doing, I'm at Alma's in the kitchen with Mari and Amelia. We haven't told Mari about the chiles being drugged. Of course what happened with Eslee isn't her fault, but I'm pretty sure she won't see it that way.

Amelia's designed the whole menu around the New Mexico chile: Parmesan green chile dip. Ginger chile spring rolls. Green chile mac and cheese. Red chile onion rings. Organic chicken and cheese enchiladas with fire roasted chile and tomato salsa. The one dish I'm in charge of is green chile stew. I have all the ingredients.

It's only when I start to prepare the stew that I realize cooking means more than boiling water or spreading peanut butter onto bread. According to the smiling woman on the website of the five-star recipe Amelia pointed me to, the recipe is easy, but when the garlic zings off the cutting board and flies to the floor where Sopapilla immediately licks it, sneezes, and gives me a disgusted look, I mutter. "Yeah, well, the theory of relativity is easy, too, if you're a physicist."

"You don't chop garlic with a butter knife, *Guera*!" Amelia snaps. With a few quick flicks of the wrist and a sharp blade, she has a new clove sliced and ready to go.

I mumble thanks and move on to the onion. "You have no power over me, onion!" I announce, but within seconds my eyes are burning, the tears so profuse I can't see a thing and I have to retreat to the other side of the kitchen where Mari's drinking lemonade, watching the whole thing unfold with an amused smile.

"Any more thoughts about 'Teen Chef'?" she asks Amelia, as Amelia takes over onion chopping.

I'm certain Amelia's going to lie, omit the detail about having aced the audition and actually gotten accepted. "They want me on the show," she says instead. "It's filming in Albuquerque on July 18th. The episode's called 'Show Me How Spicy You Can Be.'" She finishes chopping the onion and swipes her eyes with the back of her wrist. "But I don't know."

Now I'm certain Mari's going to give Amelia a hard time about her indecision, tell her she has to accept. Again I'm wrong. "I guess you should only do it if you really want to. What's that movie?"

"*Like Water for Chocolate*," Amelia says, reading her mind.

When nobody explains the meaning of the reference, I say, "What about that movie?"

"Tita, the main character can only express herself when she cooks," Mari says, her eyes still on Amelia. "And she totally loves the food she makes. I've always said Mia's like Tita, and that's what makes her food so good. It's not just that she's a really freaking good cook, it's that she loves it. You can taste the love. She affects people that way." She shrugs and looks down at her drink. "But if she's not feeling it, then she shouldn't go on the show because she'll just tank."

I'm not sure if Mari's pulling some kind of reverse psychology trick or if she's just being honest, but the meat for my stew needs browning, and I'm too stressed out by my inability to do the browning and not give someone food poisoning from undercooked meat to care. I go to the stove and stare at the meat. I've never actually handled uncooked meat. Meat comes in perfectly round, cooked patties sandwiched between two buns.

"Earth to *Guera*!" I hear Amelia say. "You've been staring at that meat for five minutes. You going to do something with it or wait and see if it cooks itself? Move over." She bumps me out of the way, and within seconds, has the meat, along with the garlic and onion, sliced and browning in a frying pan. "Can you handle the rest? Chopping chiles and putting it all into the pot with some potatoes and a little water?"

"I'll help." Mari pitches in, thank god, because even though Miss Like-Water-For-Chocolate makes it sound so easy, I'm afraid of being the world's biggest recipe moron if I get it wrong.

"Thanks," I say to Mari when the stew is happily cooking on the stove.

"No prob. You excited?"

"Totally." I hide my eyes because what's in them is apprehension about my plan, not excitement, and I don't want Mari to see that and ask why. "It's going to be great."

Once the meat-onion-garlic-chile concoction appears cooked (appears being the operative word, because really I have no idea) I pour it into a bowl. The way I'm sweating, you'd think I'd just run a marathon (or jogged around the block). Not Amelia. She has not a drop of sweat on her brow. Not a glob of meat, a peel of onion, or some other food ingredient smeared on her apron, arms, or (how'd it get there?) face.

At two o'clock, when Amelia pulls the final pan from the oven, I decide miracles are real. My green chile stew is complete, and the kitchen smells are to die for. Mari goes to her room to rest, and Amelia and I agree to leave for SCPG at three, which gives me an hour to put the finishing touches on my plan—the one detail I've left for last, timing being everything. While Amelia goes to get ready, I take out my laptop, which I brought with me, and e-mail Virg.

Dear Officer Virgil,

I think I know how Eslee was poisoned and I think I can prove it. Meet me by the back door today at SCPG at 3:30. I'll explain everything.

Faith Flores

I attach a summary of the data I got from Esha's computer and press send, then change into the clothes Dahlia lent me for the occasion. Suited up in a black skirt, white tee, and black shoes, I go to Amelia's room and knock.

"If you say a word I'll kill you," she says when she opens it.

I have no intention of dying at sixteen, so I keep silent.

Her hands fly to her hips. "Well? Aren't you going to say anything?"

"You said not to."

"Anything bad, *Guera*! Just say something nice."

I take in her clean white linen pants and jacket, her poofy, white chef hat, the lack of facial piercings. "You look ready to kick some serious chef ass," I say. "Where'd you get the hat?"

"Chef Anthony, the guy I did the internship with last semester, gave it to me. He said someday I'd be the head chef at one of the best restaurants in town, but after the whole *mole* fiasco, I threw it in the closet. I thought today would be the perfect day to wear it."

"If only Red were here to see you."

———

We arrive at SCPG just before three-thirty. Esha's already there. While she and Amelia bring the food from the truck to the kitchen (minus my chile stew, which I tell them I'll handle) I excuse myself and race to the back door to wait for Virg.

At four, there's still no sign of him, and I start to panic. My plan calls for police backup. I'm gnawing my lip to pulp when my phone rings. I jump, thinking it's Virg, but when I check the screen my heart sinks. It's Esha.

"I can't find the soup spoons anywhere," she informs me. "Amelia says you're bringing stew. We can't eat stew without soup spoons! Where are you? We really need those spoons. Do I have to go and buy some? Should I send—?"

"No. I'll be there in a second," I say, faking a calm I don't feel.

I trudge back up to the small kitchen through the back door, commanding myself to stay calm. As opposed to Esha whose shit is falling straight out of her ass. "Where are the soup spoons?" she repeats like a brain-addled dementia patient the second I walk into the kitchen. "We only have teaspoons. How can we eat stew with teaspoons? It'll be a disaster!"

"It's okay," I say, producing the appropriate spoons. "The board isn't going to cut funding because of our spoons."

"What about the napkins? I only see paper. I thought we agreed on cloth? Paper looks cheap."

"They're right here. Everything's going to be fine," I say, repeating my mantra, willing it to be so.

At five, boardmembers start to appear in the conference room where we're serving dinner. Amelia walks around with a tray of ginger chile spring rolls, fire-roasted salsa and chile sauce, Parmesan green chile dip, and homemade tortilla chips. I listen to the sounds of gastric contentment as people go for seconds and thirds. I even hear one of the boardmembers asking Esha for the name of the caterer.

"Looks like they love your food," I say to Amelia when she comes into the kitchen to restock her tray.

She shrugs me off, like it's no big deal, but she's humming to herself and smiling as she goes back into the room.

At five-forty-five, appetizers are over and still no Virg. Dr. Richmond clinks her glass and asks her guests to be seated. "Welcome," she says to the smiling posse of PhDs, the intellectual per-capita of a small nation. "It's a pleasure to have you all here. Tonight we're celebrating our New Mexico chile projects." She looks around the table with her dazzling smile as everyone claps, then lifts a hand and continues. "While there are those in the community who are against the progress we are making at SCPG, we cannot let fear and politics get in the way of good science. We here at SCPG have a solution to a problem plaguing New Mexico. A solution that could revive an industry and save thousands of jobs. A solution that merges the tradition of the past with the progress of the future. Yes, we've had a setback, but we will not let renegades stop us. Tonight we celebrate the growth of SCPG and we dine in honor of the New Mexico chile."

Applause, applause, happy congratulations. While the feel good banter continues, I set bowls of my green chile stew around the table, wondering if my plan has any chance of working without a cop here, or if I'm about to humiliate myself, destroy my reputation, and lose any chance of a future in science. I glance at Esha as I set her bowl in front of her, but she's busy talking to a suited boardmember and doesn't meet my eye. It's now or never.

When I've set the last bowl, I stop at the head of the table and clear my throat. "May I have your attention, please?" The room goes quiet. A drop of sweat slithers down my neck. "Hi, everyone. My name's Faith Flores. I'm an intern here at SCPG. As Dr. Richmond said, tonight's meal is all about the New Mexico chile, but before we get started with the main course, we have a little surprise." Another drop of sweat meets up with the first, making for a perspiration party. I notice Amelia's stuck her head out of the kitchen and is looking at me nervously. "While we can't taste Dr. Richmond's engineered chile tonight because it's not quite ready for the market, we can taste Esha's chiles, which she's been harvesting for several months. So to honor her hard work I made green chile stew using her genetically modified extra-hot chiles."

Esha laughs politely without taking her eyes off me. "That's a great idea, Faith, but unfortunately there were no chiles left after the fire, so I don't see how this is possible."

"Ernie was able to harvest some before the fire," I say, placing a hand to my heart and feigning gratitude.

Esha clears her throat and looks around. She's still smiling, but her eyes have changed. She no longer looks so smug.

"Dig in and enjoy!" I exclaim.

There's a clinking of silverware and a rustle of napkins. I'm on the verge of death by nerves as people raise their spoons. *Come on, Esha!* I scream in my head. *Are you just going to stand there? I'm counting on you to tell them not to eat it!*

Just as a woman in a yellow dress touches her spoon to her lips, Esha jumps up and shouts, "Wait!" A few surprised boardmembers drop their spoons, others pause, spoons mid-air. "Nobody move! Don't taste anything!" Esha snaps her fingers, as if summoning a butler to clear away the dishes. When nobody comes, she starts collecting them herself. She races around the table grabbing over people's heads, slopping bits of soup onto silk shirts and linen blazers.

"Ouch," Dr. Richmond cries when hot liquid spills onto her arm. "Esha, for God's sake, what's gotten into you?"

"Why shouldn't all these people taste your chiles?" I call over the chaos. "Don't you want to share with the board the work you've done?" Esha's eyes bore into me. "It's not because you engineered liquid gold into your so-called extra-hot chiles, is it?"

"That's insane!" Esha shoots back.

"No," I say, speaking softly now. No need to shout. The room has gone quiet. "What's insane is that you didn't grow a chile. You grew a drug." Dr. Richmond sits frozen at the head of the table, Jonah beside her. "Are you afraid someone will die if they eat it? Like Eslee? Like Mari, my half sister, almost did?"

"Okay, Faith, that's enough," Dr. Richmond says to me, but she sounds shaken.

"There's proof!" I'm back to shouting now. "And you can see it on the central server in Esha's data. You're all scientists. You'll understand it."

"This is ridiculous!" Esha sounds calm, but there's a storm behind her eyes.

"If it's so ridiculous, why don't you taste it yourself?"

Little clusters of bombs detonate around the room as everyone starts talking at once, but it's Esha who penetrates the uproar. "You are an attention-seeking child," she says to me, commanding everyone's attention with the threat in her voice.

"You're wrong on both things," says a familiar voice in the back of the room. I spin and see Virg standing in the doorway, holding up a badge. "She's a teenager, not a child, and she's not seeking attention." He walks toward Esha through the now dead silence. "You're Dr. Margolis?"

She clears her throat. "Yes. That's right. I'm the lab director. I hired Faith."

He nods thoughtfully, then turns to me. "Hi, Faith. How're you holding up?"

"You know each other?" Esha asks, crevices of doubt cracking her smug expression.

"Yes, not only do we know each other, but Faith invited me to be here." I'm too nervous to take his smile for anything more than a physical anomaly, a tick, an uncontrolled movement of muscles, and I keep quiet. "I read your e-mail and the information you sent me. Took a while to find someone who understood it. Sorry I'm late." He turns now to Esha. "This morning, you might be interested to know, we took a young man by the name of Cruz Sampson into custody on charges of dealing liquid gold. He had a very interesting story to tell us about how he came to be dealing the drug, and how liquid gold has been made to grow inside a chile pepper. At first I thought his story was crazy, but then I received Miss Flores' e-mail, and it looks to me like his story might just have some truth to it. More than that, it appears that this drugged chile was ingested by one girl who died and by another one who almost died."

I finally breathe. My shoulders drop about a million miles.

"Esha Margolis," Virg says, stepping toward her, "you are under arrest for the manufacturing and distribution of a Schedule 1 illegal substance and for the death of Eslee Dominguez. You have the right to remain silent. Anything you say can and will be used against you in a court of law."

Everyone starts talking at the same time. As Virg cuffs Esha and leads her out of the room, I know it's just a matter of minutes before the attention goes to me, a million questions I'm not ready to answer. I slip into the kitchen where Amelia's standing by the microwave.

"Come on," I say, grabbing her hand. "Let's get out of here."

She doesn't move. "You're totally insane!" she says, bumping me with her hip. But she smiles as she says it. "I never thought this was going to work. Missy dumping skull and bones hot chile sauce into my *mole* was nothing compared to what you just did. I'm going to go on 'Teen Chef' and show that girl she's got nothing on me. I'll win that contest and then we'll see who's laughing!"

"Great," I say, glancing nervously at the door. "But can we celebrate that later, like back at Alma's?"

"Yeah," she says. "Let's go. Just one sec." I'm about to protest and tell her we don't have a second, but she grabs two pots of food, one in each hand. "Someone should eat this. We can't let it go to waste."

Can't argue with that. I grab another two dishes and together, hands full, we slip out the back door and hurry to Amelia's truck.

As we drive away from SCPG, away from the immediate chaos, the seriousness of what just happened sinks in. "Do you think Esha'll be charged with murder?" Amelia asks.

I look out the window as we head north. "I'm guessing the charge will be manslaughter. I don't think she intended to kill anyone."

"Well, what the hell did she think was going to happen?" Amelia snaps, approaching a yellow light too quickly and slamming on the brakes.

I rest my cheek against the window. "I don't think she knew they were deadly."

"Oh yeah? And how'd she figure that?" she asks, blasting through the light the second it goes green.

I sigh and tell Amelia what I think happened—everything I've been mulling over, the clues of the past few weeks and the story they tell. "Esha screwed up. The plan must have been for her and Cruz to grow liquid gold in the chiles so nobody would detect the drug," I say, closing my eyes. "Then they harvested their crop and Bulldog extracted the liquid gold, like we saw him doing in his trailer, and sold it. That's why Virg said it was coming in cheaper and why the cops couldn't track it. Then when Eslee died, things changed. She realized the chiles themselves were deadly."

"But how did Esha know it was the chile that killed Eslee?"

I hear the emotion in Amelia's voice, the venomous cocktail of anger and betrayal and shock. I recognize it because I feel it, too. "I think I had something to do with that," I say, recalling the conversation I had with Esha the day Eslee died. "I told her about Rudy disappearing and the party and Mari's liquid gold overdose. Cruz would've told her that Rudy had taken some of the chiles. She must have put two and two together and figured out that her liquid gold was somehow responsible for Eslee's death. And she wanted out."

"What makes you think she wanted out? Maybe she was a psychopath and didn't give a shit about who died."

"Right after Eslee died, I saw this text on Esha's phone saying 'it's over,'" I say. "At the time I thought it was a breakup message, but now I think it was a message to Cruz saying that growing the chiles was over. She didn't want to do it anymore, but it wasn't just the text that makes me think that. It was finding the necklace in Bulldog's truck that she told me a boyfriend had given her. She gave it back to him when she decided not to do it." Something else occurs to me when

I say this. As Amelia turns off the main road onto the silent side street leading to Alma's, I go on. "Maybe Bulldog wasn't going to let her stop. I mean he could blackmail her to keep making the drug. Maybe that's why she burned the fields, so there wouldn't be any chiles left."

"Man," Amelia says as she pulls into Alma's house. "People suck sometimes."

"Not all people," I say, meeting her eye as we climb out of the truck. A slow smile stretches the corners of her lips and together we carry the food we salvaged inside.

Thirty-four

"You're home early," Alma says, meeting us at the front door. She looks from Amelia, to me, to the food we're carrying, and her eyebrows shoot up, seeming to intuit that something bad happened.

"What smells so good?" Mari calls from the other room, and a second later she too is standing by the front door, wanting to know why we're back so early.

"I think," I say, not knowing how else to begin, "we should all sit down and have something to eat."

"Come then, *Mijas*," Alma says, without asking questions. "It's a beautiful evening and it's still light out. We'll eat outside." She takes one plate from Amelia's hand, one from mine, and tells Mari to bring dishes.

When we're settled at the table on the flagstone patio, surrounded by Alma's garden, I realize what happened tonight means telling Mari what happened to Eslee. If she hears it from someone else, as gossip or on the news, it'll destroy her. I glance at Amelia, but she seems to be in a sort of posttraumatic stun from the evening and doesn't speak. It's up to me to explain to Mari about the chiles.

"There's something I need to tell you," I say to Mari as she serves herself a helping of green chile mac and cheese.

"Okay," she says, her expression changing from ease to anxiety. "What?"

I take a gulp of cool evening air and begin. Instead of starting with what happened at the board meeting, I tell her that the chile she took from Rudy had liquid gold in it, that she cooked the liquid gold into the stew that both she and Eslee ate, and that's how she got drugged and how Eslee OD'd. "It wasn't your fault," I say, the second I finish telling her. "There's no way you could've known."

But she's already disappearing. She pushes away her plate, her face dark and shadowed. "I'm going to my room," she says. She gets up to leave, but Alma stands up and stops her.

"No, *Mija*. You're not going anywhere. You're staying here. We're your family and we're going to help you get through this. Faith is right, child, this wasn't your fault."

With those words, Mari's face crumbles and she starts to sob. Her small body folds into Alma's arms. And suddenly I get that the sobs aren't just about Eslee. They're about losing Alvaro and her mom; about all the sadness and loneliness she's been holding inside.

Alma cradles Mari against her breast and gestures for Amelia and me to join. As we squeeze into the circle of Alma's arms, I get something else—something that I hadn't really understood until just now. Even though I'm leaving for Philly in a few weeks, these people will be in my life forever. These people are my family.

We stand cradled in Alma's arms until a cell phone rings—two lines of "Under Pressure." A call from Rudy ruins the moment. We untangle as Amelia reaches into her pocket. She turns her back and the two have a short conversation while Alma leads Mari inside.

"So, you guys make up?" I ask when Amelia hangs up. She nods and stares at her hands, as if not wanting to admit that she and a guy I spent the last month thinking was a drug dealer are back together again. "I'm sorry for anything lame I said about Rudy. He's not such a bad guy," I say, desperate to move forward and not have some other negative thing lingering between us. Still she doesn't say anything. I worry that I owe her more of an explanation, or maybe I'm just unnerved by her silence. Whatever it is, I keep talking. "I guess Rudy and I got off to a bad start. I thought he was giving you pot at the Farmers' Market when he gave you that box."

Amelia looks up at me when I say this, a wild expression in her eyes I can't read—anger? Shock? I have no idea, but then a new awful thought unfurls. Maybe it *was* pot in that box. Just because he didn't deal liquid gold doesn't mean he doesn't still dabble in dope. Maybe Amelia's pissed or defensive or…

"I'll be right back," she says, suddenly jumping up from the table, interrupting my thoughts.

She dashes toward the house, nearly knocking into Alma and Mari who are just coming back outside.

"You are not excused, *Mija*," Alma says as Amelia blasts past her.

"I'm not leaving. I'll be right back." She darts into the house and returns a moment later carrying the shoebox Rudy gave her at the Farmers' Market. "Since we're all being so touchy feely this evening and having telling-the-truth time, I might as well tell you something." She's trying to sound tough, but she just sounds scared. "If I'm going to tell *Guera*, I might as well tell you all. Then you can all hate me together."

"I guess we should all sit down then," Alma says. "Hating takes a lot of energy."

I feel a wave of confusion as I take a seat and Amelia hands me the box. If there had been pot in it, why is she bringing it outside now?

"Open it," is all Amelia says.

I slowly remove the lid. The box doesn't smell like weed. I reach inside and pull out a piece of paper. I read the first line out loud. *"Dear Faith."*

My internal organs react immediately to these two words, understanding something my brain hasn't yet computed and rearranging themselves into geographically awkward places. My heart travels to my throat. My stomach takes up residency by my feet. I don't know what's up with my bladder, kidneys, and the rest of the life-sustaining crew, but whatever they're doing, I feel sick.

I read on. "I don't know what you know about me or what your mom's told you. She doesn't know I'm writing to you. I had a lot of problems when you were born and before that, too. Drugs mostly. I was messed up in some pretty bad stuff. But I'm better now. I want to see you, but only if you want to see me. Here's my address. Write if you want to. Your father, Alvaro Flores."

"Mija!" Alma exclaims, but Amelia doesn't say anything.

I read the next three letters to myself—all variations on the first. The only real difference is the last line of what I gather from the date is the last letter.

I don't blame you for not writing back or wanting to talk to me. I respect your decision. I won't write again.

I'm too stunned to cry, to move, to do anything, but sit in a catatonic state as my lungs join the organ mutiny and stop drawing air.

"I'd hate me too if I were you," Amelia says in a dry voice, not looking at me, not looking at anyone.

I stare at the final letter, as if willing it to say something more, to tell me a different story. One in which I didn't miss my chance to meet my father, the man I've spent almost seventeen years hating, thinking he bailed and never gave a shit about me. Now it's too late. The story ended. And it didn't end with the biggest line of crap in the history of story telling: happily ever after, except for one happy part—I don't have to blame my mom for taking the letters.

Amelia keeps her eyes on the garden, as if her words are hiding in one of the flowering plants. "When I was seven I heard him talking to Mom. He told her he was ready to write to this other daughter, to this girl named Faith," she says, but her voice is so quiet, so tiny and transformed, I have to look to make sure it really is her speaking. "Sometimes he was so distant when we were kids. He'd just check out. I thought it was because he was thinking of his other daughter. I thought he loved you more than he loved us, and that if he went to see you he'd never come back. I was just a kid, okay?" Her voice rises to a sharp, defensive tone, but beneath the bite, I hear the effort it's taking not to cry. "So I kept watch over the mailbox. I checked every day to see if he'd written the letter. Then one day I found an envelope with your name on it, and I stole it. I was seven. I didn't have a plan. I just did it. I took all his letters, and the ones Gran wrote, too." I hear Alma gasp, but she keeps quiet. "When Mom died I finally realized what I was doing. What I was taking away from you. I knew I had to tell. But I couldn't do it. I mean, what if he left us for real?

I was too afraid to take that chance. I told myself I'd do it when I was older. Then he died, and I didn't see the point." She closes her eyes and takes a breath. "I hated having them around, reminding me what I was doing, but I just couldn't destroy them. Rudy offered to take the letters, but when he found out you were here, he gave them back to me and told me I had to tell you."

She opens her eyes and waves her hand around as if shooing away a fly, then spins around to face me. "When you showed up I was so pissed. You were that other kid. The one I thought he was going to leave us for. I was afraid you were my competition for so long I believed it. When you came over for dinner, I just wanted to hate you." A bird sings off in a bush somewhere. I close my eyes and take it all in. "The thing is, I don't hate you," she says, softly now. "I hated myself for what I did, and I took it out on you and avoided telling you the truth. I'm sorry. I'm really sorry, Faith."

I open my eyes when she says my name, the first time she's ever called me Faith and not *guera*, but I don't say anything. I want to hate her as much as she hated me. I want to throttle her and pummel her into the ground, but deeper than that, there's another feeling that keeps my fists safely in my lap. Even though her words blister, even though she stole something from me I can never have back, I get how that kind of hurt can drive you mad, can make you do stupid shit like stealing letters. I get why she avoided telling me, too. After all I'm the master of avoiding hard shit. Avoidance must be a shared thing. Part of our genetic code. More than all that, though, I get that I don't want to be stuck in the past. I want a half sister, not an enemy.

I'm too raw to speak, so I just nod, hoping the words will come when they're ready.

"Oh my God!" Mari suddenly exclaims. I think she's late in reacting to Amelia and the letters, that she's about to sock her sister in the face, but when I look at her, she's pointing at a hummingbird buzzing between patches of small, pink flowers. "It's the calliope! The one I've been waiting for. Dad's bird." She points at the rock she painted. "I have to get my camera."

As Mari charges off to the house, Alma rises. I'm suddenly afraid of what her reaction to Amelia's betrayal is going to be, but Alma takes Amelia into her arms and hugs her. As Amelia softly cries into our grandmother's shoulder, I get, maybe for the first time in my life, what forgiveness is. In that moment I forgive Amelia, and my mom, and yeah, even my dad. Because I need that foundation to look forward to the future I want so much: a future full of hope for this new family.

Thirty-five

I get back to the dorm Saturday evening smelling of onions and garlic and chile and march straight to Clem's room. I stand outside his door for a moment gathering inspiration from Amelia. If she found the courage to come clean and tell me about the letters, I can have the courage to freaking carpe diem. For once I'm going to live in the now, not in the "what if" worry of the future. Clem and I can do this thing. We can be together for the rest of the time I'm here. I'm leaving in a few weeks anyway. I'll sort things out with Jesse when I get back to Philly.

Clem opens the door and I decide to show him what I'm feeling, not tell him—my lips have better use than talking. As soon as we start to kiss I can tell something's wrong.

"What?" I say, pulling away. "Oh my God! The onions. Do I stink?"

"No," he says. "We have to talk."

"Oh. That." I look down, disappointed, wishing talking had never been invented.

"I'm going to Julliard in September. I just found out yesterday that they're giving me a full ride," he says. "My mom said

I should go. In fact, she said I have to go, that she'll disown me if I stay around here and try and babysit her."

"Are you going to listen to her?" I ask, and then quickly add what should've come first. "I mean congratulations!"

"Thanks and hell yeah!" He laughs, then leans over and kisses me on the cheek. It's just a peck, but heat radiates down my spine and those darned toes tingle again.

It finally dawns on me how this affects me. Julliard is in New York. A short hop away from Philly by train. "So, that means we'll be closer?" I say softly into the dark silence of the moonless night.

"It does," he says just as softly. "It also means that while I'm an hour away, you'll be back with Jesse." I try to say something, but he keeps talking. "I've been thinking about this a lot since I found out. You're an amazing person. You're all I can think about. You're brave. You're smart. You don't take shit from anyone. I really like you. And that's the problem."

I nod, hating that there's a problem, worse, hating that I'm the one causing it.

"If we get any closer and then I'm in New York and you're in Philly, it would just be too hard if you're with Jesse. Before I thought okay, I'll be in New Mexico when you leave. We can just have a fling. There's no future, but now..." Instead of finishing his thought, he gets up, picks up his violin, and starts to play. Impossibly sweet notes slip into the room. "Sometimes music is easier for me than words," he says when he's done. "I wrote that song for you. It's called 'Friends.'"

He looks at me for an answer to the question asked with his violin: Can we go back to being friends? NO! I want to shout. Platonic friends was then, before we kissed. This is the post-kissing phase. But the truth is, he's right. Getting involved with Clem is too confusing. I can hardly manage a relationship with one guy. How could I possibly deal with feelings for two?

"Okay," I manage to say. I get up to go, thinking that's it.

"Wait!" Clem blurts as I reach the door. "There's something else." He grips his violin, as if he wishes the something else could be music and not words. "When you go back to Philly you can decide what you want. After you spend time with Jesse. I'll wait for you." He looks into my eyes and says, "You're worth it."

This time my throat is too tight to say anything. I nod, and slip out of his room, wishing I, too, had music to express my heart.

To receive a free catalog of Poisoned Pen Press titles, please provide your name, address, and e-mail address in one of the following ways:

Phone: 1-800-421-3976
Facsimile: 1-480-949-1707
Email: info@poisonedpenpress.com
Website: www.poisonedpenpress.com

Poisoned Pen Press
6962 E. First Ave. Ste 103
Scottsdale, AZ 85251